MW01715245

"YOU DON'T MIND THE ISOLATION?"

Cooper gave Maggie one of his long looks. "For years I didn't. In fact, solitude was what I wanted. I was content, in my way." He reached out to stroke her hair. "Until a lady lawyer came to town. I need very little for happiness, and what's lacking, I may have found." He stopped, probing her eyes with his. "Please, Maggie. Don't tempt me into saying more than you're ready to hear."

"Then don't talk, Cooper. Hold me."

He put his arm around her, drawing her close until they were touching everywhere, side to side, and his strength had become her strength. She laid her head in the curve of his neck, allowing herself an almost inaudible sigh. She needed him. Lord, how she needed him...his strength, and even more, his love.

ABOUT THE AUTHOR

Ann Meredith Wills is the pen name of an unusual writing combination: Maralys Wills and her daughter-in-law, Betty-Jo. Maralys has written several works of nonfiction, including a book about hang gliding, but when it comes to concocting romances, she enlists the help of Betty-Jo, a "master plotter." Together they manage to bring a two-generational viewpoint to their stories. Maralys, mother of five boys and a girl, grew up in Mount Shasta, California, and is therefore particularly sensitive to the environmental issues of that locale.

Books by Ann Meredith Wills

HARLEQUIN SUPERROMANCE

62–TEMPEST AND TENDERNESS
164–MOUNTAIN SPELL

These books may be available at your local bookseller.

Ann Meredith Wills

MOUNTAIN SPELL

Harlequin Books

TORONTO • NEW YORK • LONDON
AMSTERDAM • PARIS • SYDNEY • HAMBURG
STOCKHOLM • ATHENS • TOKYO • MILAN

Published May 1985

First printing March 1985

ISBN 0-373-70164-0

Printed in Canada

To Betty-Jo Wills,
my coauthor and plotter par excellence.

CHAPTER ONE

"YOU'RE A CON ARTIST, Maggie! A conniver! I might have known you'd pull something like this, going to Meiers behind my back!" Ben Graves's pale blue eyes, usually remote, seemed brighter than Maggie had ever seen them. "So you want that job so bad...why didn't you just say so? Why didn't you come to me and say, 'Ben, I've gotta have it...give me a chance,' and I'd have probably given it to you. But the way you did it... Honest to God, Maggie, I find it hard to believe you're someone I once respected. Damn you!"

He stood in the doorway of her small apartment, a tall man, almost painfully thin, his face all angles in the indirect lighting and his blond hair so pale it was nearly colorless. He pushed his glasses toward his eyes and grilled her visually.

"Sit down, Ben," Maggie said. "I'll try to explain."

He shook his head. "There's nothing to explain, Maggie. Nothing left to talk about. You went to old man Meiers himself and it's done now. The guy believes that tale about your superior knowledge of the Mount Shasta area. Tell me, Maggie—" he leaned forward menacingly "—what does it feel like to con someone with a bald lie?"

Maggie McAllister winced. She'd never imagined Ben could be so implacably cold. But then she reminded herself Ben was stretching the facts, a good lawyer all the way. Build your own case, make it look better than it was, that was what they'd all learned to do—those who did more than survive.

"It wasn't actually a lie, Ben," she said. "I have been doing a lot of reading lately." She smiled, hoping to win him over. "I boned up on Mount Shasta." Her dark, slate-blue eyes widened. "Honestly, I didn't know the assignment meant that much to you."

For a moment he stared at her. "Don't look at me that way, Maggie. Don't use those big, lovely eyes of yours on me, it won't get you anywhere. Not anymore. You've just lost your innocence." He paused, gripping the edge of the doorjamb so hard the tendons stood out on the back of his hand. "You know what you are? You're nothing but a shyster in skirts!"

She was shocked, then angry. She found herself responding as a man might. "Graves, you've gone over the line. Get out of my apartment!" She glanced around her well-appointed living room, trying to think of something worse to say, something that would diminish him as he'd tarnished her.

He had his hand on the doorknob, his foot over the threshold.

"Take your wine!" She flung the words at him. "It's still in the fridge from last week." *Hurt him, Maggie. Let him have it.* "You may need it for someone else. . . if you're lucky."

"I don't bother with leftover wine," he said bitterly, "from leftover girlfriends." The door slammed and he was gone.

After he'd left, she sat stone still while she felt the apartment reverberate with ugly sound. Shyster in skirts! God, he couldn't mean that. It wasn't true. Never, ever, would she think of herself in that light. Ambitious. . . oh, yes. But not a shyster. The term was abhorrent to her.

Oh, damn, she thought, fighting tears. She rose

from her pale blue velvet sofa and crossed to the stereo, staring at it distractedly. How had Ben found out? Surely old man Meiers hadn't told him...?

Her hands trembled as she reached for one of her records, and she stared at her fingers as if they belonged to someone else. What was the matter with her all of a sudden? Why were her hands doing this, the second time in a week?

Distraught, she picked up her recording of Mozart's *Requiem* and almost slammed it onto the turntable. But at the last second she held back, fingering the record gingerly; a wrecked stereo wouldn't make her any happier. She had to get the music going, stop that conversation ringing in the room... or worse, in her head.

She held on to herself until the music started, trying to erase the image of Ben and the look of disgust he'd leveled at her. Why had he come on so strong? She hadn't done anything so terrible. He had to know it wasn't personal, nothing meant to hurt him. Lord, if she'd known he was going to overreact like this...

Violins swept through her living room, and gratefully she padded in stockinged feet across the thick white carpet to her minikitchen, hit the light switch and turned on the electricity under the coffeepot.

A cup of hot black coffee warmed her hands; she cozied the cup in her palm before drinking. Had she really hurt Ben's career? The specter of guilt rose and she fought it back, hating the word, even the sound of it. *I'm not guilty,* she thought, *because I didn't mean to hurt him.*

She drank, feeling the steaming liquid sear her throat on its way down, and knew she should have waited a bit longer or taken a smaller sip.

Don't think about him. He's replaceable, she told herself, but relentlessly her thoughts raced on, and she couldn't stop them. Ben was one of the intelligentsia in her law firm, perhaps the fellow lawyer she respected most, often witty and always a mental challenge. She'd relished sparring with him and sensed an inner intensity about him, warm depths of feeling that he'd always masked in wit. She wondered what else, in time, she might have enjoyed with him. But now she'd never know.

She set her lips. She mustn't look back. What was over was over. She hadn't become a lawyer by being soft and letting small things throw her.

She stared into her cup. Ben wasn't such a small thing, but that's how she'd have to look at him now. Too bad they were in the same law firm; it was going to be awkward running into him in the staid halls of Meiers, Meiers, DeCaro and Kosinski. Yes. . .rough from here on. Maybe she shouldn't have done it, or somehow done it differently. Lord, why did Meiers have to tell him?

She sat quietly, drinking her coffee, trying to understand what had happened. Nobody, she thought, nobody was ever going to look out for her except her. No one had ever reached a hand down to pull her up before, and it was obvious no one ever would. Only Maggie was responsible for Maggie, and that's how it would always be. Her father had seen to that. Years ago.

I'm sorry, Ben, she thought, *but that's how it is.*

TWO DAYS LATER, Maggie McAllister glanced automatically out the window of her fifth-story apartment in Newport Beach, California, before deciding what to put on. For a moment she forgot she'd be getting on a plane. The Park Newport complex was only a few miles from the ocean and it was possible to step out into some chilling and unexpected fog, even in the summer. But now it was late March and the mornings were predictably cold. Beyond the tennis courts she saw a mist hanging low, shrouding faraway buildings with a diaphanous veil that would trail away to the ocean.

Without analyzing why, Maggie knew she liked the mist, recognizing subliminally that it softened harsh outlines, even the steel and concrete that made up so much of her surroundings. Ordinarily she turned from the window immediately, feeling she had no time to muse about such ephemeral matters as mist, but this morning she paused to look a little longer. Indistinct shapes, dimly apparent in the vaporous air, stirred her imagination, and for just a moment she imagined she saw hills. Scotland? Heather? Then came a swift inner rebuke. *Maggie, come on! You're on a tight schedule.* Reluctantly, she turned away.

Around the corner in her generous walk-in closet, she rummaged until she found her soft, cherry-red wool suit, which conformed smoothly to her lithe figure whether she sat or stood. Perfect for traveling. Its vivid color reflected the way she felt about journeys—bold and assertive, ready for adventure.

In front of her bathroom mirror she briefly wound a strand of her dark hair around her curling iron, then another, softening the locks nearest her face. The rest hung to her shoulders, glossy and thick, in marked contrast to her white skin. Her complexion had a delicate, indoor look, almost startling against her dark hair and even darker eyes—a combination known in the fashion industry as "high color." Yet it proved useful in the legal world, as well. Women were sometimes put off, but—it came as a small comfort—hers was a world of men.

A few minutes later Maggie slammed the door to her apartment and headed downstairs to her waiting taxi.

THE ANNOUNCEMENT permeated the waiting room. "Air California passengers. . .last call for Flight 43 to Sacramento." Maggie stood and picked up her plaid overnight bag, her purse and the briefcase full of notes and papers about the community known as Mount Shasta. As she shifted the heavy briefcase to her other hand, feeling the weight of the work she'd done preparing for this trip, she felt a sharp pang of regret. So this was what she'd traded for Ben Graves—this briefcase full of notes and this plane trip. For these things she had given up ever being close to him again. Suddenly it hurt.

She crossed the Tarmac to the waiting plane. Its steps reached down to her, beckoning, and a stewardess waited expectantly at the top. Maggie had only to ascend the stairs, step into the plane and be on her way to adventure—to the next move in her career. She began walking faster. *On with your life, Maggie. Ben is just another man.*

IN SACRAMENTO, Maggie rented a red Celica, let Hertz Rent A Car load her bags in the trunk, and then drove down a short access road toward Interstate 5. Because the airport was some miles north of the city, she quickly left Sacramento behind and found herself on a nearly empty freeway traveling fast through fields that stretched left and right to distant, white-capped mountains. Suddenly she felt freer, somehow cleansed. The March air was crisp and windy. And the visibility! How long had it been since she'd been able to see in every direction like this with no impediments, no structures. There were just fields full of winter grains greening up in the March sunshine; all those straight rows whizzing past like spokes in a bicycle wheel.

Funny. She'd never thought flat open land could hold such appeal. Was city life beginning to pall?

Her Celica seemed to drive itself on the broad straight road, and she began to plan her course of action for her arrival in Mount Shasta. First, she'd contact Gordon Hamilton, the energetic, forceful man who'd retained her firm. She knew he'd be waiting impatiently because he struck her as a man in a hurry; his letter confirmed that.

> Send someone up as soon as you can. We environmentalists are in trouble. We've got to stop those skiers before they invade Mount Shasta and destroy it. They're about to ruin the mountain and everything around it. I'm retaining you, Meiers, to get an injunction.

Mr. Meiers, Sr., nearly bald and hawk nosed, hadn't let Hamilton stampede him. He'd handled too many cases to go running off like a skittery heifer.

"It's a perfect situation for one of you," he'd said at the firm meeting, looking from Ben Graves to Maggie. "You'll be taking statements, beating the bushes for evidence. A chance to see what you can do. Test your wings, eh?"

Maggie glanced at Ben and found his face unreadable, then looked down and noticed him rubbing his pant leg nervously. In the back of her mind she knew Ben really wanted the job.

"Well," Meiers had gone on, absently pushing his glasses back, "I'll give the situation some thought and talk to you both next week."

Sitting there at the firm's conference table in the Los Angeles office, Maggie had let her mind drift. Meiers went on with the agenda, but she was no longer tracking the conversation. Instead, she was listening to an inner voice, feeling the same drive to make something of herself she'd felt that day, at fourteen, when she suddenly knew for certain her father was never coming back. Her reaction had been a compensation, a putting down of despair. *I'll show him.*

Now, inexplicably, the emotion surfaced again. *I'll show Meiers what I can do.* This would be her vehicle, she thought, her chance to rise above the other fledgling lawyers with her own assignment, her own, Maggie-directed project.

She glanced at Meiers, making a half effort to listen to what he was saying. But her attention drifted again as her own thoughts intruded. Sometimes new lawyers had to wait years for something like this. Years to try a case, years to be put in charge of something.

Yet here it was, one of those rare opportunities.

She'd hardly given Ben another thought.

Without telling anyone, Maggie had rushed to the library and read everything she could find on the northern California town of Mount Shasta—learned about its lumber industry, its geography and geology, its peculiar problems. Then she'd studied other environmentalist cases until she knew exactly what tack she ought to take. And in the course of analyzing one of those mountain fights the thought came to her.... Her case should be easy!

With her chin in her hands, her dark eyes luminous with the thrill of discovery, she read the pretrial depositions about that mountain and felt her excitement growing. Here was her model, the proof that she was undertaking a winnable case.

It wasn't enough to be put in charge of something...you also had to get results!

Well, when Meiers brought it up, she'd be ready.

But something else had intervened. Another lawyer told her Meiers was already leaning toward Ben.

Panicked, she'd searched out the old man that night and found light under his office door. Knocking hesitantly, she responded to his booming, "Come in," with a moment's reluctance that she quickly pushed back. "Mr. Meiers," she began engagingly. "If you're not fully decided on who will handle the Mount Shasta case, I think I can offer some expertise that will help our firm look good to Mr. Hamilton." She told him she knew the area inside and out and dropped a few statistics to prove it. Suddenly, impulsively, she said, "You see, I once lived in the nearby town of Dunsmuir."

The lie had come out so smoothly even she was amazed. But she found her hands trembling. She clasped them firmly and went on, telling him she knew the issues firsthand—whom to see and what questions to ask. "So unless you've already made up your mind..." Almost without conscious effort, she felt her eyes widening and sensed the effect they were having on the old man.

Mr. Meiers cleared his throat quickly. "No, no. Oh, no." He smiled at her. "I want you to go. In the field of the law, my dear, nothing is ever final. There's always a higher court." Smiling, Maggie accepted his verdict without knowing what on earth he meant.

Only later—the day after her confrontation with Ben—did she learn what Meiers's cryptic comment was all about. As she issued her final pretrip instructions to a secretary in the front office, the girl smiled at her knowingly. "You really must have wowed old man Meiers. A couple of days ago I heard he gave this trip to Ben."

The Celica sped past a grain silo, a field of cows. Maggie sensed the passing miles as steps, each bringing her closer to the goal she'd set for herself—a partnership in the firm by the time she was thirty-three. That gave her five more years. But what a price she'd paid for the steps so far.

As Maggie approached the town of Redding, California, an hour from Mount Shasta, she remembered the last thing she'd heard from Gordon Hamilton. "Your biggest obstacle will be an individual called Cooper Smith. Watch out for him. He's a big man and as immovable as the damned mountain."

MAGGIE LEFT REDDING and started up the wide, four-lane highway that led to Mount Shasta. Gone now were the unlimited vistas that surrounded Sacramento, and instead she found herself in a broad, curving canyon whose road hugged its steep sides. A glint of sunlight on water revealed the reason she drove so high above the canyon floor. Deep in the gorge, Shasta Lake lapped at the canyon walls.

Maggie slowed her Celica to look. The lake seemed to be endless, fingers of it reaching into all the hollows of the terrain. Here and there she saw evidence of man's affection for the lake. On its sapphire-blue surface scattered motorboats drifted on their tethers like lily pads; houseboats snuggled up to small, pine-covered islands.

Maggie wanted to stop and soak in the view, but she dared not. Gordon Hamilton would be waiting for her promised call. She continued up the canyon, her eyes riveted on the boundless water, her heart wishing there was someone else with her to see what she was seeing.

Oh, Ben.... She lifted her chin and gripped the wheel tighter. *You can't look back.*

Instead of diminishing as she drove, the vista became lovelier. With each upward mile the pines seemed taller, more luxuriant, as if to retain supremacy over the other species of evergreen now crowding between them. Spruce, firs and cedars, each a subtle variant of green, arranged themselves showily at the feet of the stately pines, and Maggie decided she'd never seen one color in so many vibrant hues.

Below, Shasta Lake had reverted to the Sacramento River and become a mere silver thread deep in the canyon.

As Maggie took in the vista she was touched by a strange thought. *A part of me, all these years, must have been dead. Is it that there's been no real beauty in my life, or only that I've never stopped to look?*

In some odd way she felt she was coming home.

The rented car tracked smoothly around broad curves and her mind wandered. Once again she began going over what she must do when she arrived. After the call to Hamilton there'd been appointments to make with others: wilderness buffs, lumbermen, geologists, Indians whose worship included ancestral burial sites on the mountain. She'd take statements from all of them—even the skiers. Even that man Cooper Smith. You couldn't organize a fight without hearing the viewpoint of the opposition. But what an interesting little fracas it promised to be. When Meiers applied for the injunction, he'd be armed with a packet of statements that would convince any judge!

She smiled. It sounded challenging, taking up the torch and marching into battle to save an endangered mountain!

And then, suddenly, she saw it. Off to her right, through a gap between two ridges, she saw the mountain itself. Frosted in snow from its double peak to its broad, pyramidal base, it loomed in the distance like the quintessence of all mountains she'd ever seen. A solitary landmark, it stood lofty and serene. She drew in a deep breath. Somehow she hadn't expected anything like this—that the mountain would be so majestic and so...alone. She felt her foot go down on the gas pedal, felt the car surge forward. The mountain had disappeared behind a ridge and she wanted another view of it before the sun went down.

The canyon narrowed and the climb became steeper. On either side the gorge seemed to close in as though to crush her to itself, while below, the canyon had deepened mysteriously and the river was no longer visible. Abruptly she reached the town of Dunsmuir, a village deep in the crack of the gorge, which she'd claimed before the moon and Mr. Meiers as her one-time home. *Well,* she thought, *it feels like home.*

It was six-thirty on a Sunday evening, the end of March, when Maggie finally saw the town of Mount Shasta. She would always remember the hour, the day and the month when she climbed that last mile, gained the last few feet of altitude and emerged on the town's plateau.

To her right Maggie saw the mountain awesomely close. The twin peaks, so clearly defined and so virginal in their white raiment, had taken on a pinkish glow from the setting sun. The mountain guarded the town. No, she thought, it *was* the town.

Left, and across a broad valley, a whole range of smaller, white-mantled mountains lined the horizon like paper cutouts. Between and above and everywhere the air was clean, so crystalline and so unlike the air at home it seemed to be an entirely different substance.

From her car window, Maggie glanced again at Mount Shasta, then left at the string of cutouts. Was this place real, she wondered. Could this set of opposing mountains—the town between them like a picture incomparably framed—belong to one tiny community?

She took a slow, deep breath. Inexplicably, she sensed that here, on this plateau, her life was about to change.

MAGGIE FOUND HER MOTEL, a small place peeking out hopefully from behind a stand of pines. Her upstairs room was modest: a queen-size bed and bright red Indian rug on a bare wood floor.

At the east window she pulled back the drawn cotton curtains. Yes, it was there, white and gleaming. She smiled.

She sat on the edge of the bed, and having kicked off her high-heeled shoes, dialed Gordon Hamilton.

"When did you get in?" he asked, his impatient tone implying criticism. She got the impression she was already a day late.

"Just now," she said. "This minute."

"A beautiful drive, eh?"

"It was...quite unexpected. Coming up the canyon, the trees—"

"I've got a list," he broke in. "We'll want to go over it tonight, at the meeting."

"What meeting?" Irritated, she let her tone match his, curt and short.

"Eight o'clock. A little debate in town." Apparently responding to her irritation, he toned down. "I hoped you'd get here in time. Important, you know. You have to meet all the—" he laughed shortly "—the fanatics. Might as well know who you're up against. I'll see you there." He gave her the address of the high school.

But you're not about to pick me up, she thought, and then shrugged. To him she wasn't a lady, just a lawyer.

"I'll be there, Mr. Hamilton."

When he'd hung up, Maggie let out a long, slow breath. Whew! A whirlwind. Around him you didn't pause to reflect, not if you were on Hamilton's payroll. You moved. Fast.

Maggie showered and powdered herself with a light

talcum, reveling in its delicate fragrance. Then, because it was chilly in her room—and even colder outside—she unpacked her burgundy cashmere sweater and a lighter-toned, pleated-wool skirt. She debated about shoes. High? Low? She chose high; they flattered her slender legs and made her appear taller than her five foot seven. She had no idea who she'd meet tonight, but she needed to make the best impression she could.

She brushed her thick hair quickly and put on a lipstick the same hue as her sweater.

Pearls?

No pearls. The collared sweater didn't need it.

A touch of rose-tinted eye shadow picked up the tone of her sweater, though she saw that this addition was nearly obscured by the moody fullness of her brows and lashes.

It was dark when Maggie stepped out of the motel. A few lights showed in the distance as she drove down the main street.

Main street, she asked herself. As far as she could see, this was the only street.

She found a small Italian restaurant, and a half hour later, having eaten some delicious manicotti, Maggie emerged and followed Hamilton's directions to the high school.

As she drove, a rounded moon was just becoming visible to the right of the mountain. Maggie parked her car in the school's gravel parking lot and for a moment sat there, absorbing the scene. The moon was growing and promised to be full; its pale light lent a halo to the giant's silhouette, adding a surrealistic dimension, she thought, that the mountain hardly needed.

Reluctantly, she left the car and turned her back on the vista, walking toward the school's back entrance where she could see others approaching a flight of stairs. She crossed the lot and started up the steps behind a very tall man. Then she turned back for a last glimpse of the haloed mountain behind her.

In that moment something knocked her off-balance.

Maggie's feet responded with a couple of quick saving motions, but the steps were narrow, allowing her no room for recovery. She knew she was going to fall.

She swayed, feeling an inevitability about what was coming. Yet somehow, before she quite left the steps, strong arms caught her from above, and she realized the man she'd been following had in some way been the cause of it all.

He held her tight, securing them both until her balance returned. In those brief moments of being in his arms she had an impression of the mountain, the moonlight and the man all at the same time.

CHAPTER TWO

SHE WOULD HAVE KNOWN from his hands alone he was a very large man.

As he supported her, strong and in a way gentle for someone so big, she looked up into his face and saw gray, gray eyes looking down at her, the edges wrinkled slightly in a smile. He said, "Sorry. I should have sounded a bell before I went into reverse. Are you all right?" He still held her, apparently disinclined to let her go.

With a different man she might have pulled away quickly, mumbled something conciliatory and left him. Instead she found herself transfixed by this man's face: faint lines strengthened a certain cragginess; a tiny scar creased his right cheek; his smile was all-encompassing—intense, alive. Above all she had an impression of character...and magnetism, too. She could feel it everywhere.

Then she came to her senses. "Of course I'm all right," she said, and pulled out of his arms. He was just a man. What was the matter with her?

She caught his scent then, a blending of woodsmoke and a sagelike men's cologne. It was the outdoors tinged subtly with masculinity, and it had a disturbing effect on her.

Her pulling away seemed not to bother him, for he guided her up the remaining steps, casually taking her arm. "The meeting's up here," he said, grinning, "and whatever I was going back to the car for doesn't seem important now." When she made no response he added, "Two minutes ago I was in such a rush I nearly knocked you down the stairs. Now I can't remember why the hurry. Can we go back and do the collision part over?" He looked down at her, merriment in the gray eyes, and in spite of her self-admonition, she laughed.

"Just so you'll remember what you forgot?"

"Actually, I thought the collision had a certain merit of its own." His tone was dry, good-humored.

She glanced up at him and saw his strong face relaxed, his expression pleasant. He continued to guide her, his hand on her arm gentle but firm. She felt she'd unwittingly slipped into his sphere of influence, yet she had no desire to leave it.

They were in a long corridor, all dark greens and grays. The place smelled of chalk and tennis shoes and old books, impressions that she absorbed only subliminally, as a background to her thoughts about him. Then she rebuked herself. It was ridiculous, she thought. Foolish. She didn't even know who he was.

As if sensing her thoughts, he slowed and looked down at her. "I'm Cooper Smith."

For just the briefest moment her breath caught with the knowledge. Cooper Smith. And then remembered words came to mind: *"as immovable as the damned mountain."* She gave him a look of recognition. "I've heard of you."

"Well...that's good," he assented, and his smile was warm and faintly quizzical. "I hope that gives me some kind of head start."

Then, since they'd reached the classroom where everyone had gathered, he dropped her arm. "Here's the battleground...." Amused eyes flicked toward the room. "We're off and fighting."

He walked to the front and sat down at a table

where a few others were already seated, and she eased sideways into one of the old-fashioned school desks, which was a desk and seat combined.

Gradually the room filled. As they waited, Maggie's attention was riveted on Cooper's table up front. Seated there was a lone woman, graceful and dark eyed, as well as three other men, one of whom she realized was Gordon Hamilton—he'd nodded at her as she sat down.

Unwittingly her gaze kept returning to Cooper Smith. Reposed comfortably at the small table with his large hands folded in front of him, he seemed too relaxed to be the agitated man described by Hamilton. Maggie decided the only thing about him that held with Hamilton's description was his size. She guessed Smith to be about six foot four.

Studying him, unwanted feelings came back to her, the same heady awareness of his masculinity she'd had when she'd been in his arms. *Maggie,* she rebuked herself.

She stared at him hard. What was so special about him? Why did his face compel her so? Certainly he wasn't handsome, not in the conventional sense. Instead she could see the outdoors on him, the sun and the way it had darkened his face and tracked it here and there with small squint creases, and the wind bringing disorder to his sandy hair. He wore a soft blue shirt—a fine wool, she guessed—which seemed wrong for him, too much an indoors shirt and not quite broad enough in the shoulders nor heavy enough for the elements. It struck her as odd that she should be critical of his clothes, a stranger whom she'd just met. Yet that was how he appeared to her.

The chairman rose from the small table and tapped a water glass with a ruler. The talking quieted.

"We'd better get started, folks. It may be a long

evening." He had a thin face and rimless glasses. "I'm Dick Larson," he began, grinning amiably, "for the few of you who don't already know." Maggie saw that his grin was wholehearted and a little lopsided.

Larson studied the crowd. "Seems we've drawn half the town tonight. Wish we could get you all out when we're discussing buying snowplows." Scattered laughter.

"Since the issue of skiing on Mount Shasta seems to interest everyone so much, this informal meeting will give you all a chance to air your views." With a half turn toward the table, he lifted an eyebrow. "You know how these folks feel. They'll address the issues briefly, but it's you we'd like to hear from."

Larson inclined his head as a tall woman in the back stood up. In a shrill voice she asked, "Why are we here, Dick? It's obvious the special interests won't pay the slightest attention to what we long-time residents want!" Her inflammatory statement provoked a murmur of approval and scattered clapping. Maggie realized that most of the crowd agreed with her.

Larson donned a patient smile. "If the town was entirely united on this, I think we'd prevail. Unfortunately, it's not."

"It's only the outsiders who think they know what's best for this place!" someone shouted. "Outsiders and newcomers!"

With that, Gordon Hamilton stood up. In spite of the graying wings at the sides of his face, he exuded youthful energy and impatience. He extended an orator's hand toward the audience. "What happens to this mountain goes beyond the narrow interests of the town. Way beyond." He paused for dramatic effect, eyeing individuals in the crowd as though to keep them focused on his face. "This mountain doesn't belong to a few thousand residents who happen to live at its base. I say it belongs to the whole state of California, in fact to the entire United States. What happens here, in this area of the country, in some way determines what will happen to other mountains in other places. You destroy and despoil this magnificent peak and you potentially destroy all similar mountains." Again he paused, this time looking intently at a man who was scribbling vigorously into the pages of a notebook. A reporter, Maggie guessed, taking down the eloquent words of Gordon Hamilton. Hamilton went on, "And I say again as I've said in the past, a horde of skiers and ski lifts and trails and resorts and condominiums will destroy this mountain as surely as a volcanic eruption. And we don't have another one of those due for at least three hundred years!" He sat down to silence. A few people applauded fervently, but to Maggie they seemed outnumbered. In spite of the clapping, she sensed a still-stronger current of outright hostility.

Before the applause had died away, a quiet, deep voice made itself heard. Maggie realized with a start that Cooper Smith was talking. His offhand manner effectively silenced the crowd. Looking around, she saw the audience straining to hear. "You know," he said, "it's a funny thing the way I've been skiing on that mountain for twenty-one years, leaving my tracks all over the place...darn near covered the whole mountain at one time or another...and I've never once been able to go back and see where I've been! And Charlie here," he continued, indicating a monkish-looking man who sat at the end, "I'm sure Charlie's been wherever I haven't and a lot of places I have, and I've never found any traces of him, either."

Laughter erupted and someone shouted, "Let'em have it, Cooper!"

His manner still offhand, Cooper added, "Of course, Charlie and I are the lucky ones. We've not only seen the mountain up close, we've been there in the trees. We've touched it and felt it and breathed its air and lived with it. That makes us unique. Most of you have only seen it."

Maggie realized Hamilton was agitated. He rose again, said, "Multiply yourself by a hundred thousand bodies, Smith," and sat down again.

Cooper Smith merely shrugged.

Of the two of them, Maggie thought Cooper Smith seemed to have the upper hand. Yet he was so casual, hardly the bullheaded individual she'd been warned about. Which proved, she reasoned, that personality was a matter of individual perception.

For the next two hours, townspeople expressed their opinions while Maggie listened, absorbed. After one particularly vehement declaration she turned to the woman next to her—tightly curled red hair above the turned-up collar of a mackinaw—and asked, "Who was that?"

The woman whispered back, "Wilderness man. A maniac."

After the next speaker the woman offered, "He's Forest Service."

Maggie nodded gratefully, and from then on the woman gave her periodic updates. "That one's crazy." "Here's the principal of our elementary school."

Quickly Maggie saw this wasn't going to be the easy task she'd envisioned. Gordon Hamilton had intimated only crackpots opposed the environmentalist stance. Now, having recognized on both sides a fervor that bordered on fanaticism, Maggie understood this simply wasn't true. She was grateful for the voices that spoke with reason and quiet logic, but she also realized lunacy was everywhere, which meant she'd have to be selective in taking her statements. She didn't want old man Meiers embarrassed in front of a judge.

With the evening drawing to a close, the lone woman at the table spoke up. She had an intelligent face—warm, with liquid brown eyes. "As most of you know, I've lived in this town all my life except for the medical-school years. When you go away and come back, you realize how special the place is. As a sometime skier, I really don't care, personally, whether you bring skiing here or not. But whatever you do, please, please, proceed carefully. Set up an architectural committee so the new buildings will fit the character of the town. You can have development and still keep beauty, you know...if you make sure the growth's consistent and alpine to fit the mountain...if you don't cut down too many trees." She smiled, her flawless skin aglow. "Actually, I'd like to see some growth here—so others can come to love this place as I do."

Just as Maggie was wondering who the woman was, her informant leaned close again. "Anne Smith. Cooper Smith's sister. They all love her. She's a lady doctor."

Maggie smiled, amused. No doubt a similar tag would identify her: Maggie McAllister—a lady lawyer.

Suddenly the meeting was over and everyone moved toward the punch bowl and plates of cookies that had appeared at another table. Maggie sat in her seat for a moment watching Cooper Smith, so easily spotted in a crowd, as he made his way toward the refreshments. She found herself admiring the graceful way he moved. In some ways he seemed the doyen of the crowd, as much above them all in manner as he was in size. Then she reminded herself she was here for one thing only: to do a job and do it well.

Gordon Hamilton approached her desk. "So...you see what we're up against." He spoke in a confidential manner. "The other side is getting more strident by the day."

Maggie stood. "Let's go out in the hall."

Hamilton's even brows rose in question, but he followed her as she explored the hall and led him into a side passage. "You see," she explained, smiling, "the opposition won't talk freely if they know what side I'm on."

"Any reason you have to talk to the opposition?" At close range Hamilton's handsome face had a certain hardness that Maggie hadn't noticed earlier. From the speaker's platform he'd exuded nothing but uncomplicated sincerity.

For a moment she considered her answer. Hamilton wasn't, after all, a lawyer. "You get some of your best help from opponents," she said. "They're the ones who reveal the weakness in their position. Strong advocates rarely see the other side clearly."

He seemed impatient. "Well, the skiers have enough crackpots to satisfy anyone. You won't have any trouble blasting holes in their arguments." He shifted position, moving closer to her. "Would you care to have a drink with me, Miss McAllister? This isn't the most comfortable place to talk." He patted his briefcase. "My list is in here."

"Why don't you just give it to me?"

"No. I'm sorry. We need to discuss each person. Some are reluctant to open up unless you approach them right. I'd like you to take notes." Behind him, Maggie could see people leaving. She wondered if Cooper had gone yet. She hoped to talk to him soon, rationalizing that his was the most reasoned opinion for the opposition, and therefore the attitude she'd have to try and understand before assembling her statements.

"Miss McAllister?" Hamilton said, and she realized she'd been unnaturally silent. "The drink?"

She considered. *Oh, damn.* She ought to, but...

Suddenly she was tired and didn't feel like pursuing this any further. "Would you mind?" she asked. "It's been a long trip. May I meet you tomorrow?"

He shrugged. Then he smiled graciously, briefly. "Of course. I get rather caught up in it, I'm afraid. Tomorrow, then? Why don't you call me?" He inclined his distinguished head toward her.

As he turned to go, she said, "Mr. Hamilton, don't worry. We'll make this good." She smiled at him reassuringly. "We'll assemble enough strong statements to ensure an airtight case. I'm sure we'll get the injunction."

He stopped. An odd, quirky smile came to his mouth. "I don't want it good, Miss McAllister. I want it spectacular."

He left.

She followed slowly, baffled. In this strange man she'd sensed a kind of determination that went beyond the obvious. Could the mountain really matter to him that much? Somehow she'd always associated environmentalists with idealists, but Gordon Hamilton didn't seem the idealistic type at all. Oddly, of all of them, she'd vote Cooper Smith the man most likely to defend the mountain. She shook her head. It was a strange cast of characters, all in the wrong roles.

At the juncture of the halls, Maggie made a quick decision. Instead of turning toward the exit, she went back toward the classroom. Maybe, by some bit of luck, Cooper Smith would still be there.

She found him in the room. His back was to her and he was picking up paper cups and dropping them in a basket. Only he and a young boy, about thirteen, and a few others remained.

She touched his arm.

He turned, and seeing her, smiled. The little lines on

his face expanded and encompassed the whole of his eyes and his mouth. The scar creased further. He exuded warmth, and in spite of his weather-touched face. . . class! The effect on her was instantaneous and overwhelming, and she found her pulse quickening. "Mr. Smith," she began, hearing her change of mood mirrored in her voice, "I need to talk to you."

"Well, that's good. Because I need to talk to you, too—about navigating those stairs." He looked down at her, teasing. "You'll need an escort."

She laughed. "You?"

"Me." He put out his arm.

She took it.

But then he said, "Wait a minute," and turned back. She heard him call, "Anne," and saw his sister turn questioningly. "Anne, would you do me a very big favor?"

"Anything."

"Take Jesse home."

"Of course."

Smith said, "See you at home, Jesse," and the boy nodded.

Maggie looked at the child, dark haired with small-boned features and an eager expression—appealing, she thought—and she looked at the father and knew he'd gotten his mother's looks. She also knew that whatever she'd hoped for subconsciously was coming up short. No good. No good at all. Her spirits plummeted. At the very best, Cooper Smith had a son, an obvious complication. At the worst he had a son and a wife.

Damn, she thought. *Oh, damn.* How quickly the game changes. How suddenly the ball ricochets into the wrong court.

When Cooper Smith again offered her his arm, she took it, her head held high to mask her disappointment. *Back to business, Maggie,* she thought. *On with the original game.*

He led her down the hall. "I don't know your name."

"Maggie. Maggie McAllister."

He smiled down at her. "It has a poetic ring. Maggie McAllister. I like it. It fits you."

"Thank you, Mr. Smith."

She felt him pause. "I don't know anyone who calls me Mr. Smith. No one in this whole town."

She smiled up at him impishly, forgetting the situation. "Perhaps I shall, then."

His other hand came up to cover hers where it rested on his arm. She'd never have imagined that such a simple gesture could be so heady, so intimate. Something in her responded and she felt her limbs grow weak and her breathing change, but she knew at the same time it was madness, utter madness. She'd known this man only a few hours. And he was probably married. The absence of a ring meant nothing.

They were down the stairs, standing outside the building. They'd both stopped walking.

She looked beyond him to the full moon, saw the mountain glowing in its light, and felt a sense of beauty, of infinite peace so overwhelming it almost brought her to tears. He caught her look, standing with her in the gravel parking lot holding her hand, and he seemed to sense her mood, for he gazed down at her and silently let the minutes pass.

It was wrong, she thought. None of it fit. It wasn't what she was here for. Somehow she had to break the mood.

"Mr. Smith. . ." she began.

He laughed, and his voice was low and resonant. "Maggie," he responded, and then added, "what was it you wanted to say to me?"

"I thought—" she started, but he broke in.

"Look," he said, "whatever it is, don't tell me here. This is a small town and there's nothing open in March. But a few miles away, in Weed, there's an all-night diner. Let me take you there. I want to know you better. Except for our names, Maggie, we're strangers."

"I might be married," she offered. "Or you might be."

"I'm not married, Maggie, and I already checked on you. When you find a woman in your arms, a ring is the first thing you look for."

Enormous relief flowed through her and she smiled. "Women put rings in their purses."

"But you wouldn't."

She didn't answer. Instead she looked past him at the shadowy mountain, at the nearby pines that hummed a night song in the wind. Suddenly she felt defiant. "Why do you think you know me so well? As you said, we're strangers."

"We are. But I know you wouldn't put your wedding ring in your purse." His flat statement closed the subject. "Shall we go, Maggie?"

Reason and hard practicality caught up with her all at once. This wasn't the way to begin a business trip, taking a moonlight drive with someone from the opposing side. She had a job to do. She was a lawyer.

Maggie shook her head and knew another objection, a more important one. In his presence she was losing her sense of direction.

"You won't go," he said quietly, and the statement was without anger, even without disappointment. It was as though he was above such things, as though he had a kind of unreasonable confidence both in himself and in her. "But you still want to talk to me," he said. "Tell me where you're staying. I'll pick you up tomorrow."

"I may sleep late." She said it unexpectedly, and then felt annoyed. Was she hoping he'd beg her? The wind increased, cold against her face. The night had a high-mountain chill.

Without responding, he took her arm and led her to her car. "Call me when you're ready," he said. "I'm the only Cooper Smith in Mount Shasta." He opened her car door, waited, then closed it after her. When she drove away, silently cursing her stupidity for leaving him there in the moonlight when she might be with him this minute, another voice brought her up short. *This man and your career are on a collision course.*

CHAPTER THREE

SHE SLEPT only half a night and woke before daylight, thinking his name. Cooper Smith. The very sound of it was both common and very uncommon, and it seemed to fit him perfectly.

She turned, and the cold night air touched her shoulders as she moved, then crept down beneath the covers. It was a different cold than any she'd experienced at home. Sharper. And with a redolence, too, like pine needles.

She lay there in the darkness and thought about him, feeling again his presence, as though he was in her room. There was so much life to him, just being with him had heightened all her senses so she'd managed only the lightest sleep. And now she was awake.

She thought about Ben after a while, too. Calling his sharp face and colorless hair to mind, she realized he'd been diminished—whited out by a brighter light. And just as well, since he despised her.

She rolled over in bed, willing herself back to sleep. But images of Ben kept coming to mind: the good times they'd had going to plays at the Los Angeles Music Center, and Ben playing critic on the way home and amusing her with his slightly sarcastic reviews. "A marvelous first act, if you're into watching two people spend twenty minutes asking each other, 'How *are* you?' " She'd always laughed at Ben's waspish sense of humor, and realized that she'd miss him most as a friend.

She pulled the covers in closer. Friends could be tough to lose. Harder, maybe, than lovers. The things you shared with someone's mind—the odd bits of humor, the little insights—those things left traces, darn it, small poignant memories. *Ben, if you'd just been a little more tolerant...* Then she chastised herself. How much tolerance was he supposed to extend her, anyway, and why was she putting the blame on him?

She fell asleep again, finally, and woke to sunlight slanting in around her curtains. She stretched and yawned. Cooper Smith. Ben. In the morning light her thoughts swiveled back to normal, and she dismissed her predawn sentiments as one shrugs off the hazy fragments of a dream. It was her first full day here. She had a great deal of work to do.

She jumped out of bed and pulled the curtains aside to view the mountain. With the sun behind it, Shasta was like an eclipsed moon, half in shadow. Yet it had a grandeur that was seeping into her soul. She'd come here not caring about it personally, concerned only with the effect this fight would have on her career. Suddenly, staring at the twin peaks, she wanted them left alone. Let the skiers go elsewhere.

Quickly Maggie showered and dressed warmly in gray wool slacks and a soft, blue-gray mohair sweater. Then she sat on the edge of the bed, spiral notebook in hand, and flipped through the phone book. As Cooper had said, he was the only Cooper Smith in town.

She jotted his number on the first page of her notebook, but she couldn't bring herself to dial it. She knew he'd be waiting, and she could almost hear his rich, warm voice. Then why didn't she call him? She didn't know.

An inner voice said, *Call him, Maggie,* but instead she dialed Gordon Hamilton at the College of the Siskiyous. His secretary came on with pleasant efficiency. "Professor Hamilton has been waiting to hear from you. Unfortunately he had to take someone else's class this morning. He asked me to make a luncheon date. Would twelve-thirty be acceptable?"

Maggie glanced at her watch. "Yes, I suppose it would."

Afterward she realized she had three hours to kill. Not quite enough time to make—and keep—another appointment, but too much time to waste. Anyway, Hamilton had made it clear he wanted to discuss all her appointments first. She decided to take a walk into town, find someplace for coffee.

As she picked up her purse and started for the door, the phone rang. Who, besides Hamilton, knew she was here?

She answered questioningly and heard, "Hello, Maggie."

It was Cooper Smith, his voice exactly as she'd imagined it would be. She felt her face grow warm.

"Is this your 'puzzled' voice, Maggie?"

"Yes." She smiled. "Nobody knows where I am. How did you find me?"

"One of the advantages of a very small town. It's not hard to call all five motels. What are you doing this morning? Have you had breakfast?"

She hesitated. "No. I was about to go look for someplace."

"Good. Come down the stairs, then. I'll meet you at the bottom."

"You're here?" she gasped, and stared at her door. Next he'd be walking into her room.

He must have read her thoughts. "I could come to your room, I suppose, except I might not want to leave. Better that we meet where I said."

His suggestive words had their effect on her. She felt

anticipation wash over her like a tidal wave. She wanted to rush out the door and down the stairs and throw herself into his arms, to soak up his strength and his energy. She wanted to feel his body against hers. And this time it wouldn't be an accident. Again he seemed to know what she was thinking, for he said, "Or perhaps we could repeat our hugging on the stairs."

She laughed and her mind reeled. They were communicating on some strange level where he answered aloud her unspoken thoughts. Who was this stranger who was beginning to invade not only her emotions, but her mind?

"Let me grab a jacket, Cooper. And I guess I should tell you. . . I only have until noon."

"What then. . . you lose your slipper, or your coach becomes a pumpkin?"

She smiled. "Mr. Smith, if you don't let me go, we'll spend all our time on the phone."

HE STOOD AT THE BOTTOM of the stairs, looking up at her. His sandy hair looked carefully brushed, but his sweater was plainly old, a bulky Irish cable knit. It seemed right for him: comfortable and unpretentious. His gray eyes warmed at the sight of her, and the scar dimpled inward slightly as he smiled. "Maggie!" He held out his hand.

When she took it, he placed his other hand over hers, and she felt as if he was someone she'd waited for all her life. Looking up at him, she absorbed the vitality in his face, and just the sight of him gave her pleasure.

She wanted the moment to last indefinitely, the two of them looking at each other. But of course it couldn't. Some remnant of her pride and ambition rose up and demanded to be heard. She pulled her hand out of his.

For a moment he gazed down at her from his great height. "If you don't want me to touch you, try not to look at me, Maggie. With those incredible eyes you could buy the world."

How odd. With other men she'd used her eyes deliberately to gain some end—the Shasta assignment from old man Meiers; an invitation to dinner when her funds were low—whatever she happened to need at the time. If she didn't watch out for herself, no one else would. But now, with Cooper Smith, she'd been oblivious of her eyes, conscious only of him.

In a moment he was helping her into his four-wheel-drive Wagoneer, which was large and comfortable as he was, and painted conservatively in cocoa brown and a contrasting light tan. As she was climbing in she noticed something else: a tiny stripe of burnt orange slipped between the tan and cocoa, almost unnoticeable. Like him, she thought—it was that stripe of orange that got you.

He took her down the main street of Mount Shasta, and seeing it for the first time in daylight she was surprised all over again at how little was there. The whole town seemed to be only a few blocks long, and most of it had obviously been built at least fifty years ago. Attempts had been made, here and there, to add a facade over the old lines, but the place still had that row-house look of a western town of the thirties. The only thing that distinguished one establishment from another was its roof, sitting atop the building like a square hat.

With a light gesture Cooper said, "The main street, in all its ancient glory. If you like 'old,' Maggie, you'll love this town. I have some of my grandmother's pictures. Most of the buildings are still recognizable."

He turned left and as the road sloped downward, she could see meadows and forests and beyond them the range of cutout mountains, gleaming white. "So beautiful," she murmured, and he threw her a quick glance.

"The Eddy range," he explained. "My ranch is near the foot of Mount Eddy. But my view is Mount Shasta. The mountains become part of your psyche, I suppose. Any separation literally hurts." He smiled at her. "You'll see."

Abruptly he turned left again and they arrived at a small shopping center. "Our claim to the modern world," he said. He parked the wagon in front of an orange-painted restaurant, less impressive than the sign reading Perko's, which towered over it on a thirty-foot pole. Without fanfare he came around and helped her out.

Even at quarter to ten, the air had a feel of frost, and the sun, almost painfully bright in the clear atmosphere, lent more light than warmth. She looked up and saw the sky was an intense cobalt blue.

She shook her head. "You must be used to the sky looking like this. I'm not."

Standing beside her, waiting for her to proceed him into the restaurant, he said quietly, "I've never taken beauty for granted." By the way he said it and the way he looked at her, she knew the words had a double meaning. Hurrying ahead of him, she tried to shake off what was happening to her. It was all so wrong and certainly at odds with what she'd intended for this trip.

Inside the roomy restaurant, bright with alternating orange and magenta booths, Maggie automatically indicated her preference for a window table and a view of the Eddy range. Certainly this would be a good time to probe Cooper's attitudes on skiing. It had to be done eventually. Unless she could stare at the Eddies, she'd have to look at him, and that prospect seemed very distracting. This trip was not turning out as she'd expected. Why, suddenly, did Meiers, Meiers, DeCaro and Kosinski seem so far away?

As soon as they were seated, Cooper leaned toward her across the table, his expression reflective. "How long have I known you, Maggie? Twenty-four hours? No, less than that. I find it hard to remember, now, what I felt or thought about yesterday before I wheeled on those stairs and caught you in my arms. Yet what do I know about you? Nothing, except your name." He smiled ruefully. "Normally I think like any man. Only the facts matter. How have I arrived at a situation in which the facts don't seen important at all? You could tell me you're anything...a doctor, a lawyer, a banker, a janitor. I don't think I'd care. Three times married with seven kids at home. A grandmother. Maggie, how do I explain to myself that the substance of things felt is suddenly a hundred times more important than the sum of things known?"

"Oh, Cooper." She stared at him helplessly. "Don't look at me like that, I—"

The waitress arrived and Maggie broke off. Cooper ordered bacon and eggs and hash browns and then said, to her astonishment, "And she'll have a Spanish omelet." He finished, "And two coffees."

The woman bustled away on thick legs and Maggie let her eyes follow, shaking her head. "Why did you order me a Spanish omelet? It's beginning to seem like witchcraft, Cooper. That's my favorite breakfast."

He shrugged. "I don't know how I knew...what told me." The gray eyes bored into her. "So who are you, Maggie? I must learn eventually."

"I'm a lawyer," she said, and was grateful that he didn't seem surprised. "I work for a large firm in Los Angeles. Meiers, Meiers, DeCaro and Kosinski. It's a general practice, and I'm the most junior member. Except for one." The memory of Ben brought a small frown to her brows. "The two of us—we handle whatever they give us." *Or whatever we push for,* she thought wryly. As she saw his eyes on her, she immediately rationalized, *well, why not, it's a competitive world.*

She was about to lead the conversation around to him when he asked, "You've been married, Maggie?"

"No. Never. I haven't had the time." She smiled. "Or the desire. And you?"

"Yes. My wife was killed in a car accident south of Dunsmuir."

"I'm sorry."

"Thank you." He gazed past her, over her shoulder. "I'm used to it now. It was a long time ago. Almost six years. Still, I'm glad you and I didn't meet earlier. I wasn't really normal for a while. I loved her a great deal. After she was gone, there wasn't much I cared about. I—"

"But you had her son."

"No." He shook his head. "There weren't any children. Jesse is Laura's younger brother. Laura's parents died in the same accident. Jesse had no one, so I took him."

Maggie murmured sympathetically, touched by Jesse's plight and the act of selflessness Cooper could have escaped so easily. How many men would have done it? Yet she made no comment, deciding one didn't compliment a man on his instincts. Cooper was what he was.

"Jesse helped," he went on, "though I wouldn't have predicted it. Thinking about him took my mind off Laura."

Their breakfasts came and she began taking bites of her omelet, a delicious concoction. Surreptitiously she glanced at her watch. Ten-twenty. It was time to begin her work. Casually she asked, "What's your real reason for wanting skiing on Mount Shasta?"

"Real reason?" He looked surprised. "I didn't explain myself very well last night, I guess. First, Maggie, it's a silly fight we're engaged in. Everyone takes it too seriously. Especially that man Hamilton, whose motives are unclear. Lately he's been beating his drum and making speeches like he's running a campaign. I don't like him. Perhaps because I don't trust him. Whatever his reasons, he's dead wrong. Skiing's not going to hurt that mountain."

"How can you be so sure, Cooper? They'll cut down trees and put up chair lifts and—"

He started to laugh. "Maggie, they've been cutting trees on that mountain for years, doing it selectively, and Shasta's none the worse for it. Even the Forest Service is beginning to see that a few ski trails in the heavy timber won't hurt logging operations on their leased land. Might help, in fact. But it's hard to change your mind publicly." He paused to study her thoughtfully. "Maggie," he said, "you're beautiful."

She actually blushed. He'd surprised her, complimenting her out of the blue. She turned her face away, hoping he hadn't noticed. In the next moments she played with her napkin and pushed her food around a little. When she finally looked up he was still studying her and she found herself gazing straight into his eyes. What she saw there was almost more than she could stand. The intensity of his look obliterated her appetite and made her yearn to touch him. She said, "Cooper...don't!"

"I've never met a woman like you. Ever. Even the first night I knew it. Tell me something, Maggie. What were you doing at the meeting? Why did you come to Mount Shasta?"

The wrong question, she thought. But it had to come. What should she say? If she told him the truth, that she was actually here to get an injunction against his cherished skiing, he'd be guarded in his statements. Even worse, if he knew she was working for Hamilton... Inwardly she shuddered, knowing how much he'd hate that. *Quick, Maggie, say something.*

She forced a smile. "I'm...writing. Writing an article about environmentalist causes." She tried to sound casual but detected the false note in her own voice.

And then she felt it. Her hands were shaking. She clasped them together, looking quickly to see if he'd noticed.

He had. He said, "Why Maggie, you're trembling." He tried to take one of her hands, but before he could touch her, she'd put them in her lap.

"It's nothing," she said lightly. "It happens."

With surprise she watched his face change, his concern covered with a look of calm acceptance, as though he were letting go and giving her the privacy she wanted. The moment passed, and she knew he wouldn't ask her about the trembling again.

Even so, she was angry at him, angry that he'd been a witness to her lying, seen the evidence of her imperfection. Why did he have to remind her that they were so different, he so magnanimous and she...she couldn't bear to admit what she was.

With the strong will she could summon when she had to, she put aside her self-recriminations and wrenched her mind back to what she must do. They were wasting time. She needed to start homing in on the issues important to her case.

While he finished his breakfast, Maggie drank her coffee and momentarily gazed out the window. If they hadn't been sitting in this modern café she'd believe they were at the furthest reaches of civilization. Outside, the stands of pines and distant mountains were as much at odds with the orange vinyl seats of the restaurant as a Hilton Hotel would be in Shangri-la.

She said, "Won't skiing change all this, Cooper, this virginal look of the area? Surely you don't want it spoiled by hordes of outsiders."

He leaned back in his chair and wiped his mouth with a napkin. "Maggie, have you ever seen people wiped out by poverty?"

"What do you mean?"

"Children in this town are suffering. They—" seeing her expression, a quick, involuntary grimace—he stopped. "Oh, they're not actually starving, Maggie, not in the sense of beggars, but the lumber industry has fallen off these past years, and families are destitute. They're losing their homes. The town, the whole area, is slowly dying. Tourists are needed to bring money. As beautiful as the area is, you can't eat scenery."

He leaned forward urgently. "But that's not all, Maggie. Even beyond explaining what the area needs economically, I'm trying to tell you that people won't hurt the mountain! Why shouldn't others enjoy it as we do? How will it suffer? You can't bulldoze away fourteen thousand feet of granite!"

He regarded her contemplatively. "Do you know who uses the mountain now, who really sees it up close in all its beauty? Mostly men. The hardy few between twenty and forty who are sturdy enough to backpack into the wilderness. So we preserve the whole thing for them. Is that fair? And the rest of the population, why they can be damned, they don't deserve to be there."

He shook his head. "No, Maggie, it's not right. In one way I agree with Hamilton. That mountain belongs to everyone." He arranged his fork and knife on the edge of his plate. "Except Hamilton takes a lopsided view. For him it's all look but don't touch.

"Well." He smiled, his casualness returning. "I've given you the whole lecture, haven't I? A strange way to entertain a lady at breakfast. It wasn't what I wanted to talk about."

"Maybe not, but it's what I wanted to hear." She tossed her dark hair back. "I'll tell you right now I disagree with you. Before I got here, Cooper, I didn't care much about the issues. I was, well, I was doing a job, that's all. The mountain meant little to me personally. I'd heard of it, of course, but I'd never seen it, so it was just a place. A name on a map." She drew in a long breath.

"And then I saw it for myself, Cooper, just at dusk. I saw the way it turned pink in the setting sun and the way it seemed to stand there like some kind of monument that was eternal and would be here after I died and after my children died. And I had these feelings that maybe it didn't really belong to us, but to some higher power. Oh, I can't really say exactly what I mean, but I knew I didn't want anything to change it. . . ever.

"And I'll tell you honestly, Cooper, I don't want you skiing on it, or me. . . or even more, the hordes of people who will be coming here if they build ski lifts." She paused. "I'm sorry about those people who are out of work." She lowered her head meditatively. "The children. They shouldn't be the ones to pay, so I don't know the answer, honestly. But I do know there's only one mountain."

For long moments his gaze went past her, out the window. Then he said, "It's true, Maggie, there's only one mountain. But you'll have to let me show you that it's not as frail as you imagine. It won't change in the hands of skiers. Even ten thousand of us would be incapable of altering it."

He stopped suddenly, his eyes on her face. He went on, "I must not have been looking at you just now, when I was on my soapbox. You're distracting, Maggie."

"I don't mean to be."

"You can't help it. It's nothing you do. Some inner largess of spirit."

Her anger returned. What did he think she was? Why was he idealizing her, when she could never live up to what he thought? Why was he trying to force her into an ill-fitting mold?

She stared at him with hard eyes. They couldn't go on this way, the great Cooper Smith dreaming that Maggie McAllister was some kind of angel. She had to shatter his illusions or be forever uncomfortable in his presence, so she said, "I lied to you a few minutes ago."

To her great astonishment, he didn't react, but merely waited.

"Didn't you hear me? I lied! I'm not writing an article. I never was. I didn't come here to be impartial about this environmentalist thing, Cooper. I'm being paid to hurt you. If you want to know the bloody truth, I'm working for Gordon Hamilton!"

His gray eyes widened and seemed to take on unfathomable depths. "Damn!"

Though his gaze seemed to be probing her intently, she could see conflicting emotions reflected in the gray—hurt, perhaps. She wasn't sure what else. And she thought he'd be angrier than he was, maybe stand up immediately and escort her out of the restaurant. But he sat quite still, and she noticed the color had drained from his face.

"So that's who you are."

"Yes."

His internal struggle continued. He was trying hard not to condemn her. It was all so obvious.

Somehow that made her angrier still, mostly at herself because she wasn't what he'd expected. How dare he saddle her with his impossible ideals?

"So you're wrong about me," she went on. "I'm not a big person at all. I'm. . . I'm puny."

She would never understand how he reconciled what she'd said with what he'd expected, or what changed when she made that idiotic last statement.

She only knew he was the oddest man she'd ever met. Because right after she told him she was puny, Cooper Smith laughed.

CHAPTER FOUR

MAGGIE SAT IMMOBILE watching Smith across the table. The laughter was still on his lips, but dying slowly from his eyes.

Strange, she thought, that he'd chosen that ridiculous statement to laugh at. She hadn't meant to be funny. "Puny" was such a silly word. But sitting across from Cooper Smith she'd managed, in a short couple of hours, to say all kinds of things she hadn't intended. She pursed her lips, holding back any response to his good-natured laughter. She'd already let herself come too far with him.

"You don't see the humor in yourself, do you Maggie?" He leaned toward her a little. "But I wouldn't expect you to. You're *inside*, and I'm out here, observing."

Absently, he picked up his empty coffee cup and rotated it slowly in his fingers. "You have a job to do, and I expect you've got to do it any way you can." His gray eyes rose to meet hers momentarily. "Even lying if need be. Which must strike you as the only way to get information, I suppose. Making up a cover. But I noticed you couldn't keep it up long." The cup continued its slow rotation. "I wouldn't have thought so. I'd have figured you'd have problems with lying." He set the cup down and looked at her hard. "Even so, it took guts to tell me, didn't it?"

"No." A pause. "Yes, of course." She felt her control returning. "I do what I have to do in each new situation." She gave him an appraising look, hoping he would see her as the restrained, businesslike attorney. "I'm afraid you turned the tables on me, Cooper. Instead of my drawing you out, you managed to elicit opinions from me. You made me. . ." She hesitated. "You actually worked on my emotions. It was a kind of mutual-confession session, wasn't it? And of the two of us, I got carried away." She tried to keep her voice light and impersonal. Perhaps he would never know she'd finally admitted the truth to him only because he'd made her angry. He'd exposed her vulnerability by seeing her as something she wasn't.

How would she ever succeed if she persisted in taking the nuances of each of her business relationships personally? This was the accusation that men always leveled at women in traditionally male professions—that they couldn't separate their feelings from their work.

Well, she wouldn't be accused of that!

She folded her napkin neatly and lifted her chin. "I have a job to do, Cooper, and I'm going to see that I accomplish it for our law firm. So I think it's best if we don't see each other anymore. You have your opinions of this area and what should be done with the mountain, and I have mine. And my attitude happens to coincide with the work I'm being paid to do."

She could see him watching her through this determined little speech, his gray eyes attentive but his expression noncommittal. Was he laughing at her? Did he think she was merely posturing?

When he waited without comment, she went on, working at her professionalism. "I know your opinions quite well, and in fact I have most of the information I came to get." She gave him a calculated smile. "Everything you said will be used against you."

He smiled back. "You know, Maggie, somehow

that doesn't worry me. In fact, now that we're known adversaries, we may see each other more, which sounds like a rather good idea."

"No. I don't think it will work that way—"

"And before you get started, I'll throw out a challenge. Eventually there will be skiing here and the mountain will be used as it should be, which will happen no matter what you do." He smiled. "But you'll be paid for it, either way, so you won't lose—however the case comes out."

"I don't work just for money!"

"Well. I'm glad to hear you say that, because I never thought you did. I just didn't think you knew it." He stood up and waited for her to slide out of the booth. Then, with his hand against her shoulder, he guided her toward the door. "In the meantime, I'm glad you've come to town to fight me."

She walked a little faster, escaping his hand. No matter what she said he seemed to be in control, always with that abominable confidence in her, a sureness that was unshakable and infuriating. And he continually threw her. It made her furious.

When they reached the door, she turned. "You aren't going to like what I do, Cooper. So there's no point in trying to butter me up. It won't get you anywhere, and you'll hate yourself later." She looked at her watch. "Blast it, I'm late! Gordon Hamilton will have a fit!" She hurried ahead of him and pushed through the door.

Behind her she heard Cooper Smith's dry reply: "That man is quite capable of having a fit whether you're late or not."

THEY SAID LITTLE going back in the Wagoneer. Maggie had the feeling he was waiting her out, unperturbed. The thought galled her but she couldn't think of any way to shake his calm, so she rode in stony silence.

Cooper left her at the foot of the stairs and waved goodbye casually.

In an unpleasant frame of mind, Maggie applied lipstick and dashed to her car.

Gordon Hamilton's directions were good. She drove through the town of Mount Shasta and started down the long incline toward the town of Weed. Staring across the highway and beyond, she saw nothing but Cooper Smith's face—earnest, and worse, honest—looking at her as if she were different, not Maggie McAllister, but someone else, another woman who was better than she was.

She felt awkward and ill at ease, as if balanced precariously on a fragile limb. At any moment it would bend and she would topple off.

The verdant forest followed the road for a short distance, then gradually thinned. Maggie navigated the curving highway with her mind only half on what she was doing. She observed that Mount Shasta seemed to be some kind of curious dropping-off point, beyond which the forest and the dense undergrowth gradually changed character. She seemed to be losing altitude, too.

Her gaze traveled across a vast, open area to the Eddy range in the distance, and she found herself longing for the town she'd left and the familiar view of the mountain, the angle that showed its two peaks as markedly discrete. The farther north she went, the more the peaks seemed to merge.

I act like I'm part of that mountain, she thought, and shook her head in surprise, then tightened her lips determinedly and focused her eyes on the road. Impossible. This was not what she was here for, to get involved emotionally with the area. What nonsense. The mountain was a hunk of granite, nothing more. The fact that she'd become so absorbed with it the past two days must have been a temporary weakness. And her fascination with him was a weakness, too.

Maggie found herself driving faster and looking at the speedometer; she saw the needle climbing toward seventy. Too fast. She lightened the pressure of her foot on the gas pedal. Escape in a speeding car was no answer. An accident would certainly work against her career!

Finding the sign that pointed her to College of the Siskiyous, she turned left under the freeway and followed a residential road to the school.

To her surprise, the low, graceful campus that spread out to her left was modern and beautiful. The township of Mount Shasta had seemed so old and untouched by time, she had supposed this would be a vintage college, as well. Instead, small new buildings dotted a vast lawn, each structure set in its own frame of pine trees. Unlike the buildings of any campus she'd seen before, these were salmon-colored stucco topped with red roofs, giving the whole place a pinkish cast. Even the large facings of stone worked artfully into the structures did little to offset the impression that an Ivy League setting had somehow acquired a salmon-colored school.

Circling the campus, Maggie passed an ungainly steel sculpture decorating the grass, and she slowed to look at it. What was it, she wondered, and shrugged to herself. Did one ever know what these modern sculptures depicted?

The road continued its gradual curve around the school, ending in a parking lot near the lofty administration building, which was adorned with cathedral-like windows and trimmed with rich brown woods. She parked, then stared at the building absently. *Well, here I am, back in school,* she thought, and regretted for a moment that her college years had all been spent in cities—in Denver, at a commuter college, and later in Los Angeles, where she'd attended law school at night. She'd never had a feeling of identification, of belonging to anything. For her, college had been a business, a way of getting into her career.

She'd kept her eye steadfastly on her goals, weakening only once when a girlfriend in Denver begged her to join a sorority.

"I don't have time," she'd said firmly, and the girl's self-assured expression had changed, her eyes widening in disbelief.

"Come on, Maggie. How much time does it take? A dinner meeting once a week, and you have to eat anyway. Besides," the girl had continued, smiling knowingly, "we get together for special weekend things with the fraternities. You know...camp-outs and ski trips. Those weekend things keep me in dates year-round!"

When Maggie frowned, Karen had made a small, exasperated sound. "Lord, is that all you want to do? Study?"

"Listen..." she'd said with an apologetic laugh. "I have to keep up the old average. You know, Karen, eyes to the road and all that sort of thing." But she'd felt herself weakening. "Really. I can't afford to spend whole weekends camping out somewhere. There just aren't that many hours—"

"You aren't giving hours to the girls, dummy. I'm talking men. You know...HUNKS. And besides, we only go for one night. And we have a blast. Singing, eating, looking at the stars. What do you think sororities are for?"

Maggie had gone home and announced to her mother that she was joining a sorority.

For a moment her mother had said nothing. It wasn't her style to make scenes. She'd gone on putting dishes in the dishwasher without comment. Then she'd said, "If that's what you really want, Maggie, you'll have to make the decision."

Maggie had decided.

In the middle of her studies that night, her mother had come into Maggie's bedroom. "If you'd had a sorority dinner, you'd just be getting home this minute. You'd still have all your work to do."

At breakfast the next morning her mother had remarked, "You know, Maggie, I look at you and I think how lucky you are. I never went to college and couldn't type, so about the only job open to me was quickstepping it around the Texas Chili House. You ought to try waitressing some time, honey." She'd put jellied scones on the table purposefully. "You want to know how people treat you? Like a waitress. They don't see you. You're nothing but a hand in front of their faces, something setting down food. Waitresses don't get treated like lawyers. For a while I was just a hand to your father, too. I had to make him notice me. But if I'd been a lawyer..."

She left the rest unsaid—that her husband had eventually left her for a younger woman who'd planned to enter law school. Maggie had already heard the story many times.

In the end, Maggie had changed her mind, thinking the decision had been wholly hers. Others could join sororities and go on camp-outs; for herself, there were loftier goals. It gave her a sense of superiority to know she was sacrificing while her contemporaries played. There were times when she even suspected the fun-loving Karen had envied her.

MAGGIE GOT OUT of the car and requested instructions from a receptionist in the administration building. She quickly found Gordon Hamilton in one of the adjoining structures. He was seated at a functional desk in his small classroom, which held thirty or forty student tables. She'd never seen a college classroom so tiny. In all her years of schooling, lecture halls had always held at least a hundred students. Her first impression of this room was coziness.

Her second impression was coldness. Gordon Hamilton glanced at her and let his eyes stray to his watch before he asked, "Did you get lost, Miss McAllister?"

Maggie smiled. "As a matter of fact, I came right to the school. Your directions were excellent, Mr. Hamilton." She hid her annoyance, letting her eyes widen as she extended her hand. She could sense his response to her warm, dark look.

He rose to his feet. "Of course. You made it, that's the important thing."

His affability restored, he again looked the part of a self-assured, relaxed man. The graying temples and thick brows lent distinguishing touches to the squared planes of his face.

"I'd planned to take you to lunch, Miss McAllister." He glanced at his watch again. "Perhaps we can still make it."

"I don't need lunch, really. Save your money for the fight ahead."

He smiled a superior smile.

It made her feel ridiculous. They were talking about a few dollars for lunch versus tens of thousands in attorney's fees. Not worth bothering about. She said, "As a matter of fact, I ate a rather late breakfast. But I'll have dessert with you, if you like."

"I often don't eat lunch myself. Most of us don't need it, you know. Americans generally eat too much, it's a national problem. We're a fat population." He patted his lean middle with what Maggie could see was pride. "The spare-tire generation, we could be called. Well." He gathered up some papers and laid them carefully in a zippered briefcase. "Let's go talk in my office, then. Students will be using this room in a few minutes."

They strolled down a pathway toward another of the one-story buildings. "My office is small," he said, "but at least I have an extra chair in it."

"I only need one chair."

As she walked next to him, Maggie realized that Hamilton was a tall man—perhaps six one—yet he seemed short compared to Cooper Smith. Even in the fresh air she was aware of his rather heavy men's after-shave—a brand she knew but couldn't quite place. She thought it must be expensive and decided she'd smelled it mostly on older men.

At a juncture of pathways, Hamilton took her elbow and steered her left. She stiffened. For some reason she didn't want him touching her. Perhaps it was because she'd been so recently with Cooper Smith, whose touch was so different from this man's.

Maggie glanced up at him without pulling her arm away; he might think she'd already been offensive enough. And what was wrong with him, anyway?

She saw the regular planes of his face and the perfectly groomed hair and realized that by any objective definition he would be called good-looking. Still, there was that hint of sharpness and something else about his expression. She ruminated as they walked and at last came up with the word—he was *calculating*.

Her attention shifted. This was really a beautiful place. Though the scattered pine trees might have seemed at odds with the rosy-hued buildings, somehow they all managed to blend. And everywhere was the vast lawn. Reveling in the parklike atmosphere, Maggie said, "This is a beautiful campus. You must love it, Mr. Hamilton."

"Love it? I don't know about that. It's a long way from anywhere. And why don't you call me Gordon?"

Quickly she found her standard response. "I'd prefer not to, if you don't mind. I think we'd better keep this as businesslike as possible, Mr. Hamilton. To go with our rather businesslike fees." She smiled. "Besides, it's hard to break old habits. I always call my clients by their last names."

"Yes. Well, whatever." He stood aside to let her proceed him into his office building. Midway down a short hall, he gestured toward a closed door, and she opened it.

The room was occupied. Behind the ample desk that seemed to fill most of the room, a graying man sat bent over a formidable stack of blue books. He looked up as they entered, smiling behind rimless glasses.

"Oh—you're here, John." Hamilton looked annoyed.

"Yes." The other resignedly lowered the pen he'd been using. "Didn't think you'd planned to be around this hour. Do you need the room right now?"

"No, no. Carry on. I can see you're all spread out." Hamilton moved a step closer. "Exams?"

"Yes. I'd planned to correct these at home, but my wife..." He smiled apologetically. "She talks when I'm there. I can go to the library, if you—"

"No need," Hamilton said brusquely. "We each ought to have our own office, John, by now. By damn, the school ought to allot the funds."

"We were lucky to get the campus, Gordon. You know that. The offices will come eventually." He smiled. "Be patient." With a glance at Maggie, he asked, "A friend?"

"A lawyer. The environmentalist thing. Maggie McAllister, John Mackenzie."

Mackenzie's smile grew. "Well, Gordon. For once I envy you that fight. Nice to meet you, Miss McAllister."

"Thank you," she responded, smiling back. "But I think we've interrupted you long enough. Nice to meet you, too." She turned to Hamilton. "What I'd really like is to sit outside somewhere. It's so beautiful. Aren't there benches someplace?"

Hamilton frowned and Mackenzie beat him to an answer. "Plenty of benches and not too many students around. Take her out on the quad, Gordon. We may be short on offices, but we're long on pine trees."

"Great," Maggie said, and found herself following a reluctant Hamilton into an open area of picnic tables and benches where students sat eating their lunches.

They chose a table a little away from the others, and Hamilton dropped his briefcase onto the middle of it. As she sat down across from him, he said, "Now, Miss McAllister..." and the "Miss" sounded faintly derisive. "What is your game plan? How long will you be here? How many documents will it take to convince the Siskiyou County judge that we have to stop these maniacs?"

Maggie smiled. "One well-prepared document ought to do it, Mr. Hamilton. And how long I stay depends on how much work there is to do. First, let me see the list of people you've gotten together."

He unzippered the case and handed her two sheets covered with typewritten names, titles and phone numbers. Maggie was amazed at how many there were.

She turned to the second sheet. "All these people are against skiing coming to Mount Shasta?"

"And more. It's a very unpopular issue around

here. Just a few rabid types want it. The selfish bozos, macho men like Smith."

She smiled. "Cooper Smith?"

"And a few others like him. They've all got their personal reasons. You'll see."

Maggie thought back to the town meeting. She remembered the town being more or less split.

Mr. Hamilton leaned across the picnic table, bringing his face uncomfortably close to hers. "This is a national issue, Miss McAllister, not local. We are going to set a precedent—an important precedent. We—" Picking up one of his papers, he said in a composed voice, "Miss McAllister, we are about to stop a movement here that is dangerous. Dangerous to all the parks and untouched landmarks in America. Dangerous to redwoods and beaches and eroding deserts. Dangerous to mountains everywhere, in all their splendor."

Hamilton seemed to have forgotten where he was. He wasn't just talking, she thought, he was orating. Maggie glanced around nervously, wondering who might be listening. Hamilton's voice had deepened and taken on stentorian volume. It was embarrassing.

From across the table, Hamilton addressed imaginary multitudes, and in spite of the quad being scantily populated, Maggie at last put her fingers to her lips and said, "Shhh, all the kids are listening."

"I want them to listen!" he said, but lowered his voice somewhat.

When she sat merely staring at him, Gordon Hamilton stopped talking and shrugged. "I get very emotional about this. It's such a big issue. National at least. . . maybe international."

You get plain loud, she thought, but murmured soothingly, "I can see how important it is. I, too, feel the mountain ought to be protected." With her peripheral vision she noticed the students turning back to their own conversations.

Relieved to have him quiet, she began looking over his lists. A lot of names, and now it was up to her to do the rest—prepare the papers that would ensure the injunction and launch her career. She, Maggie McAllister, the lawyer who was about to help the environmentalists save Mount Shasta!

For almost the first time Maggie realized how alone she was. None of the big bosses from Meiers, Meiers, DeCaro and Kosinski would be around to check on her work; the injunction would rise or fall almost entirely on her brain power.

Suddenly she found herself hoping Gordon Hamilton would leave her alone. Unwilling to share the credit with him, she had another, larger worry: the man might make mistakes!

Somewhere a band started playing.

Maggie looked up. In the distance across the open lawn was a group of uniformed students beginning a loose rendition of "Stars and Stripes Forever." Even from here she could detect discordant notes and unscheduled solos. She smiled.

Hamilton caught the smile. "Very few of them take private lessons. Not enough teachers around here. The band leader has to do it all. Rather provincial." He shrugged. "But part of the charm."

Maggie asked, "You like it here?"

"I like teaching. But this hick..." He caught himself. "I wouldn't be defending the place, would I, if I didn't?"

"I don't know," she said suddenly. "Would you?"

Hamilton looked at her hard. "Without me, Miss McAllister, Mount Shasta...this whole district... would be overrun. I consider this project my personal undertaking. My mission. Here is a region trembling on the edge of disaster. An avalanche poised to run away with itself." His voice was growing louder and deeper.

Maggie felt new apprehension.

"A virgin paradise about to be desecrated by selfish hordes. The western territories in the predawn of Lewis and Clark—"

Maggie quickly held up a hand. "Mr. Hamilton, I think we should discuss the lists."

"Yes. Well." He coughed and adjusted his necktie. "Well. . ." He pointed to the first name on one of the sheets. "This man is one of the chief environmentalists. He's a backpacker. Knows the mountain firsthand. Hikes up the west face in tennis shoes. Famous for that. He knows the devastation that could occur. . ."

The music and its shortcomings swelled as the band, with even stranger harmonies and more untimely beats, attempted to perform the "Colonel Bogey March."

Maggie's attention shifted and she suppressed a giggle, but Hamilton went on. "And then there's Mills, a logger with a passion for the Shasta redwoods, though one nearly killed him a few years ago. . . ."

Silence came at last to the playing field, and with an effort Maggie wrenched her attention back.

One by one, Hamilton went over the names with her, his concentration unbroken. Besides the environmentalists, there were ex-employees from the former ski operation, representatives from the Sierra Club and Forest Service spokesmen. Hamilton had been gathering them like pinecones, squirreling them both on paper and in his memory. He had stored odd bits of data about everyone. Rapidly, she scribbled notes next to the names, once asking him to slow down so she could catch up.

She began to feel good about it. This man really had done an enormous amount of background work. It was as if she was faced with a horrendous college exam that suddenly turned out to be open book. All she had to do was follow what he'd written down, page by page. The ferreting out was already done. She smiled at Gordon Hamilton, suddenly seeing him with new respect.

"You've worked hard at this, haven't you? And the extra detail you're giving me—that's going to be a great help." She was tempted, suddenly, to let him call her Maggie, then checked herself. No need for that.

Gordon Hamilton looked pleased. "I've been working on it for months. I don't believe in a sloppy approach. As I told you the first night, I don't want good results. I want 'em spectacular."

"Why?" she asked suddenly.

She thought she saw him redden slightly. But perhaps not. "Miss McAllister," he said, and his face was so sincere she knew she'd been mistaken. "If you knew this area as well as I do, you wouldn't ask that. Just live here awhile. The answer will be obvious."

"Yes." She pushed her yellow tablet aside. "I can see how that might be."

Her enthusiasm was growing. She was eager to get out there and begin working. What an opportunity this was! And how wrong she'd been in her first impression of Gordon Hamilton. The man was a gold mine! He'd made it nearly impossible for her to fail.

"Mr. Hamilton, I truly appreciate this." She waggled the papers at him. "You deserve a lot of credit. You've been awfully thorough."

He nodded. "But there's still the aspect we haven't discussed. . . the people who are opposing us. Cooper Smith and others."

Quickly she put in, "They won't be much trouble. We'll—"

"There may be information on some of them, too. You should know it. It could prove useful."

"What do you mean?" She wanted him to say it, not her, in case she'd gotten the wrong impression.

"I think you know what I'm getting at."

Maggie waited.

"I'm not talking rumor. I'm talking facts. But some of them aren't... pleasant."

She raised her eyebrows, curious.

"Take Smith, for example. I've always suspected his motives—that they weren't lily white. The man holds himself up as above reproach. People around here treat him like some kind of god, listen to everything he says." Hamilton's voice had taken on a tinge of bitterness. "But he's overrated, Miss McAllister, and he's got enemies. Frankly, I have reason to suspect..."

"Suspect what?" She found herself leaning forward, then noticed what she was doing and deliberately sat back again. Why should she seem more interested in Cooper Smith than anyone else?

Hamilton sounded evasive. "Nothing concrete. It's just that everyone who pushes hard for the skiing seems to have private motives...some kind of personal gain in mind. I'm looking for Smith's angle. I thought maybe you could find it."

She felt instant revulsion. "I don't know how I'd do that."

"There must be things he's not telling everyone, and I've always suspected he's tricky, not as up front as he'd like everyone to think."

"But you're not sure."

Gordon Hamilton cleared his throat and looked away. From the strange expression that had just come over his face—anger poorly suppressed—Maggie knew there was more to the story than he wished to tell. And she sensed indecision in him, too. She decided to wait him out.

Hamilton played with the zipper on his briefcase. Slowly he moved the tab along its track. Then he faced her again. "If you're willing to do it, I know who can tell you everything!" The hardness had come back to his face.

"Who?"

"If you're clever enough...ask the right questions...Cooper Smith's sister!"

Maggie stared at him, then shook her head in disbelief. It was the dumbest idea she'd ever heard of.

CHAPTER FIVE

FROM THE COLLEGE of the Siskiyous, Maggie drove south once more, glad to be coming back to familiar land. As the pines and firs grew denser, marching in stately formation along the sides of the road, she felt a sense of peace, of relief, almost. And Lord knows, she thought, she needed it. The afternoon with Gordon Hamilton had been scratchy and sometimes uncomfortable, ending on a dubious note.

After he'd told her to visit Dr. Anne Smith, Maggie voiced her objections immediately. "Surely you're joking! Why would Cooper Smith's sister throw dirt on him? I may not be perfectly perceptive about people, but I saw that lady at the meeting, and if she isn't a person with scruples, she's nothing!" Her impatience had been perfectly obvious. "There must be some other way!"

"I know Anne Smith will talk to you," he persisted. "You. . .you're likable. A couple of years ago, Anne and I clashed." He cleared his throat again. "Since then she hasn't wanted anything to do with me."

"But she's not going to discredit her brother, no matter how lovable I am." Nor would there be anything to discredit him with, she guessed. From what she'd seen of Smith, she supposed he could be called lots of things—idealistic, too trusting—but surely devious would never be one of them.

Or would it? Why did Hamilton harbor such a strong grudge against Cooper Smith? Every mention of him sounded like a vendetta. Why?

"We don't necessarily want anything dirty," Hamilton had gone on carefully. "Just reasons for his great interest in public skiing on that mountain. I'm sure he has them, because I haven't seen a thimbleful of altruism in this whole town. Not on the proskiing side, anyway." From across the table he radiated his familiar sincerity. "The sooner you're convinced, Miss McAllister, that our side has a corner on the market in altruism, the sooner you'll see the importance of our mission." She hadn't answered.

A FEW MILES from the town of Mount Shasta, the road climbed to a summit marked Altitude: 3,917 feet. Not very high, but it gave her a mild feeling of satisfaction. Mount Shasta had its own private plateau—its own altitude. It was a place set apart. She thought of *him* again...a man set apart and so unlike this professor she now found herself working for.

Ever since she'd left him near the administration building, Maggie had been filled with uncomfortable impressions of Gordon Hamilton. He'd shown her more of himself than she ever wanted to find out. Not only was he more complex than she'd imagined, but she'd sensed a relentlessness about him...and something else. Was it secretiveness?

She wasn't sure.

But in some ways she and Hamilton were alike. They both had goals, insistent, all-consuming goals, which would keep them bound together for as long as she was here. She might not like him very much, but they were a team, and they needed each other to achieve their mutual ends. But while she knew perfectly well what drove her, she wasn't quite sure what drove him.

BACK IN HER MOTEL that night, Maggie took a long, hot bath. The tub, with the shower protruding from the plaster wall, had evidently been built into the corner as an afterthought, and not done very well, either. A ragged separation had started between its edges and the wall.

She threw a small gelatin bubble-bath tablet into the hot water, waited a moment for it to dissolve, then swirled the liquid around with her hand. Bubbles foamed up immediately, twice as much froth as she'd ever seen back home. She wondered why, then remembered how delicious the water tasted. Obviously it had good qualities beyond its wonderful taste. Watching in surprise as the suds continued to grow, Maggie knew this must be the most mineral-free substance on earth.

She sank down into the tub with an inward sigh, feeling the burning sensation of very hot water as it climbed along her bare skin. Leaning her head back against the cold porcelain tub, she let relaxation wash over her until it encompassed her whole body. She stretched, breathed deeply and sighed audibly. Sometimes it was nice to be utterly alone!

The telephone rang.

Bother! She didn't need this intrusion, and who would be calling her, anyway? Surely she and Gordon Hamilton had had enough of each other for one day!

She let the telephone ring again, then reluctantly climbed out of the suds and grabbed a towel, dripping her way across the wooden floor to the bedside phone.

On the sixth ring she said, "Hello?"

It was Cooper. "Maggie!" The deep, rich voice filled her senses and brought her warmth and a rush of pleasure. "What did I catch you in the middle of?" Cooper's question was natural, without guile.

She smiled before she answered. "You'll be pleased to know I'm standing here naked. Or almost. There's a towel, but it isn't doing much good, and not catching much water, either." She looked down. A shiny puddle had collected at her feet. "Actually, what I'm doing is ruining a perfectly good hardwood floor."

He laughed. "You were in the shower?"

"The tub. I hope bubble bath is good for varnish, because the varnish where I'm standing is getting a large dose of it."

"Sorry. Let me call you back."

She hesitated. That would be the sensible thing to do. But hearing his voice again, she didn't want to let him go. "Never mind. I'll mop up as I stand here. It can't get any worse—I've already dragged half the tub with me." Bending over, she began sopping up the worst of the water, panting somewhat from the awkwardness.

On the other end, she could hear the resonance of his quiet laughter. "You're puffing," he said.

"I'm mopping," she answered. "You talk and I'll puff."

There was a moment's silence, as if he was forming his words. Then he said, "When am I going to see you again?" When she didn't answer immediately he persisted, "How about tonight? For dinner?"

Maggie straightened abruptly. Her first impulse was to cry out, *Yes. Oh, yes. I'll get dressed immediately.*

She almost said it, but at the last moment held herself in check, trying to think it through. No good. She couldn't think with him on the other end of the line, waiting. "May I call you back, Cooper?" she asked, her words more breathless than she wished.

"Yes. Of course." He gave her his number and said goodbye casually.

Maggie got back into the tub; her tranquility had vanished. Soaping a washcloth, she rubbed it over herself absently, thinking about this morning. She'd been a fool with him at breakfast. Everything she'd done had gone against her long-range plans for herself: becoming emotional; telling lies, then immediately retracting them; thinking more about him than the job she was to do.

She'd regretted it finally, of course...but what would happen if she met him again tonight?

She climbed out of the tub and pulled the damp towel around herself. More regrets, that's what. Another detour from her chosen course.

It was no good. Especially seeing him at night.

She dialed his number, feeling both reluctance and a lurking triumph that once again she'd held on to her vision of larger goals. When Cooper answered, she said calmly, "I really would have liked dinner with you, but I start my interviews tomorrow and there's a lot of organizing to do. Calls I should make and that sort of thing." It was at least partly true, she thought. "I'm afraid I can't take the time. You understand."

He said, "I understand," and when he paused, leaving a long silence, another part of her wished he'd responded differently, persisted a little and given her a forgivable excuse for relenting.

But he didn't.

He asked, "Is there some other night this week I can take you to dinner, Maggie? Because I'll be gone over the weekend. I have to attend a cattle auction in Yreka." His tone was matter-of-fact, without regret. Cooper Smith would never beg; that much she already knew about him.

Again she paused. She had the perfect excuse to see him, since she guessed there were things Smith could tell her about Gordon Hamilton. She almost relented, but held firm. "No, Cooper, I don't think so."

Silence. She had the uncomfortable feeling she owed him more explanation. "I tried to tell you this morning. We're working against each other, and it doesn't make sense to see each other socially. Everything I'm trying to accomplish, you're against. And everything you stand for, I'm trying to undermine. Which means I'll do my darnedest to see you never get skiing on that mountain. Why would you want anything to do with me?"

He laughed. "I can separate what you do from what you are. Your job is not you. It's only how you earn a salary."

"But I believe in it!" she cried out.

"None of this would prevent you from coming to dinner if you really wanted to." She could almost feel him smile. "But I leave your wanting to up to you."

She wavered. The voice, the strength of him, reached her just when she thought she was strongest. She wanted to see him.

Abruptly, she broke down, stretching for a justifiable way to be with him. "I do need to see the area. Would you have time—maybe in a few days—to show me around? Say, Thursday?"

He laughed. "It's you who have busy days, Maggie. Mine are flexible. I'm beholden only to cattle." He paused. "They never miss me when I'm gone."

She smiled ruefully. "I like to think my clients would miss me, but perhaps they wouldn't. Let's steal a day and see."

He promised to pick her up at nine—two long days from now—and then he said goodbye.

As soon as Maggie got off the phone, she determinedly took Gordon Hamilton's list and began making calls and appointments, keeping her mind focused on her work so she couldn't think about what she'd just done.

But it was hard. She dialed, and while she waited for someone to answer the phone, and that someone went to get the person she was calling, her mind flew back to Cooper Smith. She heard his warm, rich voice in her ears and felt his presence in the room.

She sat on the edge of her bed, holding the phone to her ear and wagging her foot impatiently. Presence, she thought. That was what he had. More than anyone she'd ever met, Cooper Smith filled his surroundings with an almost-tangible aura, so that she felt acutely his being there, even when it was only by telephone.

She was trying to analyze why she would throw over a day's work to be with him—she, who'd always been so controlled—when a man's voice came on the phone and said, "I'm Joe Landover. You wanted to meet with me?"

"Yes," she said. "How about nine tomorrow morning? I understand you represent the Forest Service in its stance against skiing on Mount Shasta."

"I'm one spokesman," he replied. "There are certainly others. Are you here to write an article, Miss McAllister?"

"No," she said. "I'm a member of a law firm working to get an injunction against any further desecration of the mountain. I need to get statements—"

The man interrupted her. "Oh, good. Fine. It's just what we've needed—someone to take definitive action. Glad you're in town, Miss McAllister." He gave her the address of the Forest Service building and declared his organization would offer all the support she needed.

Maggie hung up feeling satisfied.

Other calls went equally well. Gordon Hamilton had done an excellent job of rounding up people who opposed skiing on Mount Shasta and though their reasons were as diverse as their names, they all responded to the interview idea with enthusiasm. Before the evening was over, Maggie had set up five appointments for the next day and six for the following. Increasingly, Maggie began to believe that the town was solidly unified against any development whatever on the mountain.

IF SHE HADN'T BEEN so busy, the next days might have dragged for Maggie. As it was, only the minutes dragged, while the hours raced by. Each appointment was a new experience for her, and each person she met kept her mind temporarily off Cooper Smith and her anticipated stolen day.

Maggie had agreed to meet Joe Landover in the front office of the Forest Service building. "Everyone knows where it is," he'd said. "You can't miss it." He was right; it was the only building of any size on that small side street west of town.

As she parked in front, she saw the sign over the door, Shasta-Trinity National Forest. But the look of the place was more park than forest. The brown wood building was set off by shimmering birches; low hedges encircled well-kept lawns. To the left, a mature cedar spread its limbs like a possessive matriarch.

Maggie walked up the wide brick path, pausing to scan the outdoor bulletin board with its posters and pictures. Pride radiated from those notices, she thought, a sense that the place felt itself important to the town.

Inside were two wooden chairs and an old-fashioned high counter.

Landover came through the swinging door. He was in his forties, fit looking, wearing what appeared to be a uniform—a green shirt and darker, forest-green slacks. His brown hair was neat and cut short.

"Nice to meet you, Miss McAllister," he said warmly, and took her into his sparsely furnished office.

She sat in the brown vinyl chair that faced his desk

and took a pen from her purse. Placing a long, yellow legal pad on her lap, she looked up with a smile, ready to begin.

"Before we start," Landover said, "may I ask who, er, whom do you represent? You must have been hired to—"

"Yes," she broke in quickly. "Our firm has been retained by Gordon Hamilton. He feels strongly enough about this issue to bring us all the way from Los Angeles. He's a very dedicated man." She crossed her long legs and balanced the pad on one knee.

"Very dedicated," Landover replied dryly, leaving the impression he was about to say more but had changed his mind. Yet the little he'd said was tinged with sarcasm.

Maggie threw him a quick look, trying to read his expression, but found nothing. Landover was watching her with interest, waiting for her to proceed.

She poised her pen over the yellow sheet. "Will you give me the Forest Service's position on the proposed attempt to bring skiing back to Mount Shasta?"

Landover leaned back comfortably before he began. "Actually, Miss McAllister, it's only fair to tell you we're not unalterably opposed to the skiing, as long as it's in the right place. Seven years ago, when skiing was high on the mountain in one of the bowls, it didn't interfere with our plans at all. The skiers stayed above timberline, so we weren't concerned. Of course, they were subject to avalanches and terrible winds, and it wasn't too surprising that an avalanche finally took care of the chair lifts for all time. Nobody was interested in replacing them—" he smiled "—especially the investors who had put up the money."

Maggie scribbled on her yellow pad as fast as she could write. "But the skiing back then was limited."

"Yes—very limited. In the area served by lifts, most

people could only ski about one day out of three. The other two days there were gale-force winds, fog or snowstorms. I'm not sure now why chair lifts were put there in the first place, because skiing was such a problematical thing." He shifted in his chair and absently rubbed his face. "Perhaps it was because the skiers faced opposition about the location of the lifts then, too. But now they've become organized and determined. They are set on moving into some of the little remaining virgin land, which might be good for them, but... well, there's not much prime forest left, and we believe wilderness enthusiasts have rights, too."

For the next twenty minutes, Landover outlined the Forest Service position, emphasizing that they had no opposition to skiing in the right places. "In fact," he said, "not all the proskiers are rabid. Take Smith, for instance."

"Cooper Smith?"

"Yes. He's a friend of mine—we go way back. We don't agree on all the issues, but at least he's fair-minded and honest—makes you wonder about some of those guys on the other side." Glancing at his watch, he suddenly stood up. "Sorry, Miss McAllister, I'm out of time. I hope I've answered your questions."

Minutes later they said goodbye.

In the short period before her next interview she found herself thinking again about Cooper Smith, wishing the day away. It seemed his name was always coming up. But she put him out of her mind determinedly, and drove to meet the next person on her list.

MAGGIE WAS ASTONISHED at the vehemence expressed during that interview.

A woman of uncertain background—her face was dark and heavy-featured, Mediterranean, perhaps, but certainly not Indian—spoke passionately about the worship rights of Indians and the need to keep the mountain free of white trespassers.

"I don't quite understand," Maggie said. "The whites have been using the mountain one way or another for years, haven't they?"

"No longer!" the woman shouted. "They must get off! It is holy land! They must get off!"

When Maggie tried to elicit explanations, the woman only shouted louder, saying the same words over and over. Maggie found her theme perplexing and narrow. From her research she had found no evidence that the Indians had actually worshipped on the mountain itself, so she was surprised to see that such an issue had surfaced at all.

"The Indians are gone," said Maggie.

"No, no. Karoks are here."

"Where?"

The woman waved her arms vaguely. "Everywhere. And white men must leave. They are on sacred ground! It is Karok church. Karoks worship the mountain! Draw inspiration from it!"

"White men love it, too," Maggie found herself saying.

"Belongs to Indians first!" The woman shook her finger in Maggie's face and glared. "They must get out!"

Maggie glared back, put the unused pen back in her purse, gathered her legal pad with a murmured thanks and quickly walked out the door.

Once in her car, she began to laugh. What had she been thinking of, she asked herself, to get into a shouting match over supposed Indian rights with a woman who wasn't even an Indian? Which side was she on, anyway? Who'd dreamed her up, Maggie wondered. Who would really believe the woman was devoted to that strange cause? Throughout the interview,

Maggie had had the impression she was talking to an actress.

For the rest of the day and all of Wednesday, Maggie's thoughts of Cooper Smith were submerged in her need to perform excellently for Meiers, Meiers, DeCaro and Kosinski. A sense of pride in what she was doing drove her to conduct each interview with care and in great detail, drawing out her subjects in a way that left her with voluminous notes. Flattered by her close attention, the interviewees spoke freely, enlarging on the details that would help her organize her final arguments.

Maggie knew that, with one exception, she'd made a good impression on her subjects. She hoped that at some later time old man Meiers might have occasion to hear about how she'd handled this assignment, because so far she was proud of her work and elated that she'd been accomplishing it without supervision.

The one exception, of course, was the woman who'd shouted for Indian rights, dragging Maggie into the argument. But she'd decided later that the interview had been of little consequence; no perceptive judge would take her seriously.

Maggie went to bed exhausted, but Wednesday her mind had just set aside the day's work and her limbs had grown heavy when a thought came thundering into her consciousness. *Tomorrow I'm going to be with Cooper Smith!*

CHAPTER SIX

"WHO IS IT?" Maggie asked sleepily, trying to wake up. With the phone to her ear, she patted the bedside table, seeking her wristwatch. What time was it, anyway? What day?

Thursday! Suddenly she remembered, and the thought brought her instant wakefulness.

"Miss McAllister, sorry to call you so early."

"It is rather early," she said, reading her watch. "What was it you wanted, Mr. Hamilton?" She resented his breaking into her sleep. Last night she'd been awake hours anticipating this day, and here was Hamilton robbing her of yet another hour. "Do you realize it's only seven?"

"Yes. But I imagined you'd be up by now. Sorry I woke you, but I wanted to arrange our next meeting so I could plan the rest of my week. Just touching base, you know."

Touching base. She hated the term. People who couldn't conjure up their own expressions always spoke of touching base.

"How about a breakfast meeting? I thought I'd catch you before you got away."

"I seldom get away before seven in the morning," she said.

He didn't laugh. "Well, I have to plan my day. Could I take you to breakfast—say, in an hour?"

"Today?" she asked, thinking, *Oh, no, Lord no, he couldn't mean today. No, no.*

"Of course, today. I'm already scheduled for breakfast tomorrow."

"Then how about another meal tomorrow? That leaves two other meals to choose from."

"You're making light of my invitation. I'm offering to buy you breakfast, Miss McAllister. It's one more meal you can put on the expense account." He laughed, and she cringed.

"I'm afraid I have plans today."

"For breakfast?" He sounded skeptical.

"Soon after."

"How soon? How much time have we got?"

"I have an appointment at nine. And...and the day is stacked up after that. Really, I'm terribly busy today. But tomorrow..." She hoped her vague feelings of guilt wouldn't show. Today was her day. Her day with Cooper. A stolen day.

"We'll go earlier, then. At quarter to eight. I'm sure I can have you back by nine. But maybe you should call your first appointment to warn him you might be a few minutes late. Who is it, by the way?"

Unaccountably, she felt her face reddening. She shifted on the edge of the bed, thinking fast. The nosy man, what business did he have asking? She was in charge of her own appointments! "It's someone I found on my own," she said too quickly. "I doubt that you'd know him."

"Try me."

Maggie forced a laugh. "No games, okay? It's too early in the mornning. Now," she said quickly, knowing she was trapped, "shall I expect you in half an hour, Mr. Hamilton?"

Dropping the questions, he agreed.

Maggie hung up, alert and irritated. An inauspicious beginning to a day reserved for Cooper Smith!

Maggie dialed Cooper's number reluctantly, not

wanting to disturb what had already been arranged between them, yet unable to do otherwise.

"Maggie!" he said, the voice that she'd already come to recognize bringing its expected pleasure. "Maggie. . . will I see you soon?"

"Yes. But Hamilton wants to have a short meeting first, so I may be late. I expect not to be late, but. . ." She took a deep breath. "You know how meetings can be. It's only fair to—"

"No problem, Maggie. Tell you what. Instead of sitting out in front of the motel watching cars go by, why don't I meet you in the park? Then if you're late it won't matter. I wanted to take you there anyway. It's a kind of oasis in the town. Sometimes I just go there to read. Do you know where it is?"

"Is there more than one?"

"No."

"Then I'll find it."

"The north end of town, Maggie."

She nodded, saying she'd manage. "But I saved this day, Cooper, and I won't shortchange it. I promise."

He laughed. "If I had only the merest fraction I wouldn't feel shortchanged. The whole day becomes—" he hesitated "—a miracle."

Touched by foreboding, she warned, "As long as you don't count your miracles before they're hatched. See you soon after nine."

FIVE MINUTES AFTER SHE settled into Hamilton's car, Maggie wished she'd managed to put him off. He drove like a fool, pushing his sports car well over the speed limit and taking the curves almost recklessly. Like an immature kid, she thought, who still liked the feel of fast cars.

She glanced up at his leonine profile with its graying

patches and felt the presence of two ages in the one man.

He spoke very little, concentrating on his driving. Once she looked down and saw they were doing almost eighty. "Slow down," she said. "You'll get a ticket."

"Very few patrols on this stretch of road," he declared, but slowed somewhat.

As they approached the town of Weed, noted on road signs to be fifteen miles from Mount Shasta, Maggie realized they'd covered the distance in some kind of record time, which wasn't all bad, she thought grimly, since it might get her back to Cooper that much faster!

By the look of it, the town of Weed hadn't changed in years. The main street had formed along a gully in the surrounding terrain, as though a river had once washed through and deposited the structures along its banks. Even more than Mount Shasta, the place was old, full of decaying buildings, clapboard houses that had never seen a coat of paint and tawdry neon signs that must have been erected in the thirties.

"Lumber town," Hamilton said briefly, waving his hand toward the ramshackle houses. "They never paint these shacks. When the wood rots, they put on more." He spoke disdainfully.

"But the lumber mills are closed now," Maggie said.

Gordon Hamilton laughed. "I doubt if these people ever notice until their houses fall flat down. They all live like this."

Maggie felt a surge of sympathy for the people here. There was an air of depression about the place. She wondered why Hamilton ever came near it. She also wondered where he was going to take her.

Emerging from the far end of the gullied street, Hamilton swung right, slowed, then entered a modern shopping center, a small, hidden square out of tune with the rest of the town. With sudden deceleration, he stopped the car in front of a brightly painted restaurant and dashed around to her side to open the door. Once more he took her arm in a proprietary manner.

The restaurant had no view, but it seemed clean. Hamilton and Maggie slid into a booth, where a marbelized though chipped Formica tried to give a look of class to the tabletop.

"Bacon and eggs?" Hamilton asked.

She thought about it. An image came to her of Cooper waiting for her in the park, and breakfast no longer mattered. She shook her head. "Just toast and coffee."

Hamilton shrugged. "Breakfast is the most important meal," he muttered, but Maggie wasn't listening. Instead she watched as the waitress—already tired so early in the morning—handed them a menu with a fixed smile.

"What'll you have?" The woman dug an elbow into one hip and leaned on it for support, oblivious of the strand of gray hair that fell over one eye.

Maggie smiled at her, suppressing what she wanted to say. *Why don't you sit down and I'll get the coffee?* Instead she asked, "Did you work all night?"

The woman nodded. "Well, not quite. I came on at one." She poised her pencil over a pad. "I'm off in half an hour."

"You'll be glad, I'll bet."

Hamilton broke in. "Let's get these orders going, all right?" He told the waitress what he wanted, not looking at her. As she shuffled away, he said, "We have to get cracking, Miss McAllister, remember?"

She remembered. And wished she were elsewhere.

Hamilton quizzed her about the interviews. His tone was reasonable and his questions intelligent, but Maggie was conscious only of time passing. She glanced at her watch. Almost nine. Then she chided herself. This was her job, this was what she had come for, not the rendezvous with Cooper Smith.

At nine-twenty Maggie said, "I really must keep my other appointment, Mr. Hamilton," and felt a stab of guilt. What if he learned why she was in such a hurry?

To her relief, Gordon Hamilton stood up. As he paid the check, he turned to her with a grin. "We'll get you back to town in record time."

"I'd rather just get back," she said, "and forget the records."

He looked at her oddly. "I thought you were in a hurry."

"I am. But I also have this yen to arrive in one piece, if it's all the same to you." She smiled. "If I'd wanted to set land records, I'd have been a race-car driver instead of an attorney."

He let her remark pass, leading her in silence toward the car. After he'd helped her in, he said, "This car was built to hold the road. But since you're so worried..." With a slight, deferential bow he closed her door and went around to his side.

To Maggie's surprise, Hamilton hugged the slow lane and drove at thirty-five. She sensed that he was looking at her, his head swiveling often for her reaction, but she ignored him.

Surreptitiously, she glanced at her watch, trying not to participate in Hamilton's game. At this speed Hamilton could burn up another twenty minutes, but she dared not say anything, nor did she want him to know she was anxious. She sat silent, forcing her lips into a slight upward curve. Not by any hint would she let him perceive she was ready to jump out of the car and run down the freeway.

The man was a child.

And then the bells started. The seat-belt chime went off first, a gentle beeping that repeated at odd intervals. She glanced over at Hamilton. "You've got a little bird in here that's trying to tell you something. Why don't you hook up your belt?"

He shook his head, puzzled. "It can't be doing this—not now. We've been on the road ten minutes." But since the beeping continued, he pulled the harness across his chest and hooked it. Nothing changed. The bird continued its gentle chirping. Then the instrument panel began to flicker, the clock lighting up, faltering, lighting again and going out. Numbers whirred by over the radio.

Maggie said, "What's happening?"

"God only knows. It's going crazy." Hamilton leaned forward to glare at the instrument panel and shake his head. "Never had anything like this before. Never. Oh, God!" A look of dismay crossed his face. "The power. We're losing power."

An oil-warning light came on, and then the whole instrument panel went dead. At the same time, Hamilton pumped the gas pedal with an angry foot but without result. The sports car gradually slowed.

Hamilton turned the wheel, bringing the car to the shoulder before everything stopped completely.

For a few moments they sat in heavy silence, staring out their own windows. *By the time I get there he'll be gone,* Maggie thought.

Hamilton roused himself and turned the key in the ignition, but to no avail. "The whole system's dead," he offered.

"So I see."

"Not too much point in sitting here."

"No, I guess there isn't." She knew with a sense of quiet dismay, that Cooper Smith would never wait this long. Their day was over. And no chance to make appointments now or do anything else. Twelve hours had just been wiped off the slate.

Hamilton cleared his throat. "You want to flag us a ride. . . in your inimitable female fashion?"

"By that do you mean skirt up and leg extended?"

He turned to grin at her. "Something like that. Maybe this event won't be all bad, Miss McAllister."

When she turned away from him, he added, "I didn't do this on purpose, you know. If I'd wanted to shut the car down I'd have thought of something subtler. Without all the bells and whistles."

Unable to help it, Maggie laughed. "Okay, Mr. Hamilton, tell me. . . what do we do now?"

He said he didn't know, but he popped open the hood and went outside to peer under it, thrusting his upper body deep into the engine.

Maggie could tell his examination was just a Sunday look and nothing more, that he was a world more conversant with economics than internal combustion engines.

She got out of the car and leaned against the trunk, watching vehicles sail by, each with a blast of warm air that seemed to strike her mockingly. "Damn!" she said aloud.

For the hundredth time, Maggie pushed away the long dark hair that flew into her face, seeing as she did it, a highway patrol car coming up the road in the opposite direction. *Ah hah,* she thought. She'd been lucky. She began waving her arms.

Without visibly slowing, the black-and-white vehicle came on, its rack of colored lights on top as proud and imperious as antlers. Thinking fast, Maggie ripped the red scarf from around her neck and waved it, but still the patrolman didn't see her and at full speed roared past. Maggie's scarf fluttered feebly one last time and dropped.

Then, astonishingly, the police car slowed, halted and began a definitive U turn.

"YOU CAN DROP ME at the park in Mount Shasta," Maggie said as she settled into the front seat of the police car. She turned around and saw Hamilton still leaning against his front fender, his body a discouraged slump. "I hate to leave him there. It won't be long, will it?"

The paunchy policeman threw her a quick look. "I've already radioed the tow truck. Your...friend will be rescued shortly." He squinted at her. "The park, you say? Did you really mean the park?"

"Yes," Maggie affirmed, folding her hands in her lap and not wanting to explain.

The man raised an eyebrow but didn't pursue it.

After a while Maggie asked, "They do have a phone in the park, don't they—in case the person I'm meeting has already left? In case he hasn't figured out that we broke down?"

Again, the policeman threw her a look. "Sure, lady, there's a phone. But I'll wait if you like."

"No need. But thanks."

A few minutes later the car swung onto the dirt road that led down into the forested area of the park. Without asking questions, the policeman drove slowly between trees and down along the green open lawns, circling and waiting for her to say something.

But Maggie didn't offer any comment. As she'd expected, Cooper Smith was gone.

CHAPTER SEVEN

"YOU MIGHT AS WELL keep going," Maggie said at last as the policeman continued to drive slowly through the park, "and I'll take a ride with you back to the center of town. I figured—I guess I knew all along—that nobody would wait nearly two hours." She turned her face toward the window so he couldn't see her disappointment.

"No, ma'am, that would look like a stand-up to almost anyone, I'd guess."

"I'm staying at a motel on the south side, if that would be all right. Would you mind?"

"No problem." He accelerated slightly, passing a small redwood information building tucked among a grouping of pines.

They'd just cleared the walkway surrounding the building when Cooper stepped out into the sunshine.

Later Maggie realized she'd been rather intemperate in the way she'd shouted, "Stop! That's him!" But it hadn't mattered to her then what anyone thought, only that he was there and she was going to have the day with him after all.

She'd run from the stopped patrol car, only managing at the last minute to curb her unladylike gallop toward the brown building.

"Made it, Cooper!" she gasped breathlessly, and he swung around, a warm smile enveloping his strong features.

Beyond her he spotted the patrol car, its passenger

door still open and the policeman turned toward them, obviously interested.

"They let you out of jail for this?" Cooper asked lightly.

"Actually, it was something pretty close to that. And now I've forgotten to thank the policeman." She turned back toward the patrol car, calling, "Thank you!"

The man waved, then reached over to close the passenger door.

As MAGGIE WALKED through the park with Cooper she had the odd feeling that she'd been on some sort of dizzying amusement-park ride. She'd been spun around until nothing seemed real anymore, and only in the past few minutes had the world reestablished itself in warm, familiar patterns. It seemed right to be walking there with him.

"Well, Maggie! The tour starts here!" Cooper led her across a grassy area toward a small stream, an effervescent bit of water that seemed to appear from nowhere out of the rock facing on a steep hillside.

"This little brook is really a giant in small clothing," he said, pointing. "It's the headwaters of the Sacramento River, and it comes right out of that rock. Before the rock, who knows? I stand here sometimes and find it hard to imagine this is the beginning of the great Shasta Lake."

"This is it?" she asked. "This baby stream?"

"Incredible, isn't it? Though I'd guess behind every grown-up lake there's an infant creek somewhere." He laughed, then dropped an arm around her shoulders as they stood looking down at the water.

She had an urge to lean against him but didn't.

"When we've seen the rest of the park we'll go to

the fish hatchery, and then I thought I'd take you out on Siskiyou Lake. Canoeing."

"I'd like that."

"Have you ever been in a canoe before?"

She nodded. "I used to be a camp counselor, summers. I'm good with a paddle, Cooper. You'll see."

He grinned. "Maybe we should skip the hatchery and go right to what you're good at."

"No, no. Let's not skip anything. If I'm going to steal a whole day I want to do everything in a day you can do."

"Everything?" He looked down at her, his gray eyes suddenly serious.

"Almost everything."

THE FISH HATCHERY was not quite as Maggie had imagined. Set into the ground outside were long rows of parallel metal tanks that reminded her of rows of string beans or carrots. It seemed an odd way to grow fish.

But then why did fish need to be in ponds, she asked herself, staring down at the rows of squirming, silver trout. In each long tank the fish were a different size, from fingerlings to two or three pounds each—and hundreds of them in every channel.

She said, "I thought the tanks would be round. And I never dreamed there'd be so many thousands of fish. They must get claustrophobic jammed in there together like that."

He grinned. "Perhaps you should speak to the director here, Maggie. Tell him the fish are getting a phobia, that they need fish analysis. That they—"

She clapped her hand over his mouth. "I'll get even with you for that one, Cooper Smith. I would be claustrophobic in that tank with ten million others just like me using up all my swimming room. I would feel life wasn't worth living if I didn't have my own private rock to hide under." She paused to watch the silvery masses swarming against a string that reached upward to an overhead container. Each time the string was jiggled, a trap door moved slightly and food dropped into the water. And each time food dropped, the fish underneath went into a feeding frenzy.

Thoughtfully, Maggie added, "I'm a city girl, but that's the trouble with cities, isn't it? You never quite feel like you've got your own rock." She leaned over the water a little. "Look at them. Fighting for every tiny morsel." She added with a wry smile, "Sometimes lawyers do that in the courtroom, scrapping like crazy over the smallest crumbs. And they look just about the same, only they're a different species."

He asked, "Why do you stay in the city, Maggie? There are other places to make a living."

Putting one foot up on the edge of the fish tanks she shook her head. "You set a course, don't you, and then it seems to follow a line, point by point. I'd always wanted to be part of a big-time law firm and this was the one that happened to hire me. When I'm offered a partnership—" she smiled at him "—it will all have been worthwhile."

He took her hand to lead her back toward the Wagoneer, saying offhandedly, "I guessed this project of yours—this fight over Mount Shasta and skiing—was about more than the principle and more than the money. You see it as the cornerstone of your career, don't you?"

"It's more complicated than that."

He held the door as she slid into the seat, then went around to his side. As though there'd been no interruption, he went on, "You're going to have problems with this fight, Maggie, because sooner or later you're going to see the justice of the other side."

"For today," she said, setting her lips, "let's not talk about it, okay?"

A SHORT DRIVE brought them to the most beautiful lake Maggie had ever seen. A dark mirror set in a frame of rich conifers, the lake reflected the sky and trees with a clarity that produced two perfect mirror images.

As Smith parked the Wagoneer near a wooden deck, Maggie saw on the water's surface the periodic moving rings that signaled trout jumping for insects. "Do you fish here, Cooper?"

"Once in a while." From the back of the vehicle he produced a handled plastic bag and a thermos, which he handed her with a grin saying, "Lunch." On the floor that served as an aisle she saw canoe paddles.

"Where do you have the canoe—under the seat?"

He shook his head. "I brought it down earlier in my pickup." He pointed to a sleek wooden canoe lying bottom up near the dock.

"And you just left it here?"

"I just left it, Maggie, where it waited dutifully until I returned."

She sighed. "In all the public places back home they nail down the pictures."

THE DAY WARMED, or maybe it just seemed warmer as Maggie and Cooper paddled their canoe. Kneeling in back, Cooper guided the craft across the lake in a straight line, each backward stroke accompanied by a short forward motion that kept the canoe on course.

Up front, Maggie also knelt, paddling vigorously and confidently because she knew she did it well. Alternating strokes on the left and right sides, she not only moved the paddle hard, but sent it into the water without any splash.

"You really are an expert, aren't you?" Cooper said admiringly.

She nodded, shaking back the dark hair that fell across her face. "I've had a lot of experience."

Stroke after stroke, Maggie dipped into the water and pulled, the work of her muscles filling her with well-being and the fast skimming of the canoe adding a sense of achievement. They seemed to be going faster and faster, their joint effort sending the boat flying over the water.

"This is great!" she exclaimed, her earlier seriousness fading. She could imagine herself paddling like this for hours.

"You're making it fun, Maggie! We've got a speed record going here!"

Sitting in front of him and facing forward, she couldn't see him, but she could feel his strength, the way the canoe surged each time he stroked.

On and on the boat flew. Though Maggie wasn't sure of their destination, they were headed across the widest part of the lake. After they'd been out awhile she could see figures on the far side, and soon the accoutrements that labeled them as golfers.

"You've got a golf course. . . here?" She was beginning to pant a little.

"An abbreviated one." He laughed. "Just enough holes to put a steady trickle of golf balls into the lake. The fish-and-game department stocks the lake with trout and the golfers stock it with golf balls. Luckily, only one of those reproduces on its own."

At last Maggie paused to rest and turned to see the sun shining in his sandy hair. The sun and the outdoors seemed a part of him, she thought, and marked him with a quality of permanence—like the trees and mountains all around. It was good just being with him.

He said, "Tell me where you did all your canoeing, Maggie."

"I was a counselor in a camp two summers." The canoe drifted lazily as she spoke. "It was kind of a poor kids' camp not far from Denver, and they didn't have much equipment, just their little site by a lake and a few canoes. We had to invent a lot of games to make up for what we didn't have." She smiled. "A challenge. You can't keep kids paddling a canoe all day long."

Cooper picked up his paddle and stroked enough to alter the canoe's direction, then laid the wooden piece across the sides of the boat. The ripples he'd created in the lake continued to rock them lightly after he stopped. "But you liked it?"

"I could have adopted some of those kids. They were so appreciative of everything we did for them, always laughing, and you knew a lot of them didn't laugh much at home. I'd make up a game and those who weren't involved would come bounding over to see what it was, then beg to play. We'd start with two or three and end up with twenty-five. You always had to be ready to move over to make room for more kids." She laughed. "Some pretty dumb games were played at that camp, but nobody cared."

Cooper sat looking at her thoughtfully. "But you only did it two summers."

She shrugged. "They raised the tuition at college and I had to get a job that paid more. I worked at a very expensive restaurant after that. Big tips. From then on my ingenuity brought me extra money instead of laughs from kids. I missed the kids, though. Well... shall we get back to our paddles?"

At a slower pace, they moved across the lake until they'd reached the far side. Telling Maggie to paddle hard for a moment, Cooper beached the boat on a small area of sand and jumped out, holding both their lunch and the painter.

On a small redwood picnic table next to the minigolf course, he laid out tuna sandwiches, bananas, cookies and paper cups for the thermos of iced tea. They ate without talking, idly watching the few golfers who came to try their luck on the course. Filtered light reached them through the trees, and occasional insects paused to make a run at their food. Maggie leaned against the table, relaxed and happy. She'd never known a man whose company made her so content. The burdens and self-imposed pressures of her adult life seemed to fade in his presence.

"Oops!" Maggie laughed. "There goes another contribution to the lake." She watched an orange golf ball sail high into the air, miss the land and arc into the water with a respectable splash.

Cooper laughed heartily. "I've seen a few balls in the underwater marshes, but this is the first time I've seen one on its way."

"There must be lots of them down there!" Maggie said, sitting upright suddenly.

"There must be, but they tend to disappear in all that silt on the bottom."

"Let's go find that one!" Maggie cried, forgetting herself. Suddenly she was very young again, playing with the camp kids. "I know exactly where it landed. I'm sure I can see it down there. The water isn't very deep." She stood up quickly. "I'll race you to the boat."

Like children they ran to the water, Maggie jumping into the canoe just ahead of Cooper. Before he'd quite settled into the back, she pushed against the shore with her paddle, then dipped into the water. "Out here, Cooper. I know exactly where it went. Paddle a little harder and we'll have it. Here. Stop us now. Quick."

All her energy was focused on finding what had just disappeared.

She leaned over the side, trying to see through the clear water and down into the bottom, but thick weeds obscured her view. "Oh, darn. I know it was right here." The boat drifted and then an unseen current below shifted the grasses a little. Suddenly Maggie saw a glint of orange.

She clapped her hands wildly, rocking the canoe in her enthusiasm. "I see it, Cooper, I see it!"

"Where?" He leaned toward where she was looking. Maggie shifted her weight quickly as the boat threatened to capsize.

"I don't see a thing," he said.

"There!" she cried. "It's orange, just a tiny bit showing. Can't you see it?" It was suddenly terribly important that he see what she'd found.

When he shook his head, an inspired Maggie pushed her paddle deep into the water and stirred it a little. The grasses parted and the golf ball swirled out of the depths and moved a yard closer to shore.

"There!" she cried.

Cooper laughed. "I saw it move, Maggie. By golly, you did it!"

"Let's capture it!" she said, her ideas racing faster and faster.

"Maggie, the water's too deep for that."

"I mean, we'll swish it toward shore and then get it. Look, I'll show you!" With her paddle Maggie gently swirled the water, rousing the golf ball once more and slowly wafting it shoreward.

Cooper paddled the boat after it.

"Hold it!" she cried. "We're losing it!" Head down, she saw the golf ball settle back into weeds and disappear once more. "Oh, darn. It's gone."

"No, it's not. I just saw it over here. I'll keep my eye

on it and you paddle. There...there...that's good. Now stop the boat, quick!"

Maggie backpaddled and Cooper thrust his oar deep. With cautious underwater strokes, he nudged the water until the golf ball took off once more and spun away from them.

"I see it!" she cried. "Paddle, Cooper! Paddle! It's getting away." Grabbing her own oar, she dipped and pushed and dipped again, the game now as all-encompassing as it was fun.

Laughing, he sent the boat flying after the recalcitrant ball until Maggie screamed at him to stop. Ordering him not to move, she yelled that she thought she could grab it if he'd just balance her weight. With her shirt sleeves pushed up, Maggie leaned over the edge and plunged her arm into the cold water.

It was right there. She could see it!

But the current moved and the golf ball slithered away.

"I lost it!" she moaned.

"Stir the water," he said. "You'll see it."

Once more Maggie sent underwater currents swirling off the end of her paddle and into the rushes. When the bright little orb finally appeared again in the silt, she shouted, "We'll get it this time!" Another swirl. "It's moving the right way. Paddle, quick!"

Another full-arm plunge into the icy water, and Maggie at last touched the little ball tentatively. Her fingers finally closed on it and she jerked it out of the water.

"Here it is!" she cried, holding the orange golf ball aloft.

"You did it, Maggie!"

"We did it," she said, laughing.

"Put it in the boat. Maggie, I saw a green one down there."

"So did I," she said, "but I didn't want to mention it."

"We got this one," he said. "Let's go after the green one."

"Okay." She laughed. "We'll call it underwater golf. I think we can get really good at this, don't you?"

"In time," he said. "How long are you going to be in town, Maggie? I want at least one orange, one green and one white golf ball."

She thought, *forever. I'm going to be in town forever.* But even as she thought it, an edge of reserve came back. "I think we can get them all today. You just watch."

Exuberant, they paddled and swirled the water and pointed and cried out as the green golf ball alternately appeared and disappeared. After a time, working hard with their paddles and their wills, they nudged and swirled the ball into shallow water.

Once again, Maggie plunged her arm in after it, missed, then ordered Cooper to maneuver the boat until she could get it. And she did.

At dusk they finally captured their third and last golf ball, a white one.

They'd been out for hours and had hardly noticed the time passing. Paddling hard and laughing, they raced the disappearing daylight to the other side of the lake.

They were still smiling about their crazy game as Cooper started the Wagoneer and drove away.

Yet Maggie began to feel she'd let down too much, enjoyed the day too much. She'd been a child for a time, but it couldn't last. She had a job to do and Cooper was distracting her—maybe even changing her.

"Are you sure you won't go out to dinner with me?" he asked a second time as they neared her motel.

Maggie shook her head. "I really can't," she said.

Moments later they were there. He stopped and with a gallant gesture handed her the three golf balls.

"Thank you, Cooper," she said. "It's been fun, hasn't it?"

"More than that," he said seriously. "It's been one of the best days I can ever remember."

CHAPTER EIGHT

MAGGIE WOKE FRIDAY MORNING with the feeling she'd been on an all-night adventure. She'd dreamed of golf balls and swirling water and Cooper sitting at the far end of a canoe, smiling. Sometimes laughing.

They'd played together, and Maggie had a strong impression that they'd done more than that, but she wasn't sure. That she now wanted to feel his arms around her—of that she was quite sure. But she shook off the thought and the subconscious yearning that had inspired it. She had work to do. Lots of work—a full day of interviews to make up for her day of truancy.

As she got into her car, prepared for an interview with one of the outspoken environmentalists, she fought down laughter and daydreams.

Oh, but yesterday had been fun! Something to memorialize. Last night, just as she was falling asleep, she'd thought of a way to do it.

Suddenly she stopped the car, backed up, and put it in Park, leaving the motor running. She dashed up the stairs and quickly unlocked the door, leaving it ajar as she crossed the room to the bureau and grabbed the three golf balls.

Moments later Maggie was back in the car heading in the wrong direction.

SHE WAS THIRTY MINUTES LATE for her first appointment, but the man had assured her on the phone it didn't matter, and Maggie knew she could get back on schedule just by shortening the interview.

For the rest of the day, she worked and tried not to think about Cooper Smith, running from interview to interview, running, really, from him and the impact he was having on her.

Yesterday had been a fantasy, a moment that sparkled like sunlit specks in her memory, yet had no more substance than they did. One saw such particles only for fleeting moments in the right circumstances and then they were gone. As the day wore on, Maggie began to think of her fantasy as threatening, and Cooper Smith as more so.

When the weekend came, Maggie stayed very busy, reading over her notes and writing summaries. By Monday she had decided that the worst thing she could do for herself would be to go on seeing Cooper Smith.

MONDAY'S APPOINTMENTS brought Maggie a renewed awareness of her goals and of the importance of what she was doing.

Finishing early Monday afternoon, Maggie remembered the souvenir of her canoeing day with Cooper. Now there was nothing left to do but give it to him as a goodbye.

Just before the trophy shop closed for the day, she stopped by to pick up the three golf balls she'd had mounted on a walnut board. The man brought it to her, and Maggie drew in her breath. It was so beautiful! The three golf balls—orange, white, green—were quite new, the walnut was a rich brown, and the plaque, which read, Underwater Golf, First Place, Siskiyou Lake, was a shiny brass and beautifully etched.

"You did a great job!" she told the proprietor, a mustachioed man in his forties. He beamed at her.

"It's an unusual idea, Miss McAllister, and we had fun doing it. What are you going to do with it now?"

"Give it to the man who helped win it." She smiled. "Something to remember me by."

"I'd imagine he'd remember you anyway. But if you're not enough, well, this should be!"

ON TUESDAY Maggie had an interview with one of the owners of the local lumber mill. As she began talking to him, Maggie could see he had few opinions about skiing. Perched on the edge of a chair in Len Briscoe's office, Maggie studied the man on the other side of the desk and saw mostly fatigue.

He sat with his chin balanced against his palm, the loose jowls pushed up by his fingers, adding to a general impression of defeat. Maggie guessed he'd once been a heavier man, and flesh had filled the now-loose skin.

"I'm not on any soapbox about skiing," he admitted. "I'm afraid my concerns are about this company... what's going to happen to it now that building is off and there's no sign of it getting better. We've got good men who haven't had a full day's work in months."

"That must be hard for you to deal with," she said sympathetically. "You must feel you're responsible for a lot of lives."

"I am." He sighed. "If the lumber industry doesn't pick up soon, it's not going to matter much about the skiing. All my people will move away."

She thought of her conversation with Cooper in the restaurant and decided to test him a little. "Cooper Smith says skiing might actually save the town by putting your people back to work."

Len Briscoe's eyes brightened. "Cooper Smith. There's a good man. Used to be one of our foremen, you know—one of the best we ever had. If he has an opinion about skiing, I'd listen to it, young lady."

Maggie felt her pulse quicken. "I didn't know he worked here. How long ago?" Now she had an urge to abandon her prior direction and pump Len Briscoe for more information about Cooper. Why did he fascinate her so? Why was she hanging on the man's answers?

"He worked here seven...ten years. Still comes in sometimes, but says he prefers cattle ranching to lumbering. He jokes that he still likes trees better than cows, but on the other hand he's never in danger of having a cow fall on him." Briscoe laughed good-naturedly.

Maggie smiled. "Cooper Smith doesn't strike me as a coward."

"Wasn't. Isn't. But he had a way of putting himself in danger. Maybe you'll hear about it somewhere else. Smith said he'll have my neck if I keep painting him as a hero."

Maggie could have gone on talking about Smith all day. Odd, she thought, that even absent the man could prove a distraction—a damnable distraction!

Shifting the yellow pad on her lap, she studied Len Briscoe thoughtfully once more. "I've gotten side-tracked," she said. "Would you say then, that you are indifferent to whether skiing is ever reinstated or not?"

"That's about right," Briscoe said. "Though if I had to vote, maybe I'd be more for it than against it. I can't see how it's going to hurt that big old mountain when it comes right down to it. Can't see that anyone's going to be worse off for it, either, and maybe Cooper Smith's right, skiing would possibly keep some of my lumbermen around longer, doing other things."

Maggie stood and thanked him. She liked the man, tired and defeated though he was. As they parted, he taking her hand in both of his, she sensed a warmth about him. His discouragement seemed edged with genuine concern. He would survive this lumber depression, but what about all those others who wouldn't?

Maggie strode briskly through the glass doors of the Cascade Lumber Mill—and nearly collided with Cooper Smith.

CHAPTER NINE

Maggie caught herself before she actually crashed into Smith, though she wondered later if that wouldn't have had some merit. How many days now had she suppressed her yearning to feel his arms around her?

Eyes widening she drew up short, her surprise mixed in spite of herself with pleasure.

"Cooper!" she exclaimed, smiling. Hadn't a thousand years gone by since she'd seen him last?

"Well, Maggie!" he grinned, then turned to the dark-eyed boy trailing him up the path. "Jesse, you haven't met Maggie McAllister, have you?"

"I saw her once." The boy came somewhat closer but stopped short of joining them.

Maggie gave him a direct look and said, "Did Cooper tell you about our canoe trip last Thursday? I think you would have liked it, Jesse."

"He said you fished for golf balls." Jesse's voice suggested he wouldn't have liked it. "That's all he said."

"It was more than just fishing, Jesse. We had a kind of contest, trying to get golf balls off the bottom of the lake. It's not that easy, you know."

"Why would you want 'em? Unless you're gonna play golf or something."

She felt as if she'd backed herself into a corner, trapped by the boy's logic. "Well..." She thought about it. "Haven't you ever done anything just because it was a challenge, because it was hard to do, even when there wasn't much point in it?"

Jesse nodded, coming a little closer. "I have this labyrinth game. You have to make the marble go from one end to the other without letting it drop in the holes. Maybe that's what you mean."

"That's exactly what I mean, Jesse!" She smiled at him. "That's us and the golf balls. Have your . . . have Cooper show you someday. It's fun."

Cooper broke in. "Jesse, why don't you go on and research the fishing pole and I'll catch up with you. Remember, flexibility is the key for this pole, not price. On your birthday we don't think about price, okay?"

The boy's sudden grin changed him. He nodded and ran off in the direction of the main street. Maggie watched him go with an ache, remembering her own father. Jesse was lucky. She hoped he knew it.

Cooper turned back to her. "How is your work going, Maggie?"

Looking up at him, Maggie was acutely conscious of the strong planes of his face and the gray eyes that searched hers relentlessly.

"Well. Very well. I'm liking it. I've met a lot of dedicated people . . . with strong and interesting opinions," she couldn't help adding.

"The lopsided view of the sacredness of the mountain," he said, grinning, as though he felt no bias toward the issue. "And are they convincing you of their rightness?"

"I was convinced before."

"Yes. Of course. I think of you as doing a job, but not necessarily personally involved. I have a strong image of your lawyerlike qualities, Maggie—the advocate who can defend the worst elements of our society without worrying about whether they're morally wrong." He gave her a searching look. "Which is the way you like to see yourself, isn't it?"

"I told you how I feel about the mountain," she

said stiffly, beginning to walk away from him. He was taunting her, trying to analyze her. "I gave you my impressions right in the beginning. Which I regretted, of course, since I don't think one's emotions should interfere. But I was honest with you and I still feel that way."

She straightened and walked a little faster, willing herself to get away from him. Whether or not they agreed on issues, his physical presence was disconcerting.

But he kept up without effort.

"We've both said all we ought to say about this case." She opened the door to her car. "We have irreconcilable positions and to discuss them any further is a waste of time. Please, Cooper. . ." she began as he put a hand on her arm. "I have more interviews now."

To her regret he moved his hand away, as comfortably as he did everything else. But he didn't remove himself, she thought, as she waited with her hand on the ignition key.

He was talking again. "Maggie, do you like to ski?"

She hesitated, remembering the scattered occasions on which she'd been talked into weekend ski trips. Unlike the canoeing, she'd never persisted enough to become expert.

"I haven't done it much," she confessed. "But yes, I liked it—finally. When I got over that 'runaway train' feeling." She looked up at him standing outside her car, his sandy hair almost silvery with the sun behind it, his shadowed face indistinct, but the warmth in his eyes discernible, nevertheless.

Maggie felt the intensity of his presence acutely, and the longer she lingered, the more her inner resolve to withdraw from him diminished. "Eventually I liked it enough to wish I'd had time to ski more," she admitted.

"Would you call yourself an intermediate, then?"

She laughed. "If having skied a few intermediate hills qualifies me. . . yes, I suppose so." The memory of one scary afternoon when she'd momentarily lost control on an icy slope came back to her. The growing speed, terrifying at first, coupled with the knowledge that nobody could intervene or save her from the consequences of being out of control, had brought her instant panic. She saw the ice gleaming everywhere, and even now her palms turned clammy thinking about it. But miracle of miracles, she'd figured out what to do—and she'd done it almost at once. Still shaken, she'd looked down on the ice and realized she was no longer afraid of it. She giggled. "What I know how to do best is stop!"

"Great!" said Cooper. "I'd ask for stopping number one." He leaned toward her conversationally. "Ever since Thursday I've had this idea, Maggie. I know you've already taken one day off, but how about doing a little first-hand research—taking a kind of congressman's junket? Let me show you Mount Shasta firsthand."

At her look of doubt he said, "I'm not asking you to compromise anything. Neither that hounding conscience that says we shouldn't be together, nor your belief in the rightness of your mission here. I'd like to take you skiing so you can see the mountain up close. Perhaps then you can answer a few questions for yourself." He leaned a little closer. "Before you answer, I have to tell you I could only find us a driver for next Monday."

"I shouldn't—" she began.

"You shouldn't?" He smiled ironically. "You're afraid you might change your mind, waver a little. Is that it, Maggie? Or are you afraid of certain subliminal thoughts you won't admit, thoughts that might change to feelings in the right circumstances?" He rested his hand on the windowsill. "Which is it?"

When she looked away, her eyes searching out the cedars across the road, he added, "Otherwise, there's no threat to your skiing with me. It's just an experience, a day spent learning firsthand why you're here and what it is you're trying to accomplish. You could very well come away stronger in your convictions." He grinned at her. "Perhaps you'll even change me."

"Unlikely," she said. "And you know it—*Mr.* Smith."

He laughed, as she'd expected. "Miss McAllister, are you by chance weakening?"

When she nodded helplessly, he said, "I'll pick you up Monday morning, at six."

He turned, and with a half wave began to walk toward the Wagoneer. Then he came back. "What's your shoe size?"

"Eight and a half."

"Eight and a half. I'll have the boots and skis. Oh, and ski pants, too. About a size ten, I'd guess."

Full of doubt, she merely looked at him, her dark eyes moody with internal conflict. *Dammit,* she thought, *I haven't even really said yes.*

He reached in through the window and touched her face. "Your eyes are beautiful, Maggie."

Before she could pull out of the driveway, the Wagoneer was gone.

THE SKI TRIP loomed ahead as an event that Maggie both feared and longed for fervently. In the moments between interviews, she found it was all she could think about. Somehow she couldn't turn him out of her mind in the same way she'd managed to push aside all prior involvements. In the past when someone seemed to be affecting her too much, she'd been able to redirect her thoughts toward her job, intensifying her efforts for Meiers, Meiers, DeCaro and Kosinski, so that she always produced some bit of work that was just a little better than it might have been otherwise. She smiled, thinking how often she'd been credited with taking unusually good depositions when they were the result of nothing more than redirected concentration.

The fact that she seemed unable to make similar use of her attraction for Cooper Smith annoyed her. It had never happened before. At least twice she went to the phone in her motel room to cancel her skiing date with him. Each time she sat on the bed, her hand reaching for the receiver while his challenge came back to her, *"What are you afraid of?"*

By Sunday her control had returned, cemented into reasoning she refused to see as rationalization. Of course she should ski Mount Shasta! How could she fully understand the environmentalists' position unless she saw it firsthand?

Sunday evening, about six, Gordon Hamilton called to suggest after-dinner drinks in his apartment, so the two could discuss her work thus far.

Sitting in Hamilton's living room while the professor mixed drinks at his sideboard, Maggie studied the room curiously. His furniture was what she had expected: ultramodern with straight lines and lots of glass. White upholsteries and dark woods. Blacks and whites. All stark contrasts. The bookcase next to the white fireplace was steel and glass and quite full. Wandering over to study the titles, she saw volumes on government theory, the essays of Machiavelli, philosophical treatises on wars and some history. She bent a little closer but could find no light reading. Evidentally Gordon Hamilton did not clutter his life with fiction.

Turning, she found him watching her, a suave man dressed casually in gray wool slacks and pin-striped shirt with a gray-and-maroon-striped tie. "Quite a good collection, wouldn't you say?" He handed her a gin and tonic.

"Yes. But one-sided."

"What do you mean?"

"You don't have any fiction."

He snorted. "I don't believe in fiction. It's a waste of time!"

"Is it?" she asked and realized how little she'd read herself over the years. She smoothed her pink skirt under her as she sat down on his linen couch. Fiction. At any given moment it had always seemed she ought to be doing something else. Or reading something else. Yet she didn't scorn it as he did, and the few classics she'd read had seemed notably worthwhile.

"You're missing some good thinkers," she said, watching as he swirled his drink in his glass, clinking the ice cubes in obvious annoyance.

"Fairy stories, that's all fiction is. If I ever have that much time to waste, it'll be because I'm sick."

Dismissing the subject with a wave of his hand, he sat down close to her and placed some papers on her lap. "Here are some additional names—influential people in Yreka and other places. Some of them have pull with senators, but more importantly, I have two contacts who are friends of U.S. Senators Drake and Whitworth." He waited for her reaction.

Glancing at the lists of names, she felt rather than saw his contained impatience, sensed his demand for her approval. She felt stifled.

"Wonderful," she said, feigning it. "And you want me to talk to these people, too?"

"Of course. Why don't you make the calls Monday...tomorrow?"

"Sorry. I can't. I'm busy tomorrow." She thought of the ski trip, wishing the hours away until she could leave with Cooper Smith.

"Do you mind if I ask what you're doing tomorrow?" Leaning away from her, he gave the impression of studying her down his long, perfect nose.

"I do mind," she said, not wanting the trip revealed.

"Surely, Miss McAllister, since I'm indirectly paying your salary, you must feel some sense of accountability. Or is this some private matter?"

"You're accounting for me every day?" she asked. "You're keeping track? Really, Mr. Hamilton. We're grown-ups, aren't we? How I conduct this investigation is quite up to me." She knew she was dodging him. "And furthermore, you're right, you are paying my salary only—" She stopped, horrified at what she was saying. He'd pressed and she'd lost control. Whatever he said to her, she *was* employed by him in the long run, because his reports on her work would go straight back to Meiers.

Coolly, she touched his shoulder and smiled. "Sorry. You're right. I am reporting to you. To tell you the truth, Mr. Hamilton, tomorrow I'm investigating Mount Shasta up close. I'm going skiing."

"Skiing?" he echoed, thinking about it. "Well. That's a novel idea. And maybe a good one, too. You'll see for yourself the stands of virgin timber and the vulnerability of the wildlife. I'm sure it'll be obvious everywhere you look that organized skiing would be a disaster. Well, well." He gave her a broad smile, radiating approval, and once more she saw the charm that he exuded when he cared to. At such moments he seemed both polished and likable. "Won't you have a case to throw in the face of Cooper Smith!"

Moving away from him a little, Maggie crossed her legs and wished Cooper's name hadn't come up. She felt uneasy and tried to cover it by clearing her throat. "Yes. Now, would you like to discuss these additional names?"

"Skiing. . ." Gordon Hamilton was still rolling the subject in his mind. "You'll need a driver, of course, and someone to guide you. Who are you going up there with?"

Maggie thought about changing the subject. She considered lying. Or she could suddenly spill her drink and make him forget the question. Then she imagined Cooper's face and the integrity that she'd found there. *He never lies or dodges,* she thought. *Why should I?*

Casually she turned to face Gordon Hamilton as though her answer hardly mattered. "We have to disarm the enemy, you know. I'm going with Cooper Smith!"

LATER, MAGGIE WONDERED whether Gordon Hamilton had reddened because he was angry or because he knew something about Smith he wasn't telling. In any case, he was temporarily speechless. In the seconds it took him to collect himself, she decided he would either fire her summarily or try to forbid her going.

For just the briefest time she didn't care either way. She was tired of his attempts to control her, whether paying her salary or not. Of the two of them, she was the professional and in charge, and he was merely the client. She had the right to manage this game as she saw fit, and if he didn't like it he could buy himself someone else to take over the rotten job.

Then she panicked. Seeing the look on his face, she realized how angry she'd made him, and at the same time knew that she was truly in danger of losing this assignment. It would mean her first significant failure—and more than that, her imminent departure from Mount Shasta and Cooper Smith.

She had to retrieve the situation quickly, mollify Gordon Hamilton any way she could, dishonest or not. Her brief fling at integrity laid aside, she smiled at him disarmingly. "Quite a good move, don't you think? Taking the lion into his own den? How better would I see what he's really up to... the places he plans to ruin with his chair lifts and hordes of skiers? Frankly Mr. Hamilton, I thought this was a stroke of genius!"

Gordon Hamilton had no ready answer.

She went on. "On this trip he'll probably reveal everything he and his ski buddies have in mind. I can think of no better way to arm myself than to learn the opposition's plans firsthand!"

"It's a lousy idea!" Hamilton grumbled.

"Oh, no!" She smiled at him fully, widening her eyes as she'd done so effectively with other men. "If we discover Cooper Smith's vulnerabilities, Gordon—" her use of his first name was deliberate "—we discover them for everybody! Don't you see?"

He shifted in his chair, thinking about it. Her ploy worked. "I suppose so," he replied grudgingly.

"So please be good about it and believe me when I tell you I know what I'm doing. Trust me, Gordon!" She smiled at him again, not liking what she was doing.

"You skiing the whole day?" he asked.

"I think so. And we're starting early." She stood up. "I really must get home now, so I won't be too tired. I understand we'll have to do some climbing."

"You sure will. It won't be pleasant. But as you say... research." He gave her a thin smile, only partly mollified. "I expect you'll tell me about it when you get back?"

"Of course. And thanks for the extra names, Gordon." She held out a soft hand to him, letting him hold it a second before she drew away. "I knew you'd understand." Her last smile was as charming as she knew how to make it.

As she pulled away from the curb she caught a quick glimpse of her fading smile in the rearview mirror. Disgusted, she stuck out her tongue.

CHAPTER TEN

THE SUN had only started edging Maggie's curtains with light when her travel alarm went off. She awoke fuzzily, wondering for an instant if there'd been a mistake. She was sure she hadn't slept long enough to constitute a night.

Then she remembered the ski trip and her mind blazed with excitement. She sat up quickly, not anticipating the skiing but only Cooper, ignoring the inner voice of her conscience. For one whole Monday she'd be with him from sunup to sundown.

Quickly Maggie bathed and powdered the soft skin around her breasts and stomach with fragrant talcum. Her freshly washed hair gleamed with highlights as she blew it dry, the dark strands falling full and clean around her face. She studied herself in the mirror and saw excitement looking back. The whiteness of her skin bloomed with high color and her dark eyes glowed with an inner light. *Happiness,* she thought. *I look happy and I feel happy. Today is my day. Our day.*

Drawing on her panties, then a gauzy bra, she reveled in her feeling of womanliness. She was preparing to meet Cooper, and it gave her tingling pleasure to be dressing for him, even though she knew he would never see these undergarments. But she would know they were there, and she would feel more feminine, aware that beneath the ski clothes were sweet talcum and soft lace.

She put on her cherry-colored robe and sat on the

edge of her bed, waiting. Inside, she cradled the delicious feeling of embarking on an affair. Whatever Cooper Smith thought of her, she was feeling the excitement of beginning something new, yet with known potential. She shivered. Waiting gave her too much time to think. Anticipation was scary—bad luck, even. She'd learned from the past to contain her eagerness, wary lest the moment itself prove disappointing. Life had a way of coming up short.

The ringing telephone made her jump. Its harsh sound jarred her already taut nerves, and she picked up the receiver hoping she could control the tremor she knew would be in her voice.

But it wasn't Cooper.

Gordon Hamilton's flat voice said, "Is that you, Maggie?"

Annoyed, her impulse was to ask tartly, "Who did you expect?" She took a deep breath, sighing. "Yes. It's me. This is pretty early, you know."

"Sorry. You said you had to get up early. I just wanted you to know I thought about you last night after you left. Thought about you quite a lot, in fact. I wanted to tell you to have a good time today. But not too good."

Inwardly she groaned. Oh, Lord. Complications. Why had she tried to curry favor with him, even for a moment? In her coolest professional voice she said, "I'll do a good job for us, I promise. Don't worry, Mr. Hamilton, I'll keep the essential purpose in mind. Okay?"

"*Mr.* Hamilton? What is this?"

"I really forgot myself last night. We have a professional relationship. We shouldn't—"

He broke in, "I thought we'd put all that silly formality aside, Mag—Miss McAllister. Isn't it just a little late to be backtracking to this Miss and Mr. stuff?"

He cleared his throat. "Then again, I may have misread your signals. Well, I'll say what I was going to say. What would you think of dinner with me tonight?"

Quickly sensing his vulnerability, she said, "Perhaps you're right and I am being too formal. . . Gordon." His name stuck in her throat. "But I don't think I'll be up to dinner, not after a whole day of skiing and all the note taking afterward. Why don't I just take a rain check?"

She wished she'd never tried to charm him, but she had and now this! From here on they were going to have problems.

A knock sounded at her door, diverting her attention from the phone.

"Rain check," he was saying coldly. "In other words, I did misread you. You were just—" Evidently controlling himself, he broke off, continuing more calmly, "When your notes are finished, I'd like to see them. Call me tomorrow, Miss McAllister."

"I will," she said hurriedly, her eye on the door. "And I will have dinner with you sometime—just not tonight." Before he could respond she said a soft goodbye.

Drawing her robe in closer, she hurried to the door and opened it to Cooper Smith.

SEEING HIM THERE, her reactions to Hamilton vanished in an instant. Smith stood tall, strong and smiling, his scar creasing inward a little. And those gray eyes; she would never have guessed eyes that color could be so filled with warmth. His happiness at seeing her was undeniable; he made no attempt to hide it.

"Maggie." His arms were buried under a mound of clothing, a load that shifted as he stepped into the room and threatened to fall. "Whoops—they're going," he laughed, accelerating toward the bed and dumping the whole pile into a heap on the bedcovers.

As much as she wished he might draw her into his arms then, he didn't.

Instead he took both her hands and said, "Maggie, it seems like a month since we set this up. All this week, and then the weekend, trying to get through the last half of the cattle auction, I was thinking about the skiing—about us." He smiled. "It might have been a mistake. When they deliver my heifers, I hope I don't find I also bought pigs and sheep."

She laughed, not wanting him to know how eagerly she, too, had waited. Lightly, she said, "You may wish you'd never thought of the skiing, after all, especially when you're pulling me out of a snowbank. I'm better in a canoe than on skis. I forgot to tell you how long it's been since I've skied." She smiled. "Aerobics don't count."

"Skiing comes back," he said. "Like riding a bicycle."

She shook her head doubtfully. "Only if you really knew how to do it when you stopped. I was only halfway competent for a week." Thinking back, she added, "It was a good week, though. I'd begun to think I could tackle almost any hill." She pulled away from his hand to pick up the ski pants on the bed and added with a wry face, "I wasn't exactly thinking of a fourteen-thousand-foot mountain."

Coming up behind her, he placed his hands on her waist. She felt a tremor move within her as he said against the back of her neck, "I won't hold you responsible for all fourteen thousand feet, Maggie. Only the small portion we're going to cover. And I'll be right with you, every minute."

His warm breath touched her flesh and his closeness threatened to overwhelm her. She moved away a little, fighting for control, and as a distraction held the ski pants against her waist, checking their size.

"Those belong to my sister, Anne. Put them on. We have to get up on the mountain. The temperature is ideal today for where we're going, but it could change if we wait too long." He looked at his watch. "Six-thirty. I promised to pick up Dan Gardner at seven."

She took the clothes and shut the bathroom door behind her. The thermal underwear he'd brought was still in a package. Ladies' medium. She ripped off the cellophane and pulled the garments on over her panties and bra. Sexless underwear, she thought. Then she put on a dark peach-colored wool sweater, and over that the lighter peach ski pants with a bib that tucked under her breasts. The last layer was an enormous, down-filled navy-and-peach parka. She ran a comb through her hair and looked in the bathroom mirror. The clothes were handsome, she thought, if you didn't care that most of your curves were obliterated. For an instant, surveying herself, she thought, *Why can't we be going swimming?*

When she emerged from the bathroom, he studied her intently and shook his head. "You're beautiful, Maggie!"

"You'll have to stop saying that!" she commanded, putting her finger on his lips. "Besides, I look like a roly-poly doll, so I know you're a liar."

Dropping his arm over her padded shoulder, he smiled. "Anne tells me this look is in. When I said the jacket and pants seemed puffy for a gorgeous woman, she assured me you'd positively never ski in a bathing suit."

She laughed, wanting to tell him what she'd been thinking in the bathroom. But she held back, afraid that their conversation was getting too intimate. How often in the past she'd encouraged intimate talk with men, and how meaningless it had seemed then. Now that she wanted intimacy, she was suddenly afraid of it.

"They're beautiful clothes," she said, wishing they didn't have to go anywhere. And yet what would happen if they stayed here? She knew. Oh, she knew too well.

She followed him down the stairs, studying him from the back. He wore navy-blue ski pants that had been in vogue once but were seldom seen now. Stretched tightly over his legs and hips, the lycra emphasized his muscular legs and the roundness of his— She stopped the thought, asking herself why she was paying particular attention to that part of his anatomy. But it was good, darn it! She liked the way he was built, every inch of him. And she thought that here was a man built for distance rather than speed, a lasting man, good not for months, but for years.

He wore a heavy wool sweater, a steel blue, which made her think of the way he'd looked standing in her doorway a short time ago, his gray eyes conveying infinite depths and absorbing her in a way she'd never experienced before.

As Maggie climbed into the Wagoneer she commanded herself to stop thinking such things. Everything about him was dangerous and worse, overwhelming. The day, hardly begun, already had an aura of unreality about it, and as much as she knew she ought to maintain an inner distance, she could not control the drifting feeling that in his presence there were two levels of consciousness: the one that responded to him and the one that stood back, observing.

A few minutes later they stopped at a small wood-frame house to pick up Dan Gardner, who was in his late teens and bounded into the car energetically. The back seat of the Wagoneer could hardly contain his restless movements. At one point Dan said, "I wish I was skiing instead of driving."

Cooper turned half around to give him a casual grin. "My turn, Dan. You've had your share of introducing young ladies to this mountain. And don't get any ideas about taking one little run and hiking back to the Wagoneer. It's hands off up there today. I want this vehicle waiting when we get down."

"No problem," Dan said amiably. "Besides, I wouldn't get far without skis."

The patchy snow that lay in the shadows under the trees grew denser when they started to climb and the road curved in endless bends as they gained altitude. It was a good road, well banked, and though intended to accommodate only one vehicle in each direction, was wide enough in places for passing.

Just beyond the paving, firs, pines and cedars crowded in close, their boughs overhanging the shoulders. Higher on the mountain, their trunks were padded in white batting. The roadside snow had been pushed into careless mounds, which grew deeper the higher they went. Maggie saw a chipmunk scamper across the crusty white surface, leaving behind tiny prints like sprinkles from a pepper shaker.

Absorbed by the richness of the forest around her, Maggie said very little, and even Dan Gardner stopped chattering in the back seat.

It was seven-thirty when Smith announced, "You can begin putting on your boots, Maggie," and had Dan pass her a pair of plastic, high-topped, navy-blue ski boots. A pair of blue woolen socks was stuffed inside. She was still struggling with them when Smith called out, "Bunny Flats," and pulled to a wide place in the road.

Maggie eased herself out of the Wagoneer and walked around, testing her boots. They were as stiff as two plaster casts—hardly comfortable for walking.

For the next few minutes Gardner and Smith unloaded equipment onto the snowbank: two pairs of skis, poles, hats, gloves, two backpacks—one large and one small—and some odd-looking bags that were made of something resembling seal skin.

Finished, Dan jumped into the Wagoneer, smiled, waved and spun the vehicle in a tight circle before taking off at high speed down the mountain. Watching him go, Cooper shook his head. "He'll probably grow up if he lives long enough. He has too much energy for a small town like Mount Shasta where there isn't enough for young people to do. They can't burn off their extra energy in community sports, like soccer or swimming. When Jesse gets a few years older I'm going to send him to school near San Francisco. I want his life richer than it can ever be here."

Maggie looked at him in surprise. "But you... you've said the place becomes part of you, Cooper, and you've let me believe your life is quite...rich."

He inclined his head toward her, gazing down at her with an intensity that took her breath away. "I'm an adult, Maggie. I don't need soccer. I need very little for happiness. And what is lacking, I may have found." He took a step toward her, bringing them so close there was almost no space between them. In one motion he lifted her chin with his hand and brought his lips down to hers.

Surprised, not expecting him to kiss her there of all places, she yielded without thinking and immediately knew that she had never really wanted anyone to kiss her the way she wanted Cooper Smith.

Was it the man...or the way he did it, she wondered in the brief instant before she was lost in warmth, moistness and intensity both soft and demanding. That he kissed beautifully, with a sensitivity that belied his obvious strength, shouldn't have surprised her, for she had never found anything in this man that didn't push her—no, catapult her away from all her strongest resolves.

The cold mountain air touched her cheek and a wind moaned sporadically through the upper limbs of the pines. Subliminally aware of these things, Maggie tucked them into her subconscious to be brought out later in memory of this moment. For now she recognized only the strength of Cooper's arms, the woodsy smell of his skin and her wanting his lips against hers, longer... oh, much longer.

Yet his kiss was brief, and as he raised his chin to look into her eyes he said, "I couldn't have done that back in your room, though I wanted to. I think you know why."

"I expected it."

"I knew you did. I expected it, too. But out here..." He smiled. "We can't get into trouble."

She heard the wind tweaking a pine somewhere overhead, saw a loose clump of snow fall to the ground soundlessly, leaving no evidence of its existence after it plopped into the whiteness across the road.

"Would that have been trouble, Cooper?" she asked.

"You don't think so now. But you might have looked at it differently then." He pulled her gently toward the bank and up its side toward the skis. "When it's time for us, Maggie, you'll know it as well as I."

She felt a protest rising to her lips, angered momentarily that he considered it his prerogative to make all decisions for both of them. Yet before she spoke she knew he was right. She'd been prepared to resist him back in her motel room. But here, where there was little chance of drifting toward lovemaking out in the open and with nothing around them but cold mountain air, she'd yielded unreservedly.

Cooper helped Maggie snap into her skis, then handed her her gloves and hat. "You might not need these yet, now that the sun's out. But you will before we get down. Put them in your pocket." Then he handed her the smaller knapsack. "Slip your arms into this, and I'll adjust the straps."

With his own large backpack secured, he turned into a space between two large pines, striding effortlessly across the crusty snow. The sun was still low on the horizon, creating lengthy shadows behind all the trees and making long, distorted images of them.

Gradually they left the open spaces behind. As Maggie followed Smith, she was aware not only of the effort of gliding cross-country, but also of the power and size of the man in front of her. He moved so easily, as though the skis had been grafted onto his boots, and the boots to his body. Yet she guessed he was holding back, because for the first ten minutes, while they were on flat land, she was able to keep up.

Their progress through the forest was nearly silent, except for the soft frictional murmur of skis on snow and the gentle crunch of ski poles into a slightly resisting surface. Maggie was exhilarated by the pervasive peace among the trees, aware that the animals who left their small tracks everywhere moved as silently as they did. She felt a part of the forest world, as though she had somehow earned a kind of woodland membership just by being there. And she sensed a similar harmony with this man who spoke little but included her in a trek across his beloved mountain.

When the way became steeper, Smith stopped and slid out from under his backpack. "We're starting up, now," he said. "We're going to need the skins on our skis."

"Skins?" she asked.

"They're a covering designed to improve the friction on your skis." He opened his pack and took out the four long strips of material, spreading them flat on the ground before sliding their skis into them.

"In the old days," Cooper said, "these skins were genuine seal, designed so that the tightly packed animal hairs would point down the hill to prevent the skis from sliding. Now they're made of synthetic material, but the principle is the same. Once these are on you can climb an almost perpendicular slope without sliding backward." He smiled. "You'll see."

Abruptly they changed course, and the path Smith took led almost straight up.

Maggie found that Cooper was right. When she slid her skis forward one after the other they held nicely, gripping the snow as though her ski bottoms were spiked. On the other hand, the act of pushing them uphill was anything but easy. It was like trying to slide up a very steep ramp that extended upward as far as she could see.

Maggie guessed Cooper could have climbed for hours with very little fatigue, but for her he turned around often, smiled and asked how she was doing.

At first she smiled back, with a little wave of her gloved hand. But soon she was breathing heavily and even waving felt like an effort.

With unflagging strength he pushed upward, picking a route among the trees with such certainty that she knew there was no chance of their getting lost.

Following in his path, Maggie found she was no longer conscious of the scenery but only of the trail left by his skis, the two perpendicular creases that she followed blindly.

The next time he turned around, he asked, "You sure you're okay?"

"Oh...I'm doing...fine," she puffed. "It's... easy! Just stop...a day or two...and I'll recover!" She had no energy left for smiling.

As Cooper turned to come back to her, Maggie maneuvered toward the trunk of a towering pine and leaned against it, gasping. Perspiration trickled from her hairline and ran along the sides of her cheeks. She gave her weight to the tree, staring at Cooper fixedly while she took in deep breaths.

"Sorry, Maggie." He took her gloved hand. "I've pushed you too hard. You fooled me when we started, keeping up like a teenage boy. I was going at a pretty fast pace."

She was surprised. "Were you?" She took a long, deep breath. "It seemed...slow...to me. I kept thinking...how the trees were going by...at a crawl."

He laughed. "When you're climbing a mountain, trees do not sail by lickety-split. But there's no hurry. We'll take it slower now." With his gloved hand he patted hers, a strangely warming gesture.

They stood in silence for a few minutes, and sooner than she would have thought possible, Maggie's energy returned. Perhaps her aerobics classes had given her greater fitness than she'd imagined.

They were high on the side of a ridge, but through scattered gaps in the trees, Maggie could see vast open fields of snow. "It's beautiful up here," she said, breathing normally again. All around them the wind sighed through the pine boughs, while close at hand she saw tender young seedlings, cedars and firs, peeking through the snow's surface.

"And you've just begun to see the mountain," he said. "This is a part of it few people have visited, which makes you special." He gave her an odd look. "But you were, anyway. Are you all right, Maggie? To go on?"

"Sure." She stretched out a ski experimentally. "I think my legs are actually going to hold me a while longer."

"Good. It's only another ten minutes to the cabin."

"Cabin? What cabin?"

"They call it Horse Camp. An unglamorous name for the Sierra Club building that's been here for years. We'll have lunch there."

"Someone's fixing us lunch?" she asked in astonishment, and then, seeing his grin start, laughed at her own mistake. "Well, I do think we've earned some French cuisine at the very least. If I'd known what was coming, I wouldn't have done it for anything less than luncheon at Antoine's."

Unexpectedly, he moved toward her and kissed her nose, then just as quickly pulled ahead of her once more, turning uphill with his easy strides. "Luncheon at Antoine's, here we come!"

On her own again, she smiled. The canoeing had been her day, but today was his, and he gave it a spirit that she'd have had difficulty defining.

While she'd invented a silly game and prodded him into playing it as if they were trying to win an Olympic medal, he brought her to all this grandeur—his mountain—and assumed she would see it as he did.

Well, maybe she would or maybe she wouldn't. But just being with him made her feel good and vibrantly alive, as though she'd been newly born into this bright, snowy world. With renewed energy and feeling stronger than ever, Maggie kept up easily, though she realized that Cooper had set a much slower pace. Ten minutes later he called out, "Here it is, Maggie," and they emerged from a thicket to find a small, protected cabin set in a clearing deep in the woods.

PARTED FROM HER SKIS, Maggie sat down on a stump to wait while Cooper disappeared behind the building, seeking the accustomed hiding place for the key.

The little hut before her was constructed entirely of mortared stone, with a stubby stone chimney poking out of a corrugated tin roof. It was very square, a no-nonsense building that Smith had described as having "weathered a thousand storms."

Key in hand, he returned and unlocked the door, turning to Maggie before he pushed the heavy wooden barrier aside. "Antoine's," he said with a gallant gesture toward the interior, "where the cuisine is positively the best to be found on this mountain."

Laughing, Maggie took his hand and swept inside, noting that the one-room cabin still retained the chill from the night before. A cold stone floor and triple bunk beds in the corner—frames minus their mattresses—enhanced the impression of barren chilliness. Along one wall a simple wooden table was flanked by two plain, straight-backed chairs.

Involuntarily, Maggie shivered. How much nicer the place would have been with cloth somewhere—curtains, a rug, mattresses—anything. But of course that would be impractical and silly up here on the side of a mountain. To the wanderer who found this place in a blizzard it would no doubt look like heaven.

Only after a second inspection did Maggie notice the fireplace, faced with more of the same stone that made up all four walls of the cabin. Some attempt had been made to outline the opening with rocks of a uniform size, but still it seemed little more than a gaping mouth, its interior blackened by the soot of bygone fires.

As she tried to envision the blazes that had once warmed the cabin, Cooper walked in with an armload of firewood. "Each user replaces what he burns," he explained, dumping logs on the uneven stone hearth. "The cabin comes with an ax and a warning. Tends to make you stingy about burning too many logs. But we're going to have a fire, Maggie. This place is cold."

A few minutes later, having achieved a crackling blaze, Cooper asked Maggie to help him pull the little wooden table around in front of the fireplace, and sitting across from her on one of the chairs, he ceremoniously opened his backpack and pulled food out onto the table. With a flourish he arranged before each of them sandwiches, apples, packets of chocolate cake, tiny sacks of mixed nuts and two squat thermoses. Picking up one of the sandwiches, he said, "Ham and cheese *du jour*. The best Antoine's has to offer!"

She laughed, placing her hand over his. "When did you do all this? In addition to finding all my clothes and skis and. . . skins? When did you have time, Cooper, with your cattle auction and. . . and everything else you have to do?"

He set his sandwich down again and lifted her hand, entwining her fingers with his. "I'd like to take the credit, but I didn't do it all. I asked my housekeeper, Mrs. Winslow, to come back Sunday night to pack this lunch. All I did was tell her what we wanted." He unscrewed her thermos and poured hot liquid into its top, then held it out to her. "Hot tea. Try it—it'll warm you in a minute."

"I'm already warm." She took the cup and gazed at the sputtering logs, feeling the heat that poured out into the room, but even more, the warmth that came just from sitting there with him.

As Cooper ate his sandwich, Maggie stole a surreptitious look at his profile, saw the straight, strong nose, the chin utterly masculine in its width. Locks of his sandy hair, ruffled from the outdoors, fell in unruly bunches over his forehead, lending him that look of enduring youth that belied his maturity. His was the kind of profile you'd search out in a crowd if you were in trouble, she thought, the face you'd turn to, because everything about it was stamped Capable. She wondered if there was anything he couldn't do.

After a few minutes of eating in silence, Cooper asked, "What made you become a lawyer, Maggie? Was it something you've always wanted to do, or did you decide much later?"

She frowned, wishing he hadn't asked. To explain would be to let him get too close. She didn't feel like rummaging around in her psyche, stirring up old traumas that she preferred to keep submerged. "I decided when I was fourteen." She hoped he wouldn't ask more.

"That long ago?"

She shrugged. "That was when it seemed most important to me."

"Why?" His gray eyes searched hers, not with idle curiosity but with caring.

"Why do you want to know?"

"Perhaps," he responded, pouring hot tea into his cup, "because I want to know everything about you, which has been the case since the moment I did that sudden about-face on the high-school stairs. I almost knocked you off your feet that day, Maggie, but it's I who've been knocked off my feet since then. I think about you all the time. Questions. I have a thousand of them."

"And you believe you have the right to have them all answered?"

He drank from his cup contemplatively. "I don't know. Probably not, from your viewpoint. From mine, yes, I think I have the right. Call it an investment of caring, which seems to confer special privileges." He smiled. "I'm getting murky. If you don't want to answer, don't."

She said nothing. Staring into the fire, she wondered why, when her mind was constantly occupied with him, she resented having him know those last painful details from her childhood. Was she ashamed of what those years had done to her?

She said, "The cake's good, isn't it?"

"Mrs. Winslow makes these once in a while. Jesse and I clamor for her cakes continually, but she won't bake, even to please us. Says someone has to guard our health. We only get cake on special occasions." He grinned at her. "I convinced her this was a special occasion."

"But you'll eat the rest when you get home," Maggie probed.

"Yes. I'll urge Jesse to have it, but I'll make sure I get my share. I don't have any willpower."

She laughed. "I wouldn't have guessed it, Cooper. Ever. All along I've been imagining you're the strongest-willed man I've ever met."

Again the gray eyes met hers. "Are you talking chocolate cake, Maggie, or something else?"

To her surprise, she blushed. "I. . . well, I'm not sure." She hated being awkward. "In every situation, every place I've seen you, I get this feeling of willpower. Of control."

He stood up, throwing her the hint of a smile. "You haven't seen me around chocolate cake." He walked to the fireplace, threw the ax over his shoulder and said at the doorway, "I have to replenish the firewood. And after that we've got the whole mountain ahead of us."

"The whole mountain?" she echoed. Then in sudden understanding added, "You mean the whole mountain going down!"

"No, Maggie. We're still a long way from Giddy Giddy Gulch. I'm afraid I mean the mountain going up!"

CHAPTER ELEVEN

MAGGIE STOOD AT THE BOTTOM of Giddy Giddy Gulch, trying to adjust her eyes to the dazzling whiteness they'd come upon as they emerged from the forest. Though the day had turned cloudy, the unrelieved snow on the great slope ahead of them had a brilliance that made her squint. Shading her eyes, she tried to imagine herself as a speck at the top of that mammoth contour, somehow making her way down. She couldn't picture herself doing it. The rise was much too steep.

She turned to Cooper. "I'm sure I can't ski down that. It's...it's overwhelming." She shook her head. "I'm nowhere near good enough for that, honestly. You'll have to understand and give up on me."

He rested his hand on her shoulder. "You'll be fine. Once you're up on top, it won't seem so steep, and going down is only a few yards at a time. Just one turn and then another, Maggie. You'll find it glorious."

Unconvinced, she mentioned her second worry. "But we have to get to the top, don't we? Up that!" Why was she worrying about coming down, she wondered, staring up at the curved, shadowless expanse, smooth and trackless. One could not come down what one was unable to climb up. "I'll never make it up there!"

"You've made it so far, haven't you? The rest is no worse."

"But we were in the trees! It seemed...safer!" For the last half hour they'd been deep in the forest, and she'd managed to keep up, following in Cooper's tracks as he picked his unerring way among the trees. But she'd never expected to come up on a scene like this!

He leaned on his pole. "Can you believe me that what's ahead is no steeper than what we've left behind? It only looks so because it's. . . naked!"

"Yes, it's naked. . . and so am I! You're looking at a plucked-clean, undisguised coward. I'm scared, Cooper!" She turned away from the hill, unwilling to look at it any longer.

He came up behind her, putting both hands on her shoulders, but when she kept her face averted and held her arms defensively, he reached for her chin, drawing her face around. "Look at me, Maggie. Do you trust me?"

"If you say I can handle that mountain. . . no!"

"I say you can ski it—climb it and ski it. But you'll have to believe me."

"I don't believe you. I think you think I'm something that I'm not; that I'm stronger than I am, more capable than I am. . . ." She was thinking but didn't add, *that I'm better than I am.* Indignant, she went on. "Sometimes you see what you want to see, Cooper. I'm not an experienced mountaineer, and that mountain up there is more than I can handle. I just know it is by looking at it."

"Maggie, I'm going to show you what you're capable of." Without arguing further, he led off, leaving her where she was.

She stood watching, amazed. He kept skiing away, not turning around, and all the time she stood there she thought he'd stop or come back, but he didn't. Five minutes went by while Maggie tested him.

For one wild moment she thought she'd try to retrace their steps and return to the cabin, but immediately she knew it was hopeless. Even if their tracks were perfectly clear, and she got there, what would she do then?

Watching his back moving away from her, Maggie grew angry, then fearful. How far would he go without her? Unsure, she knew she had no alternative but to follow him, and quickly.

Grabbing her ski poles, she moved across the bottom of the great white slope after him, skiing as fast as she could. When, in the distance, he started up a steep slope, she pushed on faster, really afraid that she might lose him. With head lowered and eyes on his tracks, she didn't see him turn around or notice that he'd slowed.

Instead, propelled by anger, she cursed him. *Damn him! Damn this man!* A litany of damns cycled in her brain and brought her speed she'd never have thought possible. Even as the slope increased in steepness, Maggie traveled with wings on her skis.

She reached the top of a small rise and started down, then stopped abruptly. Cooper was right in front of her!

"Well! You caught me!" He grinned down at her.

"Oh, shut up, Cooper Smith!"

"Do you know how fast you went, Maggie?"

"Was I supposed to be running a mileage check or something? Thirty miles an hour? Forty?"

"You were magnificent!" His grin widened. "We don't have much farther to go. I've decided not to take you clear to the top."

"Oh, great! Great! He's not going to send me over Victoria Falls, after all. He's settling for Niagara. Big of you, Cooper!"

"But you could do it. You could make it clear to the top and ski all the way down." His gray eyes were thoughtful. "If you want to, Maggie."

She was still angry. "Okay then, prove your point. Take me to the top. Dammit, take me all the way up. It's what you intended to do anyway. Go ahead, what are you waiting for? You know I can do anything—Maggie McAllister, iron woman, the lady who's never found anything she can't accomplish!"

"You're on," he said calmly, as though her outburst was serious. "Come on, now. It's not far."

AN HOUR LATER they stood at the top looking down.

To her surprise, Maggie's anger had dissipated as she climbed, replaced slowly by a sense of her own fortitude, then by a growing awareness of her physical strength. As they came closer to the top she began to feel truly happy. Taking those last few glides that brought her to the ridge had been pure triumph, an accomplishment that was hers and hers alone.

Cooper slipped his arm around her shoulders. "Not bad, Maggie."

She looked up at him and smiled, grateful he hadn't patronized her.

For a moment they stood in silence, looking down at the great white bowl spread out below them. Then he said, "Why don't you unhook your skis?"

Before she had quite straightened, he took her in his arms. Drawing her in close, he brought his face down to hers, and she felt the excitement that was already in her veins augmented by the headiness of his breath and his lips and his tongue becoming part of her.

Suddenly she needed him for support. Melting against him, she experienced his strength in ways she never had before. His arms held her upright, and she gave up her sense of self to a profounder knowledge of him. Maggie was happy, but more than that, she was utterly content.

When he released her, smiling, his face mirrored the

happiness of her own. "Maggie, promise me something. Never again sell yourself short."

She shook her head. "I can't promise you that, Cooper. I'm not on the outside looking in. I... . I don't see me as you see me. I'm in here." She pointed to her chest. "In here peeking out, and it's a different view from yours."

He laughed. "Well put. Point taken."

Saying he was warm, Cooper took off his jacket and spread it on the snow for both of them to sit on.

Maggie sat down gratefully, and drawing her knees up, gazed down at the swale that was Giddy Giddy Gulch. It seemed to extend below them for miles, wide, white and steep. Unbroken by trees, the slope could have accommodated a thousand skiers at once. Far below, miles away, the tree line began.

"Is this what you call a bowl, Cooper?"

"Yes. It's one of the finest ski bowls on this mountain. But this is only one. There are many others."

She caught herself wondering how skiers would do it any harm, since there weren't any trees to disturb, nor any noticeable wildlife that would be affected, though she supposed the animals had been keeping out of sight.

She sighed. It was time to ask a few questions. "Is this the area of the proposed skiing, Mr. Smith?"

He threw her a quick, startled glance, then laughed warmly. "Time to do your homework, eh, Maggie? Well. . . part of the skiing would be here, sure, but not all. The bowls above treeline are excellent for good weather, like today, but other times—during storms, whiteouts and blizzards—they're unskiable. We've got to have the protected areas, too, down in the trees. As you can see even from the relatively small area we covered today, the possibilities are endless. You've seen only a small bit of one face of the mountain. But there are three hundred sixty degrees of face to consider—a lot of territory, huh? Certainly enough for everyone."

She was silent.

"But you're going to have problems, talking to me. If I really convince you I'm right, what will you do?"

She answered defensively. "I'll go on doing my job, of course. Lawyers are advocates—we plead others' causes and not necessarily those positions we believe in. When we're hired to do a job, we do it, leaving our feelings somewhere else."

"But for you that's difficult?"

"It isn't!" She pulled away from him and stood up. "What kind of lawyer do you think I am? A namby-pamby emotional woman who can't separate her feelings from her job? Don't be ridiculous. I found out in a hurry that what I believe doesn't really matter. I went through my period of caring too much, trying to defend indigents for Legal Aide when I was just out of law school. But the system isn't geared for indigents. Clients who can't afford to pay seldom win. And the lawyer can't afford to cry about it, either."

Maggie tossed her long hair back defiantly. "You learn, Cooper, you learn. Now I'm pragmatic... pragmatic enough to know that only results count, results that suit my client." In the silence her voice sounded oddly strident.

Slowly, Cooper got to his feet and walked over to his equipment, then squatted to remove the skins from their skis. He stuffed them into his backpack.

She'd overreacted, Maggie thought, glad he had let it drop. The best lawyers *did* get emotionally involved with their cases; they did care. It was a matter of how much and whether they chose the issues themselves or chose them for the money. She smiled to herself as she leaned over to put on her boots. A big fee had its peculiar way of making you care.

Feeling stiff, Maggie straightened slowly, imagining herself a workhorse reluctantly reshouldering its traces. It was obvious she'd been sitting too long.

"Ready to start down?" Cooper asked.

She nodded.

He skied up next to her. "Sometimes I think you know yourself even less well than I do." He raised one of his poles, pointing. "We'll head over to the edge where the snow is nice and even. It's corn snow at this time of year, easy to maneuver in. I'll pick out the easiest way down, and all you have to do is follow. Now comes the dessert, Maggie."

Unexpectedly, Cooper leaned toward her and kissed her lightly on the forehead, saying, "Come along, my child. Follow me."

And he was off.

For the first time, Cooper's kiss angered her.

As he began his long, slow turns, leaving a wide, gradual figure S in the snow, she had a burning desire to overtake him and scream in his face, "I'm not a child! And you *don't* know me!"

His manner infuriated her. How dare he presume to understand her better than she did herself? What business did he have calling her "child" and ordering her to follow him? Who did he think he was?

Seething, Maggie skied as fast as she could, the skills she'd once acquired returning to her with surprising speed. Before they'd gone far she was executing her turns with greater ease than she'd ever done before. The corn snow under her skis crackled satisfactorily, but best of all, it held her edges in a way that made her feel secure. Letting go a little, she picked up speed, which had the effect of making her turns still quicker and smoother.

In front of her, Cooper traveled faster, too, his knees moving from side to side with the grace that was the hallmark of an excellent skier. Effortlessly, he narrowed his turns, choosing a smaller path and sending blowing snow behind him in a fine white spray.

He must have known she was right behind him! Still angry, Maggie tried to catch him, but he never allowed it. The faster she went, the faster he went.

Breathless, with knees suddenly tired, she at last decided she had to rest. Throwing her hips to the right in an exaggerated gesture, she swung her skis left and gripped the snow hard, sending a flurry of snow behind her in a white cascade. A few yards down the slope, Smith stopped, too.

Below, the hill gleamed white and inviting, and Maggie imagined herself skiing down it unrestrained—perhaps even faster than him! She saw him there waiting, not prepared to go, and on impulse she suddenly pointed her skis down the hill and sped past him. Down into the endless white bowl Maggie sent her skis flying, negotiating turn after turn, feeling her mood change until she skied with a new spirit of abandon. She'd never experienced such limitless, unobstructed motion.

On and on she went, her anger swept away by the rush of wind in her face, exhilaration taking over until she felt a near-mystical union with her skis.

It was only after many minutes of such freedom that she saw in the distance the beginnings of the timberline. Slowing a little, Maggie expected Cooper to overtake her, but he didn't, and she was just as glad. She liked leaving him behind.

At last, regretfully, fatigue caught up with her once more and Maggie drove her skis into a stop. Immediately, Cooper arrived in a snowy wake. "Well, Maggie. Looks like you're a convert to bowl skiing!"

Maggie shrugged, her annoyance surfacing anew. "Yes. I like it."

"I knew you would."

There it was again. She faced him, now genuinely angry. "Why did you know I would? How can you presume to speak for me, to tell me what I'll like and what I won't like? What do you think you are—a mind reader?"

For the first time in their relationship, Cooper was taken aback. Surprise crossed his features, then a kind of closing in that was unfathomable. His jaw hardened and his eyes narrowed before he looked away. Maggie had no idea what he'd do.

His eyes fixed down the slope away from her, he said, "We have to get going. Will you lead out, or shall I?"

"How far down this bowl do we go?"

"All the way."

"Then I'll go first. And leave you back there to pick up the pieces in case I fall."

Unsmiling, he looked at his watch. "Dan will be meeting us soon. Are you up to skiing all-out like you did before?"

"I think so."

"Better start, then."

The sound of his voice hadn't changed, she thought as she again pointed down the hill, only the look on his face. He'd put space between them, without obvious anger or hurt. She felt the separation acutely.

For a short time Maggie let her skis have their way, but the thrill had lessened, since her mind was occupied with Cooper.

After a while she realized she was tiring, and in place of that carefree feeling of letting go, she found herself holding on in her turns, gripping the snow as though any minute she'd slide out. *I'm tight,* she realized. *This is what is meant by "skiing tight."* Overcome by an ache in her knees, Maggie stopped again to rest.

A flurry of snow, and Cooper was beside her. "You want me to lead?" he asked matter-of-factly.

"After a minute. . . yes." Maggie was panting.

"Tired, huh? Or am I not allowed to notice?"

"You. . . you're allowed."

She tried to read his face. There was nothing there, neither sympathy nor contrition. Maggie wished she hadn't blown up. Had he really done anything so terrible? She guessed not, but pride wouldn't let her apologize.

She glanced at her watch and saw it was three-forty. The air was turning colder and their bodies left noticeably longer shadows on the snow. Foraging in her pockets, she drew out her gloves and hat and put them on.

Cooper waited, finally saying, "Maggie, we'll have to go. Once we get down into the trees I'll have to break trail because it's a tricky pathway. Can you negotiate a narrow trail?"

"I don't know. It's been so long."

"I'll be aware of how you're doing," he said, starting out again.

She followed, regretting acutely what had happened. His words were the same, his voice the same, yet everything had changed. Cooper had withdrawn from her, and she wondered if she could ever get him back.

COOPER AND MAGGIE EMERGED, two hours after they'd started down the bowl, at McBride Springs. The last half hour they'd been in deep forest, and though down here they were protected from the wind, the lateness of the day had brought a new and sharper chill to the air. Maggie was glad they'd been in constant motion. She knew the minute they stopped she'd be cold.

Cooper found the road where Dan would pick them

up, and having unfastened his skis, walked out onto it and looked down the cleared highway as far as he could. But neither had to say they were quite alone. If Dan was here, they'd see him.

"That kid was supposed to be back half an hour ago!" Cooper slid his pack from his shoulders and rotated them in a gesture of fatigue before consulting his watch once more. "Forty minutes ago," he amended. A strange expression crossed his face. "He wouldn't...there's no way he would have come and gone...."

For a fleeting moment as he turned to Maggie, puzzled, Cooper seemed unsure of himself. Had he misjudged Dan Gardner, Maggie wondered, and was he now questioning himself? Was there some flaw in Cooper Smith, after all?

"You're not sure of that boy," Maggie offered.

"I thought I was."

"You've always considered yourself a good judge of character?"

Smith paused to study her thoughtfully, weighing his words before he spoke. "I realize you find this hard to accept, Maggie. But yes, I've always relied on that as one of my talents. Judging character isn't difficult if you have a feel for it." He picked up his backpack and rummaged deep inside, pulling out a thermos. "There's some tea left. Go ahead and drink it, Maggie. You're going to need it to stay warm."

"And what about you?"

His gaze went once more to the road. "If Dan doesn't show up in the next five minutes, I'll be too busy to notice whether it's cold."

The air temperature dropped rapidly and the wind rose, keening in the trees above them. Smith abandoned his search for Dan, and ordering Maggie to wrap up in the parka he carelessly shucked off, strode into the woods, looking for fallen pine boughs.

Trip after trip brought them an even-higher pile of needled boughs, which he began arranging into a kind of shelter.

"What can I do?" Maggie asked.

"You can place these so that they're interlaced, bottom-top, top-bottom, letting the needles fill in the gaps. We need a shelter just large enough so the two of us can stretch out and still be protected."

"From animals?" she asked.

Stopping midstride on his way back into the woods, he turned to smile at her for the first time since they'd reached the bottom. "From the cold. If an animal wants to come snuggle with us, he's welcome."

In spite of the extra parka, Maggie shivered. So Cooper was planning on their spending the night in the woods. He'd said nothing about walking out, which she supposed he'd already dismissed as impossible. How many miles were they from civilization, anyway, she wondered. Somehow she preferred the idea of walking, of doing something besides just waiting.

And it was going to be so cold. Already she felt the chill on her face, realized it was creeping inside her clothing. The prospect of a confrontation with wild animals no longer concerned her. Cooper knew the real risk—that they might freeze to death.

As the daylight faded, Maggie and Cooper worked feverishly to strengthen their small shelter, piling up boughs on three sides and the floor, leaving a fourth side open to a bonfire. Working now at even-greater speed, Cooper gathered the wood they would need to keep flames going throughout the night. Just before darkness settled over them altogether, Maggie appraised their woodpile as sufficient for several nights. But she said nothing.

Concentrating, Cooper arranged his wood in stacks, his words as few as they'd been during the lingering twilight, so that Maggie wondered whether his quiet was inspired by her or the situation. She sat watching him work, dreading the long night that would keep them cooped up together in leaden silence.

By seven, the last glimmer of light had disappeared from behind the trees. Maggie sat on the pine boughs, her legs drawn in close to her body, her hands deep in the pockets of Cooper's parka.

Cupping his hands around a match, Cooper touched the tentative flame to a fragile twig and hovered over it to shield the sputtering flame from the wind. The match went out.

Again he rounded his body around a flickering match, huddling even closer, and this time the flame caught a few pine needles, flared briefly, caught again, then ignited the twig. Maggie held her breath as the twig continued to burn, the flame gradually inching toward other twigs, which began to sizzle from the heat. The fire grew.

Ten minutes later a modest bonfire burned in front of their shelter. Quickly Cooper pushed back all the loose wood, isolating their fire so it was contained within a small area.

"We should have made a ring of rocks," he said, crawling back into the shelter to join Maggie, "but we were lucky to do what we did." He sat down as far from her as the space allowed. "Provided we don't burn down the forest, we're probably going to be all right the rest of the night."

Gratefully, Maggie felt the heat that flowed into their little structure from the flames. "The trees won't burn this time of year, will they?"

He was emptying his backpack onto a space beside

him, not looking at her. "It all depends on the snowpack. Usually not."

Maggie sat in silence. His terseness made her uncomfortable, and she yearned to have him again as he'd been earlier—warm and chatty, willing to reveal how he felt about her. Yet she could blame this situation on nobody but herself.

Maggie opened her mouth to apologize, then closed it again, unable to say the words. Damn her pride, she thought. Why did she let it get in the way? Tired of sitting up straight, she leaned back on one arm and propped her head in her hand.

"Ah, that's better." Cooper stirred the contents of his pack. "Now I can see. Here, Maggie." He held up a little sack of nuts and an apple. "These were left from this morning." He tried to hand them to her, but she drew back, averting her eyes from the food.

"No, I don't want them. But thanks. You've been doing all the work, you eat. I'm not especially hungry." It wasn't true, but she wouldn't eat the food he needed more than she.

"You have to be hungry. . . it's been hours."

"And you?" she asked. "Tell me what you've been eating all this time, while you were running back and forth from the woods with logs and branches. Besides, I had the tea. I'm okay." She saw his profile against the firelight; the fine, strong features turned partly away from her, so appealing that she longed to touch him with her fingertips, stroke the tousled hair back from his forehead. He still held the food in his hand; she realized then he wouldn't touch them as long as she didn't.

"All right then. Give me half the nuts, Cooper. And I'll take a bite of apple, too."

He tore open the little packet with his teeth, and then as he leaned toward her, ready to pour nuts into her open palm, she was overcome by his closeness and full of contrition. Fighting her pride, she impulsively kissed him on the forehead.

Nuts spilled onto the ground. He jerked upright, swinging around to face her, a question in his eyes.

"I meant to do it," she said.

"Good," he answered. "Here, Maggie, have some of these. I'll deduct the spilled ones from my half."

"The hell you will!"

Amused, he said, "Well." In the light of the fire she could see his starting smile, the whiteness of his teeth accentuated by the fire's glow. Relief took over, the joy of something lost returned. Maggie let out a long, slow breath.

"You'll be glad to know there's another packet of nuts here somewhere," he said. "And I brought candy bars, too, which I snuck into the lunch pack when Mrs. Winslow wasn't looking. She considers candy an even greater evil than cake. We won't starve before morning."

When they'd finished their small snack, he took her hand. "This will be our first night together. I hadn't envisioned it like this. A makeshift shelter. . . the cold. But it doesn't matter, does it?"

Without answering, she dropped her head onto his shoulder. Cooper put his arm around her, drawing her close, and she snuggled against him, fitting into his contours. His arms were strong, comforting. She felt him kiss the top of her head, as she gazed at the fire. Her eyes followed the flames that rose skyward, but she saw them only abstractly, her concentration focused on the man who encircled her with his arm.

To Maggie the night seemed warmer, yet she knew it to be a false perception when the wind, howling suddenly, brought a whip's lash of cold air to her face.

"Are you warm enough?" Cooper asked, his face against her dark hair.

"Yes. Are you?"

"Of course." He brushed her cheek with his lips, then asked, "Tell me about your childhood, Maggie. What is your mother like?"

Maggie thought a moment. "She's. . .well, she's a strong lady. Determined."

"And your father?"

"I only knew him as a child."

She could feel his next question, momentarily curbed. Then, "Do you feel like telling me about your father?"

She'd held back once before, reluctant to delve into old hurts, but that had been a different situation. That had been ages ago—this morning—when the sun had been out and they'd been ready to go on with their skiing. Tonight would be a long night, and she felt the need to be close to him.

As Maggie looked into the fire, her past loomed up strongly and painfully, bringing words tumbling out of her. She said, "I never loved anyone more than my father. Until I was thirteen he took me everywhere, told me his thoughts, let me in on everything he cared about. It made me feel grown-up and important and I adored him. The only part of his life he never mentioned much was his relationship with my mother, perhaps because he felt it would be disloyal to criticize her. I could hear them arguing sometimes, when they thought I was out of earshot. Mother would tell me he didn't give her much respect, but dad. . .he never put her down at all, not to me.

"One night I heard her crying, but I tried not to let it upset me. She'd cried before. The next morning when I got up dad was gone."

Deep in her throat Maggie felt the tightness that preceded tears. It was the last thing she wanted to do... cry. Yet when she allowed herself to think about it, the shock of that morning could still produce the same sharp impact as it had then.

She plunged on; he might as well know it all. "When mom told me he was gone, I didn't believe her. I went to their room and looked in his closet. Half the closet was empty, and his shoes were gone, too. His wallet wasn't on the chair where he always left it. He even took the little framed picture of me. That was the only thing that gave me any comfort. I thought, if he has that, he won't forget me. He'll come back.

"Except he didn't. He never returned. Never called or wrote, so we didn't know where he was. For a whole year..." She stopped and took the deep breath that would keep her from breaking down. "For exactly a year, until just past my fourteenth birthday, I watched for him every day, and after that I gave up. I finally knew he'd deserted me as much as her."

Wordlessly, Cooper stroked her forehead.

"That was when..." She stopped, composing herself again. "That was when I knew I'd have to prove myself. In case he ever heard of me, I wanted to be *somebody*. To show him I didn't care and didn't need him. I meant to prove to...to that bastard...that it didn't matter what he did to me, I'd turned out fine without him." She sighed. "Not the best reason for making your life a success, but the reason doesn't matter anymore. Your drive to succeed becomes ingrained, I suppose. It takes on its own importance and pushes on without the original reason."

Cooper said, "I guessed part of it. Not the details but your being driven. One senses it about you. It isn't a bad characteristic, Maggie, if you keep your perspective."

"I shouldn't have told you," she said sharply.

"I knew anyway."

"But it makes me vulnerable to you."

"Is that so bad?"

"It is if you get me off track. Don't you see, Cooper, I think it's important to make something of yourself. If you don't become worthy in your own eyes, how can you be respected by anyone else? I have to be a good lawyer. I have to do it, and then...then I'll see what else I have to do."

His hand slid gently across her forehead, down over her eyelids, closing them. "I hope you don't wake up someday and find you've lost other things that you didn't know were important—until they were gone."

MAGGIE WASN'T SURE when she'd dozed off, but the sound of an engine woke her up. She was still in Cooper's arms, awake before he was, listening to the distant revving of a vehicle coming up the mountain road. She sat up quickly.

Dawn was encroaching on the forest, showing itself as a pale light filtered by trees. The fire had burned down to small, glowing embers, and even in their shelter it was bitterly cold.

The engine sounds grew louder. Beside her, Cooper stirred, then sat up with a crackle of pine boughs. Maggie wished she'd looked at him before he woke up, but still she saw the small sleep wrinkles that creased his face, and in that brief moment before he noticed the approaching car, the relaxed look of an awakening boy—puzzled at first, with his gray eyes slowly absorbing the wonder of finding her there.

In the distance the engine whined, and Cooper's expression changed. "Someone's coming," he said.

"That's what woke us up."

"I'm almost sorry. Oh, Maggie, I was so happy to see you here." He smiled at her. "How did you like our first night sleeping together?'' He reached out and gathered her in his arms.

''There was only one thing wrong with it,'' she murmured. ''We slept.'' She snuggled against him, trying to block out the cold that numbed her nose and fingertips.

He said, ''That's what can happen when you've had too much exercise. I was still talking to you when suddenly you were gone. Then I must have fallen asleep, too. Whatever...I don't remember.''

''Didn't we blow our opportunity?'' she teased, feeling safe. ''And now it's too late, since we're about to be rescued.''

''God forbid!'' He made a face, listening to the heightening engine sounds.

''Does it sound like the Wagoneer?''

''Probably. And if it's Dan, he'd better have a very good excuse—'' he grinned ''—besides my bribing him not to come back.''

She smiled. ''If it hadn't been so cold out and we'd had more food, I might have thought it deliberate. As it is, I'm starved. Aren't you?''

''Yes, I'm starved, Maggie. Ravenous.'' He pulled her to her feet, holding her away a little so he could see her face as he spoke. With an expression in his eyes that warmed her through the bitter cold, he said softly, ''But part of what I'm hungry for has nothing to do with food, my love.''

He spoke to her of physical yearning, but Maggie heard more than that in his tone. For one beautiful moment she yielded to her feelings and immersed herself in the wonder of being in Cooper Smith's arms.

And then Dan Gardner came into view.

CHAPTER TWELVE

MAGGIE CLOSED THE DOOR of her motel room and looked around as though she'd never seen the place before. The bed was still as she'd left it, with her cherry-colored robe thrown over the end, and the drapes were still half-open to reveal a partial view of the mountain.

Yet her room looked different, as though she'd been away for years. A streak of bright sunlight highlighted the wooden floor, and dust particles danced merrily across the rays, adding to Maggie's perception of the room being cheerier and larger than she remembered. Had she come back to this room a different person, or had something else changed?

Puzzled, she sat down on the edge of the bed and slowly removed her heavy parka. Anne's parka. She must get these clothes back to the doctor soon. With anticipation, she removed layer after layer of ski things, imagining herself and Anne discussing the all-night adventure, and inevitably, Cooper. Suddenly she wanted nothing more than to talk to somebody about him, and especially someone like Anne, who knew him well.

What was he like as a boy? Whom did he admire, and what sports did he play? What sort of woman had he married? Full of questions, Maggie turned on the faucet in her tub, ready to immerse herself in hot water while her mind roamed over the things she still didn't know about Cooper. How much there was to learn!

Yet she wondered if these were merely the unimportant details about a man whose character she already knew well.

With enough hot water in the bottom to take the chill off the enamel tub, Maggie let herself carefully down into the vapor and wriggled her toes under the hot stream still pouring in. Ah! It felt wonderful! The first time she'd been thoroughly warm since early yesterday.

Relaxed, Maggie relived the events of the day before. Already some of the insignificant nuances were beginning to fade as she concentrated on the highlights: her feelings as she drifted to sleep in Cooper's arms, followed in a wink of the eye by their mutual joy at finding each other the next morning, and their unspoken disappointment that Dan had shown up when he did. Why hadn't the snowbank held him prisoner a little longer?

Yet not all of that day had been wonderful, had it? She picked up a bar of soap and absently rubbed her arms. The discord had been there, an important part of the day, perhaps more important in the long run than the rest, if she was to come to any understanding of their relationship.

At times she'd been furious: the moment Cooper had skied off without her; later, his declaring she'd never be able to work wholeheartedly on a case she disagreed with.

Baloney, she thought, scrubbing the bottoms of her feet. She'd work on anything, as long as it advanced her career. Moralizing was for lawyers who were already rich!

She splashed water over her soapy arms, feeling again some of the annoyance she'd felt yesterday. That was it! That was what was wrong with Cooper Smith. He was blind, never seeing her as she really was, perceiving only an idealized Maggie, someone she hardly knew.

But why should this surprise and annoy her? Was it because he made her feel substandard, somehow? Well, one thing was certain: he made their relationship impossible. She could never live up to his rose-tinted images. Yet, as she thought about Cooper, Maggie knew she'd lost some of her sense of direction and surefooted progress toward a partnership in the law firm. More than that, her whole life seemed off-balance. She climbed out of the tub, discouraged.

Toweling herself off, she felt the tightness in her throat that signaled suppressed tears, and took in a long, stubborn breath, fighting them. There was no point in crying; she wouldn't give in to tears. Instead, she'd retreat to what she understood best. She stood for something, she was making something of her life. Wasn't that a good enough goal all by itself?

She could still rescue what she'd had, retrieve her career and her own sense of self by giving up Cooper Smith. That was her only salvation, she thought, as she fell onto the bed for a quick nap. She had to stop seeing him. . . now and forever.

GORDON HAMILTON was incredulous. "What do you mean, you spent the night out there in the woods? What kind of fool do you think I am, Maggie? I tried to call your motel over and over. You weren't in your room at midnight!"

Still groggy from the interruption to her nap, Maggie held the phone farther from her ear, trying to adjust to the sudden, harsh voice that had followed the insistent, jarring ring. She could swear the phone rang more stridently when Gordon Hamilton was on the other end.

But when she heard his last bit of logic she burst out

laughing. "You're right, I wasn't in my room at midnight, since it's impossible to be in one's motel bed and also be lying on a bed of pine boughs at the same time!"

"Pine boughs!" Hamilton laughed unpleasantly. "Oh, come on, Maggie, what kind of euphemism is that?"

"I mean, that's what I was lying on. Compared to a mattress they aren't what you'd call deluxe accommodations, but they were better than lying in the snow!"

"Look, spare me, all right? I told you once I'm not into fiction, and besides, this isn't any of my business. If you want to spend the night with our avowed enemy it's your affair, as tasteless as it is. But don't try to make me swallow this—"

She broke in, "Of course, I wouldn't expect you to believe the truth, Gordon. It's always so much more titillating to imagine something worse. But as it happens, I did spend the night with Cooper Smith, though not in the way you imagine—since we were stuck in the woods without a way home. You didn't come rescue us and nobody else did, either.

"Together we shared one little corner of the forest—a very cold corner, I might add. Instead of spending your time on the telephone, why didn't you just drive up the mountain and find us? We were right at McBride Springs. Do you know where that is? And we were by the edge of the road, too, in plain sight, with a very obvious bonfire, trying not to burn down the whole darn mountain." She no longer felt compelled to jolly him out of his petulance.

"No doubt part of somebody's grand plan—yours or Smith's."

"Hardly." Her anger was building. "What I really planned was to be in my own little bed last night." In the coldest possible tones she told him that Dan Gardner, who had driven brainlessly considering the conditions, had buried Smith's Wagoneer in a snowbank on his way up the mountain, and it had taken him all night to dig out, adding, "The only reason others in this town don't spend their nights in snowbanks is that there aren't enough snowbanks to go around."

"You mean me, I suppose," he said sourly. "Well, my car tracks beautifully, fully capable of handling anything they've got here."

But you're not capable, she thought, and kept it to herself. Now that she'd started, she could hardly stop lashing out at him; he was such a small-minded man. Besides, it almost gave her relief. Inflicting her anger on Hamilton meant she wouldn't have to dwell on her own unhappiness. Already the thought of not seeing Cooper again was working into her psyche, leaving a dull ache at the pit of her stomach.

Realizing she hadn't heard what Hamilton just said, she asked, "Repeat that, please?"

"So why don't you just give me your overall impression of the damage skiers will do to that mountain. Something I can jot down right now for an article I'm writing. It's due late this afternoon."

"My impressions? You still want them after all this? And you want them this minute? Well, for one thing, skiing's no good at night. I can tell you positively they'll never push through moonlight skiing. What else would you like to know?" She was now too angry to be reasonable.

"Haven't you made light enough of this?" he asked, his voice imperious and harsh. "I wouldn't call this professional behavior, Miss McAllister. In fact I think you've taken a cavalier attitude from the moment we got on the phone, and your superiors at Meiers—"

"As for you, Mr. Hamilton," she interrupted without caring, "I can either treat you lightly and assume you feel thwarted and have temporarily lost your good judgment, or I can take you seriously and conclude that you're a boor. Now, if you want a report from me, I think you'd better concentrate on our business and leave my personal life alone." She added, "I think my firm would find it unprofitable to replace me with someone else. And they wouldn't be disposed to offer a refund, either."

To her surprise, Hamilton coughed and was momentarily quiet, his breathing the only audible sound for several seconds. She could almost feel his painful efforts at control. "Perhaps," he said mildly, "I have overstepped a bit. If you'll accept my apology, I would like to see you this evening for a short time. Would that be possible, Miss McAllister?"

She thought about it and decided she'd done enough, that henceforth she'd be pressing her luck.

"What time, then—and where?"

"My place okay? About eight?"

"Yes. Your place at eight. And may I suggest that from here on out we simply start over. We may be working together a long time, and it won't be made any easier by rudeness."

He took a moment responding. But his answer was dry and almost pleasant. "As far as I'm concerned, Miss McAllister, I've forgotten it already."

LATER THAT DAY Maggie found Anne Smith in the uniquely modern hospital, which belied the town's general feel of antiquity. Situated on a quiet back street, the sprawling medical complex was all angled roof lines and uncluttered facades. An orange wind sock at the highest peak and an adjacent helicopter landing pad placed it squarely in Maggie's era.

Having parked near the emergency entrance by mistake, Maggie wandered past beds of tulips and crocuses looking for the main lobby. Dotting the lush lawns on either side of the path were young trees, mostly spruce and birch, marked as memorial gifts to the hospital. Everywhere the place was trimmed and cared for.

Entering the small front lobby, Maggie was instantly aware of its cathedral ceiling, perhaps thirty feet high. She had just paused to scan her fellow visitors when Anne entered across the room, holding her hand out.

"Maggie McAllister!" Anne's dark, warm eyes and gracious manner radiated friendliness. "Come in, come in. My office is just down this hall." She wore a dark blue dress with a soft ruffled collar that feminized her professional white jacket.

Feeling a little silly carrying ski clothes through the lobby, Maggie followed her quickly, glad to turn into the hallway where she was out of sight of the people who waited there. She could feel them eyeing her curiously.

"I've brought back your clothes," Maggie said, placing them on a side table in Anne's office before she sat down. "They fit perfectly. You were generous to lend them to me. They looked brand new."

With a smile and a dismissing gesture, Anne said, "I don't get to ski very much. I think I invested more time buying the clothes than wearing them. Was it fun?"

Memories of pleasure lit Maggie's eyes. Before she could stop herself she said, "More than fun!" Then, to lessen the effect of her unrestrained enthusiasm, she asked, "Didn't Cooper tell you? It was a twenty-four-hour ski trip!"

"You mean you stayed overnight at Horse Camp?" Anne looked surprised.

"Not exactly. Our ride never came for us, so we

camped by the side of the road at McBride Springs. Cooper must have been a Boy Scout, because he knew exactly what to do. It wasn't a minute before he'd built us a pine-bough shelter, and then a great, roaring bonfire."

Anne smiled. "My brother's never been at a loss when it comes to solving problems. I think I'd vote him The Man I'd Most Like To Be Shipwrecked With!" Anne gave her a quizzical look. "But it must have been bitterly cold up there on the mountain!"

"It was." Maggie nearly added, *"Your brother took care of that, too,"* and felt warmth rise to her cheeks at her unspoken thoughts.

Across the desk, Anne waited quietly for what she had to say next, and her look of interest might have brought confessions from Maggie had she not at that moment told herself sternly she was through with Cooper Smith and such reminiscences were pointless. Her only purpose in being there, besides returning the clothes, was to find out something that might discredit Anne's brother. Only then could she finally forget him and pour her energy into her work.

But how was she to go about it? Thinking quickly, she asked, "Has Cooper told you why I'm in town?"

"Nothing specific, just that you're a lawyer here on business." Anne smiled. "Judging by his tone of voice when he mentions you, Miss McAllister, I don't think your reasons are really important to him."

Warmed, the other said, "Please call me Maggie."

"Sure. Of course. And why are you here, Maggie?"

Maggie hesitated. If she told Anne too much she would never cooperate. Yet she liked Cooper's sister instantly and felt at ease with her. Perhaps the information she sought would simply come out unasked.

She said, "I'm doing some legal research. I have clients who are interested in stopping the skiing before it starts, before the mountain is spoiled." Briefly she described her interviews and documentation, waiting for Anne's reaction.

Anne nodded, then with the trace of a frown said, "You must know how Cooper feels about this."

"I do. I'm afraid we've discussed it more than either of us wants to. We're not getting anywhere. It's always there between us, and I don't think either of us will ever budge." She pushed back her hair. "It's been a divisive issue, hasn't it?"

"I'm not sure your problem bothers Cooper very much, Maggie. I'd guess your conflict, to him, is rather distinct from your relationship."

"But how can it be, Dr. Smith? How can you separate—"

"Call me Anne," the other said softly.

"Don't you see, Anne, I'm working against him, trying to undermine something he believes in fervently. And I'm being paid to do it. It's my job. So even if I came around to his viewpoint, I'd still have to carry on with this project they've selected me to do. And I know he doesn't understand that. He can't see it my way, that I can't throw over my whole career—" she snapped her fingers "—just like that!"

Suddenly, embarrassed that she'd said so much to a total stranger, Maggie stopped talking, acutely aware of how close she'd come to pouring out all her inner conflicts. And to Cooper's sister, of all people!

In the moments of thoughtful silence that followed, she saw Anne's dark eyes on her and a look of understanding that seemed to bridge any differences between them.

Absently, Anne played with the ball-point pen lying on her desk, making doodles on a prescription pad. "You know, Maggie, I can sense that it's more than the mountain getting in your way." She laughed.

"Though with a mountain that size, it could be conflict enough. But isn't there another issue cropping up here?" Her dark eyes were direct and probing. "I think I picked up on some things you weren't quite saying—subliminal feelings—that maybe Cooper doesn't understand because he isn't a woman. He isn't us and he hasn't faced any of our problems. But I have—oh, Lord, have I!—and I recognize a fellow agonizer."

Maggie was silent, trying to hold back, though she sensed Anne Smith was close to broaching their last thin barrier. Odd, how quickly she'd come to feel allied with Anne Smith. It was as though they'd picked up on an old friendship and had no need of the usual getting-acquainted amenities.

Abruptly Maggie asked, "What did you do about medical school, Anne? All the dates and guys who thought you were wasting your time and wanted to turn you into a sweet and loving—and stay-at-home—wife?"

Anne laughed. "There weren't that many, Maggie. Just one, and maybe one or two near misses. But you can see..." For a moment her eyes held regret. "Well, here I am. I just had to decide as the issue arose, that if the relationship could survive my dedication and my impossible hours, it was meant to be. And if it couldn't, I guessed it wasn't really strong enough anyway. Unfortunately, there weren't any men I cared about who were willing to go the whole road with me."

"But what if you'd decided you had to have that one man no matter what? Would you have quit and opted for marriage? I know it's none of my business, Anne, but I know so few women in our situation. And I feel like...well, like I can talk to you."

Anne smiled. "You know, Maggie, if you're having

a problem, I can't help you even if I wanted to. Because we're all different. For me, medical school was something I had to do for myself. And at the time I believed I'd be going into research and had to qualify for a fellowship, too, so my grades had to be ninetieth percentile. It wasn't even a choice. I saw myself a certain way and I had to become the person I envisioned. I simply had to. And if I never met a man who fit..." She shrugged. "It's internal, isn't it? How you see yourself and how important that image is? And I've never faulted the women whose careers fell by the wayside, or those who compromised a little careerwise and fitted into a marriage. I'm not even sure most of them aren't happier in the long run. But it's quite individual, Maggie. Quite."

"Yes." Maggie's eyes dropped. "Yes, I guess it is. But such a debate can tear you apart, can't it? You keep feeling you're making the wrong moves either way." She smiled suddenly. "It's kind of like the bandit who sticks a gun in your side and says, 'Your money or your life.' I've known people who would hang on to their money. I wonder sometimes if I might not opt for my money, too. Because I just have this blasted, unshakable feeling about myself."

Anne smiled. "That's the old syndrome, Maggie. Welcome to the club."

The two laughed companionably.

Maggie said, "Anne, while I'm here—" She made a little "what can I do" gesture with her hands. "Here's my career raising its sinister head again. Can you answer a few questions about Mount Shasta? I won't ask you to compromise yourself—or Cooper."

The other shrugged. "We think for ourselves. And I consider him a bit biased."

"Is the town growing at all, do you think?"

"No, I would say hardly at all, and it won't unless the skiing goes through. People have invested in land around here, of course, hoping something would happen. So far nothing has. Everyone keeps fighting, but nothing really changes."

"Well, the land investments," Maggie suggested quickly. "Maybe the investors will do something with the land even if the skiing never comes."

"Not likely." Anne shook her head. "All those investors are just waiting. And hoping. Even Cooper won't do anything with his property unless skiing finally makes it."

Maggie's heart raced. She was on to something, and now she wished she wasn't. Dreading what she would learn, she knew she was about to find out more to discredit Smith than she'd ever really wanted.

"Cooper owns land, too?" she asked as casually as she could.

Anne looked at her curiously. "I imagined he'd already told you."

Maggie laughed, hearing it echo hollowly in her own ears. "He's told me so many things in these past few weeks, Anne. Perhaps he did tell me that. Was it..." She took a wild guess. "Was it acreage somewhere at the base of the mountain?" She held her breath, wondering if the bluff would pay off and intensely disliking trying to fool Anne, who'd been so honest with her. Damn, why was she doing this? But now the question was out.

Suddenly she blurted, "Don't answer that if you feel you shouldn't."

"It's no secret," Anne said quietly. "If Cooper spoke of his land in terms of acreage he used the wrong word. It's actually a half section, right off the highway leading up the mountain itself. A beautiful half section that had been Laura's before she died." A look of regret flicked over her serene features. "They had such big plans for that property. They'd intended making a resort of it, back in the days before the avalanche took out the chair lift. But she was killed before they could do it. Then the avalanche ended the whole idea, once and for all."

Anne sighed. "I suppose I do have some bias, partly for Cooper's sake. Unless skiing comes to our town, that land of his is really just useless property. Lots of pretty trees and not much else."

Maggie looked away, trying not to show what she felt. She'd found out, after all, what she'd come to discover, but now the information saddened rather than elated her.

So Cooper had the same ulterior motives as everyone else, motives that lowered him, put him on hard, dirty ground, level with every other person she'd ever known. She hadn't thought it possible. But Anne had no reason to lie to her.

She stood up, looking at her watch. "Gosh, I didn't mean to take so much of your time, Anne. I'm sorry." She edged toward the door.

"Maggie, not to worry," Anne said graciously. "After everything Cooper has said, I've wanted to get to know you a little. This afternoon I happened to have a spare hour." She smiled warmly. "He described you accurately."

"Is Cooper in town?" Maggie asked suddenly, explaining that she still had some unanswered questions about logging.

"No, he isn't. But I can direct you to the second-most-knowledgeable ex-logger in the business. His name is Ed, and he works for Cooper. Why don't you go out there and talk to him?" She brushed back her dark hair. "Cooper won't be back for several days, but I know he won't mind."

Maggie nodded, smiling, and gave Anne a little wave as she left.

Through the lobby and out the front door, Maggie walked slowly, deep in thought. She'd felt a strong kinship to Cooper's sister and wanted to know her better. The time with Anne had been comforting, thanks to her perceptive analysis of their very similar problems.

Unfortunately, Maggie thought, as she stared absently at the beds of white and purple crocuses, there was still an element missing: Anne didn't have any of the solutions.

CHAPTER THIRTEEN

THAT NIGHT MAGGIE FELT too tired to meet with Hamilton and rang him up to say so. But he insisted, his mood almost jubilant as he dismissed her protests about fatigue. "I've got something you have to see right away, Maggie. Meet me in my office instead of my apartment and I'll let you go early."

Halfheartedly, Maggie drove to the college, her disillusionment with Cooper Smith weighing her down like lead. All that was finished, now; she'd decided that morning, even before she'd seen Anne. Anne had merely provided the final reason. While she pondered, her car seemed to find its own way along the road that led to the salmon-colored buildings of Siskiyou college.

Hamilton paced his office as she entered, and she could see from his expression he was no longer thinking about that morning.

"Maggie!" He whirled around excitedly. "Look at this!" He pointed to a paper held in his hand. "I just discovered something in the county courthouse in Yreka. This is the official record of a legal partnership formed for the purpose of opening a ski chalet in Mount Shasta. Look at the names. Look who holds himself up as holier than thou, except he's been waiting like everyone else to make money off the skiing!"

Maggie leaned forward to see, knowing who it would be. Even as she read his name, plain as could be, Hamilton gave her the information.

"Cooper Smith!" he said jubilantly. "Our nobleman charging forth on his white horse isn't exactly what he pretends to be, is he?"

"Does this automatically make him suspect?" Maggie asked dully. Then she thought of something, a bit of information she'd hardly noticed while she was scanning the paper for names. "Let me see that sheet again, will you?"

He handed it to her and she looked it over carefully. The date. That's what she'd passed over the first time, but there it was, the date that told her when the partnership had been formed. She read it again, a bit of tiny print down at the bottom of the page next to the signatures. Without saying anything, Maggie studied it silently and felt a growing smugness, as though there'd been a bitter conflict between her and Hamilton and suddenly she'd gotten the upper hand. Cooper Smith had formed that partnership more than ten years ago, while both the skiing and Laura Smith were still alive. With all the events that had intervened since, the partnership meant nothing; it had no bearing whatever on his present stance on the subject. She suspected Cooper had just never bothered to dissolve it.

Only his present ownership of the land was important, she realized. But Maggie had no wish to disclose any of this to Hamilton. He might be her employer, but he didn't own her, and she had no intention of handing him any real weapons against Cooper Smith, or trying to make Smith look good to Hamilton, either. In some strange way, she wanted minimal dealings between the two.

"Well, what did you find out?" Hamilton asked after her long silence.

She shrugged. "You were right. The paper looks official."

"So you've got to suspect his motives if the guy's going to make money on the deal," Hamilton crowed.

"Yes, I suppose so," Maggie said. "That's what you'd suspect, isn't it?"

Hamilton sat down behind his desk, waving her to a chair. "There's more, Maggie. A little digging, and I found out that when Smith was a logger he fought against the indiscriminate logging of Mount Shasta. But now that he's part of this conglomerate, he obviously no longer gives a damn what they do to Mount Shasta. Some dedicated man, eh? His values last about as long as it takes him to spend a paycheck."

Maggie gave him a wintry smile. "Well, we can put this in our report, can't we?" She started to tell him some of the details about her ski trip, but Hamilton only half listened, giving her occasional perfunctory nods. She was nearly through when a young male student holding a newspaper approached Hamilton's door tentatively, then backed away when he saw her there. "Oh, sorry. I thought you were alone."

Maggie stood up quickly. "I was just leaving," she said, glad to have an excuse to go. "He's all yours." She smiled at Hamilton. "I'll get some sleep tonight, Gordon, and go back at this hard tomorrow. I still have a great many interviews ahead of me." Suddenly she yawned. "That night in the woods is still with me. Talk to you later."

"Much later. I'm scheduled for Sacramento all next week."

Maggie hurried away, but outside the office she paused, trying to decide which way to turn. She badly wanted a drink of water and guessed there might be a drinking fountain somewhere in the hall. But would it be left or right?

As she stood silently just beyond the open door, caught in a moment of indecision, she heard the young man say excitedly, "They call you the 'great environmentalist.' Hey, isn't that what you wanted?"

Suddenly interested, Maggie inched closer to the open doorway.

"Yeah," came Hamilton's voice, tense with excitement. "I couldn't have put it better myself. The reporter caught what I was trying to do, didn't he?"

"But he called you 'great,'" the boy persisted. "Did you ever expect he'd say that?"

"Well...that's about tops, I'd guess, from the *San Francisco Chronicle*. Not too bad, Mark." Hamilton laughed shortly. "Not too bad for now."

Sick at heart, Maggie walked quietly away. So it meant that much to him, Hamilton being called the "great environmentalist," as though it was some kind of goal he'd planned for, counted on. What was he up to, anyway?

She shook her head, baffled and upset. What a horror this assignment had turned into! She began to walk faster, turning down the nearest hallway so she'd be out of Hamilton's reach as quickly as possible. What kind of mess had she gotten herself into? Everyone involved in the skiing issue seemed tainted in one way or another.

Maggie started her car and turned onto the main highway, wanting to escape to her motel as a kind of sanctuary from bewilderment. But she knew there would be no escape and no one to trust, because now everyone's motives were suspect—Smith's, Hamilton's and her own!

ALL RIGHT, she still had her job, Maggie told herself the next morning. She was still being paid to accomplish something and it would still be an important step on her way to a partnership if she did it right. So what did it matter whether she really liked or trusted Gordon Hamilton?

For that matter, she no longer trusted Cooper Smith, either, so she could hardly worry about the moral issues or the lack of them in this ski-Shasta fight. Meiers, Meiers, DeCaro and Kosinski had trusted her to get an injunction, and that was what she was there for, she told herself sternly as she got dressed. Nothing else.

Hair brushed and curled, Maggie looked over the list she'd made in the beginning, two and a half weeks ago: thirty-two interviews, each one important, and six issues she'd felt it necessary to research. To her chagrin, she saw that she was only about half finished. Yet the time she had allotted for this case was running out. Old man Meiers expected her back next week.

She studied the list once more. Two or three weeks' work left, even if everything went perfectly. And so far nothing had. How was she to know she'd lose two and a half days on all her junkets with Cooper Smith?

There was only one solution: she had to ask for a time extension. Maggie dialed her Los Angeles office and they put her right through to Meiers.

In his usual gruff tones he asked, "So you need more time, Maggie, eh?"

"About three weeks," Maggie said quickly, asking for what she knew was the moon. Perhaps he'd then give her two.

"Three weeks!" Meiers's surprise came through all too plainly. "Oh, no, my dear, we can't spare you that long around here. There's another case that's come up that I'd intended you to handle. Right down your alley. Rental problem in Los Angeles. Tell you what—" he cleared his throat "—why don't I send Ben up to help you finish? Ben's been itching for a trip out of town, anyway."

"Ben?" Maggie tried to hide the dismay she felt. "You sure he wants this particular assignment?"

"Of course, of course. He nearly had it once, remember?" Meiers chuckled. "Nearly had it, didn't he? Ben'll be glad to come."

"I'm not so sure he will."

"Well, Maggie, you just leave Ben to me. He'll be there, within the next day or two. And those tapes you sent...excellent, excellent. Your interviews are going well. Keep it up."

Ben! Maggie put down the phone, hardly believing what she'd heard. Ben was coming, and she couldn't imagine anything worse. Complications...oh, Lord! Not only would he diminish her solo performance here, he would...well, what would he do? What would he expect of her? They hadn't been speaking when she left. But they'd have to now. Somehow they'd have to communicate, and speaking was the accepted way of doing it. Ben! She should have worked faster, not let this happen.

Thinking quickly, Maggie studied her list once more. The rush was on! She'd try to get as much of her remaining work done as possible—cram it in, if she could—before Ben arrived. Why should he have any of the credit for what she'd done? This was her assignment. She'd worked it up into something noteworthy, and now to have Ben come along and steal it out from under her...

Feeling greedy and mean and not liking herself very much, Maggie decided on the deforestation issue as today's first project—especially with Cooper Smith out of town. She could go out to Smith's ranch and meet Ed, find out once and for all if self-serving reasons had caused the environmentalists' greatest foe to change his mind about logging. Perhaps, too, she'd find out enough to lessen Cooper's hold on her.

She spent the morning making additional appointments, dictated a few tapes and then left.

AFTER NOON, Maggie headed north once more in her Celica, following the instructions of a gas-station attendant who'd said, "You can't miss the Smith ranch. Just take the Old Deetz Road west and you'll run right into it. End of the road."

Old Deetz Road, to Maggie's relief, was paved. For the first mile or so she found herself in open range land, broken only by scattered houses. Then abruptly everything changed. Beyond the railroad tracks the road took a sharp right, rounded a vast, open meadow, then lost itself in deep forest. With luxuriant pines, firs and cedars on either side of her and the road gradually climbing upward, Maggie had a sudden feeling of déjà vu. What was there about this trip that she'd experienced before?

Looking left, then right, she tried to take in all the beauty at once—the very tall, very old trees that reached skyward, forming a canopy for the smaller, younger trees that crept among their gnarled trunks, and below, spring's first wild flowers in purples, oranges and blues, tiny things that hugged the ground and were almost hidden by thick-growing ferns.

Through an opening in the trees she spotted the meadow again, and realized the road had circled and followed it. And then Maggie saw a deer. Startled, it came out of the meadow, leaped in front of her car with a quick, brown-eyed glance in her direction, then bounded in one great stride over a fallen log and into the forest.

Maggie's foot had already brought the car to a skid. Stopped, she sat watching the animal in disbelief as it catapulted over obstacles and disappeared among the trees. She took a deep breath before easing forward once more. How beautiful it had been!

Suddenly she understood her sensation of familiarity. It was a repeat of the experience she'd had that first day as her car found its way up the long, beautiful canyon that led to Mount Shasta. The same feelings, the same nostalgia. Then, as now, Maggie felt she was coming home.

COOPER SMITH'S RANCH was marked by a huge sign that hung from a timber that crossed the entire road, Red Cedar Ranch. A simple sketch of a cedar was burned into its lower-right corner.

Beyond the gate, the paving gave way to gravel, and Maggie's car left a trail of fine white dust as she drove the last half mile toward the ranch house.

To her right, a large fenced meadow lay adjacent to the house, and in its upper section cattle grazed peacefully, the bells around their necks sounding a variety of muted notes.

In a turnaround circled by towering pines, Maggie parked her car. She got out and started down the path to the old house, a two-story wooden structure with a steep, shingled roof, freshly painted dark brown wood facing and a bright red door edged with narrow white trim. A fine-textured lawn, parklike with random cedars, surrounded the building.

As she approached, the door opened and a man stood there. "Are you looking for someone?" He was an indeterminate age, perhaps fiftyish, overalled and lean, his face deeply seamed by years in the sun. His hair, still brown, was short and sparse. Blue eyes watched her steadily as she came closer.

"Are you... are you by chance, Ed?" Maggie asked tentatively. He hadn't smiled and she felt his open scrutiny intimidating.

"I am."

"I. . . I'm Maggie McAllister." She waited, hoping for a reaction, but there was none. The man continued to look at her without blinking.

"Cooper Smith told me something about you," she offered.

"Smith isn't here now. You want to come back?" He stood as though barring the way, and Maggie's first inclination was to retreat to the car and depart.

Instead, she took a resolute breath and smiled. "I really didn't come to see Cooper Smith. I came to see you."

"Why?"

His taciturn manner stopped her momentarily. The smile wavered. "Well. . . you know a great deal about logging, perhaps more than anyone else. I thought you could answer some questions."

"Smith knows more than I do. Why don't you talk to him?"

"As you said, he isn't here." She smiled again. "But his sister, Anne, said you could tell me anything Smith could. And there are things I need to find out about logging on Mount Shasta. How it's done, what you think—"

"Who are you?"

"Maggie McAllister."

"You told me that. What are you, then? Why all the questions?"

Maggie hesitated. A quick lie came to her lips, something that would appease Ed more than telling him the truth.

She smiled and started to tell him she was writing an article about logging on Mount Shasta, and she wanted to know what it was like in the old days. But her hands started to tremble. Even before she began to speak the shaking started, and so did an inner revulsion at what she was about to do. She looked at the man, his blue eyes fixed on her face stubbornly, his expression uncompromising. Somehow, in a way that was direct and unsophisticated, he reminded her of Cooper Smith. He was Cooper without polish.

Maggie's inner revulsion grew and she decided she couldn't proceed with the lie. She said, "I'm a lawyer, and I'm trying to learn all I can about skiing on Mount Shasta. Part of that has to do with logging on the mountain, what has been done there and why." Even in this more honest vein she couldn't quite mention the injunction.

He came a step closer, stopping on the last of the four stairs that led to the front door. "What side are you on?"

She hesitated. "Uh...I'm against the skiing." She shifted her purse, expecting to leave. That, of course, would end it.

But Ed's expression didn't change, and Maggie gave him a moment more. He said, "People have come up here from everywhere, running around town lying to get folks to talk. At least you didn't do that. I figure you know I'm for it."

"Yes."

"Well, what do you want to know? Nothing I say will help you."

She blinked in surprise. "Have you ever logged the mountain yourself?"

"Sure. Anyone who's logged this area has been on the big mountain. A good part of our timber came from there. There and the Eddies." He jerked a thumb toward the mountains that cradled the Red Cedar Ranch from behind.

"You and Cooper...you both logged there?"

"Years ago. We was a two-man team then."

"And the timber taking...did it hurt the mountain, do you think?"

"Then or now?"

"Well...then."

"Then it wasn't too good. Me and Cooper didn't like it, because we was taking out trees that shouldn'ta been took out. Leaving big bare patches and no cover against the rains." He shook his head. "It wasn't good then. I didn't care much, but Cooper railed about it all the time. Threatened to quit if we didn't change our ways."

"Then what happened?"

"What happened? Nobody could see it his way. Cooper wanted to get out of logging, but he couldn't do it then, didn't have enough money saved, so he told them he'd log anywhere else, but not Mount Shasta. So they put him on the Eddies. And I went, too."

"He's changed his mind, lately, hasn't he? About logging on the big mountain?" She tried to keep her voice casual, hoping he wouldn't see the trap. This was the big question, the one that would tell her most about the motives of Cooper Smith. And this would be the answer she'd be forced to use later in her written summary about people who pushed for skiing on Shasta.

The man came down off the steps and sat on the bottom riser. "No, I wouldn't say as he's done that. You want to know, has Cooper Smith gone back on what he used to believe, just so he'd help the skiing along? Well, he hasn't. Because logging isn't a stripping operation like it used to be. They got different methods now. They don't take out everything and leave them big bare patches. So they're doing it without all that erosion."

Maggie sat down on the grass nearby. This interview wasn't going as she'd expected. Instead of painting

Cooper Smith as a turncoat, Ed was merely confirming his character as she'd seen it.

Wavering in her purpose, she decided to take a different tack. "Why did Smith get out of logging, finally?"

Ed's lined face softened into a near smile. He waved his arm in a large arc, indicating the ranch. "If someone left you all this, wouldn't you take it? Cooper never pictured himself ranching, he says, but when his parents died it was make the ranch pay or sell it. Well, he wouldn't sell it because he claimed he couldn't part with all these trees. Besides, Laura liked the place, too."

Maggie sat quietly for a few moments, imagining Cooper here with Laura. Somehow it was a peaceful image, not threatening, because love of the sort Cooper expressed could never be a disturbing thing. Laura must have been a wonderful lady, Maggie thought.

Then she wrenched her mind away from him, wishing she hadn't come. Nothing had worked out as she'd imagined. Her case against Smith had been weakened, and so had her personal resolve to put him out of her life.

She stood up. "Are you ever sorry you got out of logging, Ed?"

He shrugged. "There was a day when I said I'd never quit, that I'd die in the timber first. Then I almost did die in it. A big tree came down the wrong way and Smith saw it before I did and shoved me sideways, catching a branch on his cheek. Maybe you've seen the scar."

She nodded.

"I kept on awhile after that, but I wasn't whistling in the woods no more. I was always lookin', lookin' up to see what might be comin' down on me next. When you're finally doing more lookin' than cuttin' it's time to get out. So I got."

The sound of an approaching car caught their attention. Far down the road, a slow-moving vehicle chattered over the gravel and sent a cloud of dust boiling behind it. The machine came closer, and to her horror, Maggie recognized the Wagoneer.

Her heart began to pound. This was awful, the last thing she wanted, Cooper Smith finding her here prying behind his back. She gave Ed a worried look as the other got to his feet. "Well. He's back two days early."

Her first instinct was to rush away, but she realized that would be pointless. Cooper's Wagoneer would block her car going the other way. There was no escape.

CHAPTER FOURTEEN

MAGGIE WAITED as Cooper pulled around the large circular area and stopped. Then she started forward almost hypnotically, as though powerless to prevent the scene that would surely follow. She'd wait until Ed had his say and then she'd be on her way. She might have known she'd do herself no good coming to Cooper Smith's ranch.

She looked up to see Cooper jump out of his car and run down the path toward her, his gray eyes alive with pleasure. "Maggie!" he shouted long before he reached her. "Maggie, this is a surprise. What are you doing here?"

She continued to walk toward him, still in her trance. It was as though, believing herself a sneak, she was incapable of seeing her behavior in any other light. She continued to walk toward him slowly, not answering, because there was no answer she could give.

Her silence must have made no difference to him, because in a split second he'd covered the distance and with one motion swept her off her feet and into his arms. "Maggie, I can't believe my luck," he said against her cheek. Round they went, and then at last he set her down.

Unable to help herself, she looked up at him and smiled, her feelings of guilt momentarily vanishing.

"So, Maggie..." He probed her face with those intense eyes. "I'd never imagined...never thought it possible that I'd find you here. Ed, have you met her?" he called over her shoulder. Taking her hand, he pulled her toward the house. "Ed, this is Maggie."

They were just words, she thought, ordinary words, but not the way he said them, not with that reverence in his voice. When had anyone ever introduced her like this? Her face flushed with pleasure.

Ed said, "We've been talking a spell. Didn't think you'd be coming back, Cooper. She was asking me about—"

Cooper broke in impatiently. "Have you shown her the house, Ed? The grounds?"

A puzzled look. "No. Was I supposed to?"

"Come inside, Maggie. Let me show you around."

He led her through the kitchen and into a dining room whose windowed wall looked out over the meadow and beyond to a very different view of Mount Shasta.

"How beautiful!" Maggie breathed. The twin white-frosted peaks shone in the late-afternoon sunlight. From here they were more distinct than she'd ever seen them, and the mountain itself reposed in a frame of towering pine trees. It seemed as though someone had planned the room to catch the mountain at that particular angle.

Cooper stood beside her, absorbed by the view. "I never tire of it, Maggie. This is where I eat and think and do paperwork. But for the past years—always alone."

Alone. Yes, of course that's how it would be. She smiled up at him. "But today it's different. I'm here." It was almost the first thing she'd managed to say since he'd literally swept her off her feet.

"Maggie." He gripped her hand tighter. "How different you make the view look." Bending toward her, he kissed her gently on the forehead, lingering with his lips pressed to her skin.

She shivered.

"I've meant to bring you here, but until now you've never seemed... willing. I've always felt reluctance, so I waited." He laughed heartily. "What do men know? You came of your own accord."

She shook her head, a sense of shame driving her to tell him the truth. For the first time in her life she felt truly contrite about something. She said, "Cooper..." but before she could get it out, he'd taken her hand again and begun pulling her through the house. "Come see the living room. I seldom use it anymore, but it's a good room, my first attempt at redoing the old house. It's designed especially for 'dinners for two,' which we'll have tonight if you trust my cooking."

They entered a magnificent pine-paneled room, whose salient feature was a sunken fireplace with built-in bench and bright orange and red pillows piled along the seat. Anyone who sat there would be just far enough from the fire to be cozy. Gazing around in awe, Maggie abandoned her attempts to explain.

Beyond the fireplace, which was on their left, an entire wall of windows formed a cathedrallike peak that framed the mountain from yet another angle. Overhead, two sides of a steep ceiling of rich brown woods met in the center above a single, rough-hewn beam.

"Where did you ever get such a beam?" Maggie asked, realizing she'd never seen another like it. The wood must have been two feet thick.

Cooper looked up. "A pine from my own property. It had to be three hundred years old. The roots had started to weaken, and one of these days it would have come crashing down. Laura said it might be the oldest thing on our land, and we ought to have it in the house." He grinned. "But when it came to honing it down to normal size, I just couldn't do it. I used most of the tree just the way it was."

"But how did you get it up there?"

He groaned. "Don't ask, Maggie, don't ask."

"But you could have made it smaller and lightened the task a little. It didn't need to be so . . . huge."

He looked at her strangely. "I couldn't compromise it, Maggie. The beam was what it was, and I could somehow make it fit into our room, or I couldn't. A lot of things in my life have been like that."

Thoughtfully, he strolled over to the great window. "The deer will be along soon. They come at dusk to share my hay. I always plant somewhat too much to allow for extra helpings."

Joining him near the window, she said, "One of them ran in front of my car on the way up here. He was beautiful, so fast and sleek, and he ran like—" she laughed "—like a deer. He thought I was going to hit him, and he gave me one of those looks with his big eyes as he crossed in front of my car. You know, 'For crying out loud, lady, watch where you're going.' "

Cooper laughed and laid his arm across her shoulders. "It must have been a female deer. Any male looking at you would have stopped in his tracks and stared, spellbound."

"Crazy man. You're an absolute zany, you know that? You've lost touch, Mr. Smith. You've been living alone too long."

"I have." He turned to her and his gray eyes grew serious. "It's true, Maggie. I hadn't known until now how much I've wanted to stand at this window with you—just to be on this place with you. I see the deer at dusk and I think of you and imagine you might like watching them as I do." He stopped, pointing. "Here comes one now. See, down there near the gate."

They watched the deer stand and sniff the air, then move tentatively into the meadow, a fawn-colored bit of movement, indistinct in the fading light. Delicately it made its way farther into the field, walking carefully, then pausing, head high to sniff and stare. Finally reassured, it lowered its head to eat.

Maggie felt Cooper's arm tighten across her shoulders, felt herself turned toward him until she was forced to look into the eyes that regarded her with an expression as questioning and hungry as any meadow creature. "Maggie, I can't believe you're here. Why did you come? Can you tell me?"

She pulled away a little, a confession on her lips. How could she let him believe she'd come merely to see him? What would ever come of a relationship built entirely on false assumptions? "Cooper," she began, "I have to tell you..." But seeing his trusting look she shook her head, her moment of bravery gone. "Does it matter why I came? Do you really want to know? Or can you just accept the fact that I'm here?"

"It doesn't matter," he whispered against her hair. "It doesn't matter at all."

THEY SAT WORDLESSLY SIDE BY SIDE near the fireplace finishing the supper Cooper had prepared for them. The fire crackled brazenly in the silence, providing all the sound, light and heat they needed.

Maggie was full. Looking down at her plate she saw that she'd made only the smallest inroad into her steak. She never ate much when she was either very happy or very sad; in the year after her father left, she'd lost eleven pounds, weight a growing teenager could scarcely afford to lose.

How unimportant food seemed now! It was enough just to be here with him alone. Her mind drifted away into fantasy. She imagined Cooper taking her in his arms, holding her, then covering her mouth with his and kissing her until she was breathless with desire. She could almost feel his cheek against hers, the touch of his hand on her breast. Somewhere deep inside her an insistent yearning began. She was glad they were here alone.

Alone? Suddenly she sat up straighter. "Where's Jesse?" she asked. Somehow she always forgot about Jesse.

"He's staying in town with a friend. He does that sometimes to save the long ride on the school bus. Besides, Jesse is fairly isolated out here, with no kids around. He says the animals are his kids, his friends, but it's not enough. I feel for him."

"Yet you don't mind the isolation and loneliness."

He gave her one of his long looks. "For years I didn't. In fact, that's what I wanted. Until recently I told myself this life was all I could expect and all that I needed. I was content, in my way." He reached out to stroke her hair. "Until a lady lawyer came into town. From that moment my feelings changed." He stopped, probing her eyes with his. "Please, Maggie. Don't tempt me into saying more than you're ready to hear."

She said, "Then don't talk, Cooper. Hold me."

He put his arm around her, drawing her in close to him until they were touching everywhere, side to side, and his strength had become her strength. She laid her head in the curve of his neck, allowing herself an almost inaudible sigh.

Filling her vision was the fire, hypnotically in motion so she couldn't take her eyes from it. She watched the sparks drifting up from a log, their incessant rise akin to the rising desire growing within her.

Here in his living room in front of his fire she felt vulnerable, different. She wanted to yield to him, to give herself and be part of him in a way that would ensure their being together indefinitely. She needed him. Oh, Lord, how she needed him...his strength, and even more, his love.

Sensing her desire, he turned, keeping his gray eyes on hers until the last moment. "Oh, Maggie," he whispered as he slowly lowered his mouth until it covered hers, and she was absorbed totally by him.

How long he kissed her, she didn't know. She was aware only of the infinitely beautiful caress of his lips, the strength and tenderness of his arms as he held her against his chest. In the background she heard the crackling of the fire and felt its heat, yet it was Cooper Smith's heartbeat against her body that she seemed to feel more than anything, Cooper's hand caressing her neck and her back and then her hips, Cooper melding her to him in a way she'd never have imagined possible.

She knew she'd never wanted a man as much, never felt as spiritually and emotionally joined with anyone. His hands and lips were her universe, all that she'd ever longed for. Yet feeling his body so much against hers and being acutely aware of the cloth that separated them, she wanted more. Infinitely more. The yearning would not be appeased until they joined completely, flesh to flesh.

Instinctively, he pulled away from her, looking down into her eyes with such hunger it was almost more than she could endure.

"Maggie," he said softly, "come upstairs with me. Come, my darling." Slowly he got to his feet, pulling her up with him. The warmth in his hand was fire now, an inseparable part of the flames that she sensed consumed him everywhere.

She leaned against him while he held her once more. His fingers rested on the buttons at the back of her dress, and with a deft touch he began to unbutton them, releasing each closure one by one so that soon she'd be out of her business dress and held against him in the fragile undergarments that changed her identity from lawyer to woman.

A sudden perception of her altered self brought her up short. She stiffened and said, "No, Cooper!"

His hands fell away and he looked down at her perplexed. "What's the matter, my love?"

"I can't do it," she said, pulling her dress together in back. "I can't, Cooper." She stared up at him miserably. "You don't understand, do you?"

"I'm afraid I don't."

"I can't surrender. I can't give up now. Don't you see? I can't let you. . . change me."

With his hand on her shoulder, he shook his head, baffled. "What am I asking you to change, Maggie, love? When have I ever asked you to be anything except what you are?"

"But I will change, I will. It's inevitable that you'll do it to me. And I'll lose. . . lose everything." She averted her face as tears filled her eyes, hated symbols of her vulnerability that she didn't wish him to see. How could she tell him she'd had a sudden vision of her career evaporating, of her chance at a legal partnership—even her identity—lost as she gave herself to him. "I can't do it, Cooper."

She sat down again on the fireplace bench, hunched over, hearing him say in his matter-of-fact tones, "You haven't explained anything at all."

For a few moments only the crackling of the fire could be heard in the room. Maggie let her misery wash over her and then subside, trying to put aside her unhappy feelings as a silent Cooper stood by. He made no move to touch her; the spell was broken.

She looked up. "I think I'd better go home now."

"All right." He smiled faintly. "Would you like me to rebutton your dress?"

She shrugged. "It's easier for you than me."

"You're not being very gallant."

"I seem to be fresh out of gallant. Besides, men are gallant, not women. Women are. . . giving."

"Yes. You're right, of course. I just experienced it. For a few moments you were the most giving woman I've ever known."

Perhaps I was, she thought, and felt again her yielding to him, her kissing him back with all the fervor she could summon. Yes, for those few moments she'd been someone she didn't recognize. Perhaps, she thought sadly, that was another reason she'd found it necessary to call a halt. Her lost identity. She just couldn't endure being someone other than the uptight Maggie she'd always known.

Cautiously, he rebuttoned her dress, careful not to let his fingers linger against her back. "There. It's done. Do you need anything else, Maggie?" He stepped away from the sunken fireplace and reached a hand down to pull her up.

Standing uncertainly beside him, she shook her head. "You've fed me, undressed and redressed me. That should be enough for one evening."

"It should be." He looked down at her gravely. "But it isn't. I'll walk you to your car."

Minutes later, he was helping her in, carefully holding the door until her dress and purse were inside. With a firm hand he pushed it closed, putting hard metal between them.

She wanted to linger, to absorb his face, dimly seen in the darkness, to make it part of her consciousness so she could never lose her mental image of it. At the moment, unable to admit very much, she could at least admit she loved his face. Oh yes, she did. And what harm was there in that? She would always love his face, but it didn't mean she had to love him.

For an instant Maggie turned on the inside light so she could find the ignition slot. And there on the floor beside her, she saw the trophy she'd had made and never given him.

She picked it up, looked at it a second, then handed it through the window. "In memory of a wonderful day," she said. "Something to remember me by."

Cooper looked down at it blankly, not reacting. In the dark, Maggie realized, he couldn't see it very well.

"The golf balls," she said. "I had them mounted."

Still he held the trophy in silence. "You had them mounted, Maggie?" he asked at last.

"Yes. For you," she said. "Because we had such an incredible day. I meant to give it to you sooner, but it's been in my car and I. . . well, I just forgot."

"You picked a strange time." He seemed to be trying to collect himself. "A strange time indeed. Are you doing this on purpose?"

"If you don't want the thing, Cooper, I'll take it back." She was close to tears.

He shook his head. "Of course you won't take it back. I'm keeping it. My trophy of mixed memories—the day on the lake and tonight."

"I'm sorry," she said.

For several seconds neither spoke.

It was Cooper who broke the silence. "Goodbye, Maggie," he said gravely, stepping back. "Drive carefully. And watch out for the deer. They're bolder at night."

"As apparently I'm not," she said, and started the car. Without looking back, she left him standing there and drove incautiously away.

IN THE MIDDLE of the night, Maggie woke suddenly with fretful dreams. In that half-awake state she saw her father standing by her bedside, looking down in love, his expression familiar and warm. As she tried to see him more clearly, the image dissolved and became

Cooper, and he, too, stood looking at her with love.

She awakened further. From her subconscious came a realization as dark as the night. *Now I know why I can't let myself love Cooper. Eventually he will abandon me, just as my father did.*

The thought struck her with the force of a thrown brick. Abandonment. That was what she was afraid of, ultimately. Trust given and used and then neglected until it eventually turned sour, like spoiled milk. And she, Maggie McAllister, left alone once more.

She turned over in the bed, steeling her mind. It couldn't happen again; she wouldn't let it happen. No man would ever do that to her, solicit her love and eventually leave her without it and without him.

It couldn't happen to her if she didn't let it. And that, she thought in a kind of grim triumph, was what her career was all about!

THE INSISTENT RINGING of the bedside phone jerked Maggie fully awake once more. She sat up dazedly, asking herself what time it was and fumbling for the receiver. It fell out of her sleep-numbed fingers, requiring some effort to bring it back under control.

Whoever it was, Maggie knew she didn't wish to speak to him. Not Cooper, not Gordon, not her Los Angeles office. But when she heard the voice, dismayingly familiar, yet projecting something amiss, she realized she wished to speak to Ben least of all.

CHAPTER FIFTEEN

"BEN! WHERE ARE YOU?" she asked, trying to keep the displeasure out of her voice. "You...you surprised me."

In nasal tones he said, "I expect I did. I'm here in town, not exactly what I intended, since I thought I'd have a few days to get ready and get well. But Meiers ran me out of Los Angeles with a shotgun, almost literally." He coughed, and she knew the reason his voice sounded strange. He was sick.

"What's the matter with you?" she asked, suddenly sorry for him. "You sound terrible."

"I am terrible. Don't know when I've been this sick. It's at least the flu. Or I may have bubonic plague, I don't know."

She laughed. "The Ben I remember. Are you well enough to come up to my room?"

"Listen, Maggie, I've already covered hundreds of miles on cough power. I can probably make it another six blocks." He coughed again. "Judging by the size of this town, I expect I could travel the distance on my hands and knees. Why did you want to get stuck in this pothole, anyway? It's not even a very big pothole."

"You can't be dying, Ben. Not with the way your mind is still working."

"My mind always works. A hundred and two, a hundred and three, a hundred and five, it's still working. Never quits. You got a thermometer?"

"Of course not. But I know a good doctor."

"Fine. You owe me a favor, Maggie. Make an appointment with that doctor, will you? And get your door unlatched, so I don't have to make the effort to turn the knob. It's your last chance to be nice to me. I feel like I'm gonna be dead by evening."

HE STAGGERED INTO HER ROOM almost exactly as he said he would. His face was flushed and his voice startlingly hoarse. Maggie had never seen him look worse. His tie hung limply around the collar of a wrinkled shirt, untied. Behind his glasses, his eyes were rimmed with red, and the bones stood out on his thin face.

"Sit down on the bed, Ben. Sit down," she commanded, taking his arm. "My goodness. You do look awful."

"Well, Maggie, those are very kind first words after our long separation." He looked at her dully. "And I quote: 'You do look awful.' I wish I could say the same of you." He hesitated. "But you don't, of course. I can hate you but I can't lie. You definitely do not look awful."

"Thanks, Ben." She gave him a sad smile, nostalgic for their old relationship. So the bitterness still ate at him.

He dropped back onto her pillow, closing his eyes, and Maggie glanced at her watch. Anne had said three-quarters of an hour. Lord, Ben looked sick. She felt his forehead and her eyes widened at the heat against her palm. His temperature must be a hundred and four.

Struggling, he opened his eyes. "Ever hear what the man said as they looked down into his coffin? 'I told you I was sick!' " He closed his eyes again.

"Macabre," she said, reaching for the phone. She waited three rings.

"Anne? Ben is sicker than I thought. Can I bring him in right now?" She made a face at the silent figure on her bed. "He's making cracks about dying on me, which doesn't sound like someone mortally ill, but he is terribly hot, Anne."

"Bring his suitcase, then, in case we have to admit him." A pause. "You know him, Maggie, I don't. Is he making sense?"

"Oh, yes. So far he's still lucid."

From her pillow came a hoarse voice. "Of course I'm lucid."

"He says he's always lucid. If it's all right with you, I'm bringing him in right away."

"I'll just shift my appointments around," Anne said.

"STOP TALKING and let your fever rise," Anne commanded, watching Ben with a thermometer in his mouth. "You haven't been silent long enough to let that thing warm up."

Shifting the glass rod with his tongue, he said, "I just want you to know I'm not delirious, I'm frighteningly alert, but you do have a healer's touch, Dr. Anne. Put your hand on my forehead again." He closed his eyes.

Anne placed cool fingers above his eyes. "Dr. Anne. Is that what Maggie called me?"

He muttered, "She just called you Anne. You deserve more respect."

Anne smiled at Maggie. "Your friend, Ben, is a city man, I can see that. We country girls aren't used to such blatant flattery."

Ben removed the thermometer and handed it to her. "I'm serious, Dr. Anne." He waited while she rotated the silvery rod back and forth. "I'm sick, right?"

"You're sick," she agreed after a moment. "Would you agree to being hospitalized?"

"Will you be my doctor?" he asked, and Maggie thought for the first time since she'd known him, Ben looked vulnerable.

Anne stood over him thoughtfully, once more laying her hand on his forehead. "We really don't have any choice, Ben. At the moment I'm the only doctor in town."

He slumped a little lower in the chair. "Then put me in, do with me what you will." He closed his eyes and gave a convulsive swallow. "I leave it to you, Anne. Maybe you can do something about these knives in my throat."

When Maggie left him a few minutes later, she saw that beads of sweat had formed a glistening chain around the edges of Ben's blond hair.

THE NEXT DAY, Maggie faced her interviews without interest, her mind on Cooper and Ben. When she returned to the motel that afternoon she found a note hung around her doorknob. "Maggie, please call me. Cooper."

She read the note eagerly, then set it down, forcing her mind to go blank. No, she wouldn't call him. What earthly good would that do?

Instead she changed her clothes and drove to the hospital, where she met Anne in the corridor near Ben's door. "His temperature's still high, Maggie. Down a little from a hundred and four and a half, but not much. It's the worst case of tonsillitis I've ever seen. But this can happen with adults. Some day he'll have to have those things taken out—when they get somewhat smaller than basketballs."

"Is he giving you a hard time?" Maggie asked.

Anne smiled. "Not at all. He's funny, Maggie. One of the best minds I've ever met."

"I know."

"He said you two used to date, but..." She took a stethoscope out of her pocket and began warming the end against her palm. "He also said that's all over now."

"It is."

"So he's telling me the truth about that. Sometimes he's so glib I don't know when he's serious." Her eyes went toward his door. "Odd that he can think so well right through his illness."

Maggie laughed. "You ought to see him when he's well."

Anne led the way toward Ben's room. "I'm glad I've got a boyfriend here in town. Ben pretends some kind of feverish interest in me, which will doubtless vanish when he recovers. But if it doesn't, he might, in good health, be almost dangerous."

Maggie said, "He's never boring, Anne. And that's more than you can say for most men."

Maggie found Ben propped against his pillow, eyes glazed with fever, yet as talkative as always. After a few minutes, afraid she'd be the cause of his wearing himself out, she left.

On her way down the hall she heard his voice, hoarse and unrelenting, and then a light laugh from Anne.

For the next day and a half, Maggie did her work determinedly, reminding herself that every distraction was another barrier to her ultimate success. Ben's illness had unexpectedly extended the exclusivity of her job, and she meant to make the most of it. With a nagging sense of guilt, she fitted in all the appointments she could, bent on making this injunction effort hers and not his.

She had, after all, not wished Ben ill. Yet by the third day she realized she wasn't being fair, that Ben could never jump into his work without some briefing from her and a look at the reports she'd already done. He might as well start during his convalescence.

Putting the material into her briefcase, she hesitated when she came to the names and contacts of the two California senators. She withdrew them. Why should he have those? They were the plums she was saving for herself. Neither senator had been available this week, but when the time came, she wanted her name at the bottom of the reports, not Ben's!

She found him sitting up in bed, still a little flushed and holding a newspaper in listless hands. He laid the paper down when he saw her. "Why am I so eager to catch up on rotten news? Have you ever seen anything to cheer about on the front pages?" He gave the sheet a disdainful thump. "It takes a well person to handle this plethora of bombings, strikes and murders."

Maggie smiled. "Brought you something that might seem more relevant. Are you up to going over some of my reports and the interviews we still have to do?"

Ben hesitated before he answered. "I was wondering if you were ever going to let me in on it, Maggie, this job being, you might say, your coveted assignment."

Ignoring the barb, Maggie sat on the edge of his bed and opened her briefcase. "Ben, this is where we're at...." She began handing him reports, letting him scan them one by one. For the next hour, they discussed their forthcoming strategy, and to Maggie's surprise, Ben saw issues she hadn't thought of, even pointed out small oversights in the work she'd already done.

Even more surprising, Maggie found she liked working with Ben. The same intelligent rationality that he brought to their dates now appeared in his approach to this job, and the same zany sense of humor, too. By hour's end he'd given her new enthusiasm, and best of all, he had the ability to keep his comments—even his criticisms—impersonal.

When she could see him tiring noticeably, Maggie stood up, gathered the papers into a pile and put them in the drawer of his bedside table. As she tidied up, Ben lowered the head of the hospital bed and pulled the covers up under his chin.

Closing the little drawer, Maggie said, "Why don't you finish up and jot me brief notes later, okay?"

Ben yawned. "Tell you what, Maggie. Right now I'm going to take about twenty minutes off."

Maggie grinned. "Okay, I'll give you twenty minutes, but that's all you get." And with a little wave she left him.

On her way out of Ben's room, Maggie spotted Anne working on a clipboard at the nurses' station, her head lowered in concentration. Maggie paused a moment, wanting to say hello, then decided against interrupting her. She'd just turned the other way when Anne called, "Maggie!"

Maggie stopped. "You looked so busy, I—"

"Just charting, but I can finish later. Have you got a few minutes for a cup of coffee?"

Pleased, Maggie said she did and walked with Anne down a flight of stairs to the hospital cafeteria.

They sat on either side of a small Formica table, sipping their hot coffee companionably.

"Ben's doing quite a bit better, don't you think?" Maggie looked down at the sweet roll she'd picked up on impulse. "I shouldn't be doing this, but here goes."

Anne smiled. "You won't like it, I predict. These hospital pastries must have been made in the nearest cardboard factory. Most sweets are hard to resist, but I have no problem with these. And to answer your question. . .yes, Ben's doing better, but he's had quite a stubborn infection, in fact so resistant I've had to switch antibiotics. Ordinarily, he would have been out by now." She watched Maggie bite into the sweet roll, then laughed when she put it down abruptly. "Bad, huh?"

"Very," Maggie said, pushing the plate aside. "Wow! In addition to the cardboard, they must use some glue. Well...what do you think of Ben, now that you know him a little better?"

"He's different. Entirely unique. And principled, too, I think. These last few nights I've spent a lot of time with him, just talking. I seem to be drawn to his room because he's so interested—and interesting." She smiled. "We've covered the oddest topics, but it all seems quite natural, as though we're operating on the same wavelength." She sighed nostalgically. "I'm quite fond of the man I'm dating currently, but we run out of things to say. It makes the future seem..." She shrugged and let the idea drift.

Abruptly, Anne leaned toward her. "How is your project coming, Maggie? I hear you're working for Gordon Hamilton. Is it...are you liking the experience?"

"The experience, yes, but not him." Instantly Maggie regretted what she'd said, wishing she could take back her derogatory words. He was, after all, the man in charge. "Look, cancel that statement, will you? Forget I said it."

"Don't worry, Hamilton will never hear your opinion. But I had to know your reaction to him, Maggie, which is rather the reason I asked you down here. I... Hamilton and I..." She frowned, obviously concerned with her phrasing. "I guess the best thing you can say is that we go way back."

"Really?"

"Maggie, I really didn't want to tell you this, and I haven't confided in anyone else, but since you're so involved with him—and I like you, which is the main reason—I think you ought to know a few things about that man."

"What, in addition to the fact that he's arrogant and unpredictable? Sometimes he seems reasonable and sincere, and other times he gets upset over nothing, and I get the feeling he's playacting." Maggie turned her coffee cup in uncertain fingers. "Look, this really is confidential. I'd hate to do anything to blow my job."

"Maggie, our confidences are going two ways, aren't they?" She took a thoughtful sip of coffee. "Gordon Hamilton was one of the first men I ever dated in this town. He came from, well, I'm not sure where, but he got the professor's job and then he apparently had some kind of deal he was working on locally, an investment or something, which of course I didn't know about right away.

"Gordon seemed quite charming when I met him. He was good-looking, of course, even more so when he was younger, and he courted me with zest and I thought, real feeling. Took me to Yreka on expensive dates and that sort of thing. He was always a little too smooth, but for a while I hardly noticed. Then about the time he started trying to get me... well, into bed, he said something about Cooper being on the County Board of Supervisors, and would I talk to Cooper on his behalf."

"About what, Anne?"

Anne shrugged. "He didn't make it clear because I told him that sort of thing was between him and Cooper. But he kept angling, and I kept telling him Cooper wasn't my pawn. He just wouldn't believe I had no influence with my own brother." She smiled. "Even if I wanted to, you don't push Cooper around when it comes to principles." Her tone hardened. "I began to think Hamilton might be using me, though I was somewhat naive then and not quite sure."

Anne pushed her cup away disgustedly. "As I started to back off, he came on, and..." She shuddered slightly. "He...one day he...he actually frightened me, he was so insistent." She stopped. "Salacious, is all I can call it. All that smoothness disappeared in one hour."

Maggie listened, shocked.

"But Maggie," Anne went on, "this doesn't mean he isn't sincere about the skiing issue. I've learned you just can't generalize about people. They'll fool you every time. But be forewarned, that's all."

With genuine gratitude Maggie said, "I appreciate this, Anne. You didn't have to tell me your...well, your private affairs, and I'm sure you'd just as soon forget all that."

"I have, mostly. But I got to thinking about you, Maggie, that you might be a bit vulnerable. I don't know how he can hurt you, but at least be ready."

For a moment Maggie considered mentioning the overheard conversation in Hamilton's office, but not quite sure what it meant, she let the subject drop.

As she sat musing, Anne asked abruptly, "Have you seen Cooper lately?"

Maggie shook her head. "Not in the past few days."

When she didn't volunteer anymore, Anne waited for a moment and then stood up. "I guess I'd better get back."

They pushed their chairs in and returned their coffee cups to the kitchen counter. Anne led the way out of the cafeteria and back up the stairs. As they reached the top, Cooper's sister turned to her thoughtfully. "If you ever want to talk to me, Maggie—about anything—I'm here most of the time."

Maggie understood. Anne's unspoken words would ring in her head for days, the offer of a sister to intercede for her brother.

ON MAGGIE'S DOOR that night was another note. "Maggie, have you got my phone number? Cooper."

The next day she found, "Maggie, are you still alive?"

She put one on top of another on her bureau. Why did Cooper's messages disturb her like this? How would she ever put him out of her mind if he continued to upset her?

The day arrived when she came home to no message. Her doorknob was empty, and in a moment's panic Maggie searched the floor around the top of the stairs and then the ground below, certain that his note must have blown off the knob. But she found nothing. And that was the most upsetting day of all.

On Ben's fifth day of illness he was ready to leave the hospital. He'd looked a little better each time Maggie went to see him, and on the last day with his temperature almost normal, she found him sitting beside his window in hospital bathrobe and slippers.

"She's discharging you, eh?" Maggie asked from the doorway, seeing how pale he looked. "You haven't quite pinked up, have you? Are you pretty weak?"

"Weak?" he asked in disbelief. "Weak would describe someone infinitely stronger than I. But what can you expect...I get a kids' disease, I end up twenty-six years younger. I'm now as strong as the average five-year-old." He made a fist and flexed at the elbow, grinning at the mound in his upper arm. "Don't tell Anne my muscles are smaller than marbles."

"I don't think Anne will ever notice your muscles." She smiled. "Not as long as you keep talking. But shut up for a moment and you're dead." She walked over to his chair and felt his forehead. "A hundred degrees cooler. You want me to get you a room next to mine so I can keep an eye on you for a while?"

"Anne's volunteered, Maggie, so you're off the hook." His voice turned somewhat acerbic. "You haven't changed much, have you? I read over those documents and I found references to material you haven't let me see. Something reminiscent of what happened with Meiers back in Los Angeles. I wouldn't ever want to need you for anything—or stand in your way. I did that once."

Maggie stiffened. "You're wrong. Everything's there. Why wouldn't it be?"

"I don't know—you tell me."

"I know what it is! You're still carrying a grudge, that's what, and looking for new ways to make a case against me. I thought we were past all that. Or were you just too sick last week to be nasty?"

He turned in his chair, eyeing her critically. "That's right. That first night I wasn't up to taking you on, and in my delirious state you still stopped me with your beauty." His gaze went past her, searching the doorway expectantly. "Five days here and I've changed my definition of beauty. This stay changed my mind about a lot of things. Not about us, though. Nothing's any different there. In case you had hopes."

"Hopes? Of what, Ben? Do you imagine I've been up here in Mount Shasta pining away for you? Is that what you came up here thinking? My Lord, you've got an ego!" She squared her shoulders, ready to lash out at him. Vicious words came to her tongue, and she opened her mouth to say them, ready for the rematch they hadn't had earlier.

Then she looked down at him, pale, bespectacled, thin, draped in his ugly hospital garments and obviously too weak even to stand. Not a worthy opponent, though he had attacked first. A new standard of behavior rose like a specter in her consciousness—a standard subliminally reminiscent of Cooper Smith.

Maggie took a deep breath. "Would you believe that's not quite true and I really have thought of you?" She shook her head. "No, I don't suppose you'd give me that much credit. Especially since I'm not very good at this sort of thing. So maybe you'll just have to go on thinking of me whatever it is you think. But I did have regrets, Ben. About you and. . ." She stopped, a new self-image beginning to assert itself. She'd never felt pangs like this, never arm wrestled her own conscience before. But now she did and the struggle was hard.

And then, finally, feeling terrible, she blurted out the truth. "So okay, I did hold back two papers. But only two, and you can believe me or not as you like."

It was as close as she could come to making amends.

He waved a careless arm at her. "That's a start, Maggie. A beginning. I'll give you credit for half an apology. You can add to the down payment later."

"Maybe." But she doubted it, and changed the subject. "Where are you going, then? What has Anne volunteered to do?"

With an effort he pushed himself out of his chair just as Anne entered the room.

Maggie started.

It was Anne who answered her question. "I'm taking Ben home for a few days, Maggie, to let my housekeeper give him a little more care than he'd be able to give himself. He's still pretty weak and I hate to send him off to a motel, where he'd have to go out for every meal." She smiled at him. "I also used to take in stray kittens."

Maggie hardly heard what Anne was saying. Her scene with Ben was still so much with her she could hardly wait to leave.

As she edged through the door, waving casually, she heard Ben say, "I'll accept any excuse for a little nurturing."

CHAPTER SIXTEEN

SHE WAS ALWAYS REGRETTING something these days, Maggie thought. Every time she saw Cooper she regretted it because she couldn't seem to control her runaway feelings. Long ago she'd regretted lying to Mr. Meiers. And this evening, she'd regretted deceiving Ben—and later regretted having to tell him the truth, because that meant she had to give him the missing papers!

She picked up the documents from her bureau, studying them uncertainly. When she brought them to Ben tomorrow, there would go the last of her claims to having accomplished something extraordinary. One senator swayed by Maggie McAllister would be worth two wins in court. Anyone would think so. And she'd imagined closeting herself with those gentlemen and ultimately bringing a lot of senatorial weight to her cause.

Darn! There was now no reason Ben shouldn't follow up on these leads himself.

THE NEXT DAY Maggie looked up Anne Smith in the phone book and drove out to her house with the missing documents.

Her house was on Old Stagecoach Road, the woodsy street parallel to the freeway west of town. Maggie had been on it once or twice and each time was charmed by the Hansel-and-Gretel look of the dwellings nestled among the trees.

At a large paved driveway, Maggie turned left and wound among thick spruce and fir trees until Anne's expansive home was revealed in its parklike setting.

The house itself, white and broad with shingled roof and diamond-paned windows, had a look of classical country charm. It seemed formal and gracious compared to the nondescript ranch style of Cooper's place.

It was Ben who answered the door wearing a long blue bathrobe and leather slippers. He seemed surprised to see her. "You miss me already?" he asked, holding aside the heavy paneled door. "I only left the hospital yesterday."

"I know, Ben. But we had some unfinished business, didn't we?"

"Did we? I figured the apology was all I was going to get. . . never imagined you were going to give me the documents, too."

"All right, Ben. All right! I'm trying, darn it. Give me a little credit. It isn't. . . this isn't easy for me!"

They moved toward the living room. "You mean it isn't easy being honest, Maggie." Ben sat down on a blue-and-white floral sofa. "No, I guess for you it wouldn't be. Just never came naturally to you, did it?"

Flushed and angry, Maggie stood near the fireplace holding the papers. One more taunt from Ben and she'd just walk out on him. One more. She stared at him coldly.

"Well, sit down, Maggie. I'll get over being mad. In fact, I'm not a grudge bearer, whatever you may think."

"You sounded like one yesterday." She leaned against the mantel, still undecided about staying.

"You make me nervous looming over me, Maggie. Please. . . ." He gestured to the blue chair on the other side of the coffee table. "I can't stand up with you, so why don't you just sit?"

Suddenly seeing herself as somewhat childish and petulant, Maggie sat down. "You know, Ben, you surprised me yesterday bringing up all that stuff about Meiers and Los Angeles." She tried to stay calm. "I honestly thought you and I were going to get past it and have a good working relationship."

"Yesterday brought it all back again, Maggie. It was inevitable. A repeat performance tends to remind you of the grand opening. But I have a great capacity to forget, and I give you credit for being here. So let's see what you've brought."

She handed him the documents.

"Senators," he said with a little frown. "Big stuff. No wonder you wanted to keep them. You bring them to our side and you've really done something noteworthy. Well...no wonder."

Ben fingered the notes on where the contacts could be found and when the senators might be reached. "So." He set the papers on the coffee table and looked across at her thoughtfully.

"So that's it, Ben. You've seen it all." In the distance, Maggie could hear a car coming down the driveway and she looked out the window to see who it was.

"Maggie, I'll tell you what." Ben coughed and had to stop. Then the coughing got worse until he was choking and sputtering. For a moment he stopped and took a breath, then broke into renewed spasms.

Maggie jumped up. "I'll get you a glass of water." She found the kitchen, found a glass and hurried back. Through the window she could see Anne stepping out of her car.

Ben drank his water quickly and set the glass on the coffee table, wiping his eyes before he spoke. "Maggie," he said at last, "what I wanted to tell you is, I think this project means a lot more to you than it ever will to me. You're into it, now, and you've done three-quarters of the work. And I think psychologically you—" He broke off. "You just keep that stuff on the senators, kiddo. It's something you'd be good at."

ANNE STOOD IN THE DOORWAY, looking at Maggie in surprise. "I wondered whose car that was out there."

Maggie stood up. "I had to bring Ben some papers, Anne—material I neglected to give him yesterday. But I think I'd better go back to work now."

"No, no, Maggie, stay. At least for a cup of tea. Then I'll let you go."

In a moment Anne had arranged bear claws and teacups on the coffee table. Glancing at her watch, she said, " 'A little something at eleven,' as Winnie-the-Pooh would say."

Ben grinned at her. " 'A little smackeral of something.' He said that, too, and it wasn't bear claws, it was a pot of honey. Winnie-the-Pooh, who as you know, was a bear, would never eat bear claws. It would be against his principles."

"Hush up, Ben!" Anne said amicably, putting down napkins. "You must have spent your childhood reading children's books. I imagined you as a youngster propped up with the *Wall Street Journal*."

"One learns more from children's books," said Ben. "Fairy tales are universal and everlasting and the *Wall Street Journal* only contemporary. Where's the tea, Anne?"

"Be a little patient, will you, Ben? I can't be off in the kitchen and at the same time standing here listening to your patter."

She disappeared and Maggie said, "Do you two go on like this all the time?"

"We get worse," Ben affirmed, grinning. "Anne is a brilliant woman—who is also warm. She knows so much she's keeping me overstimulated. My brain's had very little rest since I've met her."

Anne, coming back with a pot of tea, overheard Ben's comment. "We're not trying to rest your brain, Ben. Just your body, thank God. If your body was in overdrive the way your mind is, that tonsillitis could have killed you." Sitting down, she said as an afterthought, "As a matter of fact, you didn't do so well with the tonsillitis. I kept culturing you and you were resistant to almost every antibiotic in the spectrum." She picked up her teacup. "Tonsillitis shouldn't keep you in the hospital six days!"

Ben swallowed hard, wincing. "My throat is still sore, Anne. Since you threw me out of the hospital—what's six days?—you'll have to keep me here until I'm able, at least, to swallow."

Anne laughed, looking at Maggie. "I bring him home like a wounded bird, and now he's talking of staying forever. Oh, when will I learn? One doesn't take pity on one's patients and then bring them home to heal. It isn't done."

"So you've brought other patients home, Anne?" Ben cocked his head at her. "This isn't the first time? I'm not your virginal bring-home patient?"

"Ben, for Pete's sake!" Anne said, standing up as the telephone rang.

She walked away quickly, answered the phone in the hall, then took it on a long cord into the kitchen where she spoke in lowered tones to someone Maggie was quite sure Anne wanted to keep to herself.

While she was gone, Maggie began trying to lay out the next two weeks with Ben, but she could see he wasn't listening. His answers were halfhearted and distracted, and when Maggie stopped for a moment, she realized he was trying to tune in on the kitchen. She gave up.

"What were you saying, Maggie?" Ben asked, dragging himself back.

"Nothing, apparently."

"Sorry, Maggie, I—" He broke off, looking up as Anne came back. "Was that Ted?" he asked casually.

"Yes." Anne sat down again, her expression carefully noncommittal.

"Does he call you often in the daytime?"

"Sometimes. He tried to reach me at the hospital, Ben, but as you can see, I wasn't there. More tea, Maggie?"

"I'll have more tea, Anne, and I'll try to swallow it. I'm making a point of getting well." Ben sounded angry. "So I can leave."

The look Anne threw him was perceptive. "Ben, Ted wanted to set something up for tonight, and I refused because I'm taking care of you, okay?"

"But you're going to go on seeing him."

"Yes, I think I am. I've dated Ted for a long time, you know. I don't plan to throw him over just like that. You don't treat a friend that way."

"But he's wrong for you, Anne!" Ben shifted angrily on the couch. "Dammit, Anne, why are you wasting your time on a man who's got no future, and who can't even talk after you've finished discussing the weather!" Ben had apparently forgotten Maggie was still there, staring at the two of them in surprise. "He runs a department store, and that's all he's ever going to do!"

Anne was plainly trying to remain calm. "Ted's a good, solid, decent man, and I'm sorry I ever told you so much about him. I never expected you to use what I said against me, Ben, and certainly not in front of anyone else. I think you're out of line, quite out of bounds. Now, do you want a second bear claw? I've got more in the kitchen."

"I do, Anne," said Maggie, though she didn't at all.

The moment Anne was out of earshot, Maggie said, "Ben, for heaven's sake, why did you do that? You embarrassed Anne and me and now she's furious at you. You can't win her by knocking Ted."

"Ted's just wasting Anne's life, and it makes me seethe to think about it."

"But you don't have any claim on Anne!"

He turned on her furiously. "Oh, I do, by God. We've got something going and she knows it. I expect her to get rid of that jerk. He's just a local hick."

"Shhhh. . . ." Maggie put her finger over her lips. "Shhh. . . ."

Anne was back, tight-lipped and distressed. "He can't be shushed, Maggie. Ben always says exactly what he thinks, whether it's appropriate or not. Nobody's going to silence Ben. It can't be done."

"I'm sorry," said Maggie. "I sometimes get into things that aren't my business. I just hated to see you two—" She stood up. "I should leave."

Ben stared out the window, shoulders set stiffly, but as Maggie headed for the door he stood. "Call me tomorrow, Maggie, when I've finished making notes on this material. Then we'll divide up the rest of the work."

Anne saw Maggie to the door, and stepped outside with her. "We've both got our problems, haven't we? I'm not sure I can ever deal with a man as outspoken as Ben. He's great one moment, but he says things that throw me completely the next. He can be terribly sarcastic and actually hurtful when he's angry."

Maggie nodded sympathetically. "You just have to decide whether you can handle his frankness in exchange for all that brilliance."

"You said once that Ben is never boring. Well he isn't—you were right. He's just infuriating. And I keep asking myself, especially at times like this, how much he is of one thing and how much of the other and whether I can stand it."

"Weighty problems all around, huh? I wish I could help, but I can't work out my own problems, much less anyone else's." Maggie stood awkwardly, wanting to ask Anne's advice about Cooper, yet knowing there was little Anne could say because the problems were all within her.

Finally, with Anne looking at her expectantly, Maggie confided, "I'm so confused, Anne, about my own life. I never meant to come up here and get myself torn in two like this. I had such a clear picture of what I wanted to accomplish here and how this would be a very big step in my overall plan for myself. This job was important to me, Anne. And now..." She shrugged helplessly. "Your brother entered the picture and I can't remain rational anymore and be with him and still go about my business. So I've had to stop seeing him entirely or I'd be lost. He must hate me. I haven't even responded to his notes."

"He doesn't hate you, Maggie. But he might give up on you in time."

"I know."

"Why don't you at least talk to him and explain?"

"I can't talk to him, don't you see? I just get swept away and—it's no good. I've got to think it through alone."

"Well, he's.... Oh, Maggie, I shouldn't interfere with you, either." She stepped back. "But call me if you want to talk."

"I will."

"Promise?" Anne smiled at her.

"You're the only one I'll call."

Maggie drove back toward town more confused than ever.

ANNE'S INVITATION came three days later, after Ben finally moved into the motel. "Maggie, can you come to my house for dinner Saturday?"

Maggie had driven back from Yreka and just arrived in her room. She'd sat down on the edge of the bed to pick up the phone, subconsciously ready to luxuriate against her pillów in case it might be Cooper, which she knew was an unreasonable hope.

When the call turned out to be Anne, she minded less than she'd have thought. More and more she found genuine pleasure in talking to Anne.

"Dinner? Sure, Anne, I'd love to. What can I bring?" Maggie was warmed by Anne's melodic voice.

"Nothing. Just come with Ben. He's already agreed to it."

"Couldn't you use some wine...or cheese?"

"Really, no. Just you, Maggie."

Anne said it too quickly and a suspicion arose. Maggie asked, "Just the three of us, Anne?"

The other hesitated, cleared her throat, then said finally, "I guess there's no point in trying to fool you, Maggie. Cooper and Jesse will be there, too. I hope you don't mind."

Maggie sighed. She'd come to no decisions, had resolved nothing. Facing Cooper again couldn't make her dilemma any worse. And yes, she did want to see him. A lot.

"No, I suppose I don't mind, not really. If I truly objected to being around your brother, how easy everything would be!"

THE PUNCTUAL BEN waited restlessly in Maggie's room while she finished applying her makeup in the bathroom. She wore a dark maroon dress with a scooped neck, wide gold belt and a heavy gold chain. Maggie had gathered her thick, dark hair in a loose gold ring that allowed the ends to fall free around her shoulders. The effect, she thought, was both sophisticated and elegant. . . and probably too much for the occasion. Yet she felt like dressing up.

With her lips slightly bowed, she applied lipstick with maroon tones, then tilted her head to study her face from a different angle. Not a bad face, even serious, but the anticipation on it helped. She smiled, her mood lighter than it had been in days.

All this week she'd been lecturing herself. *Your work is absorbing, Maggie, you and Ben are getting along fine, and Gordon Hamilton has taken himself off to Sacramento. Be happy!*

But she wasn't, quite.

Her work was now going as she'd imagined, her interviews smooth and professional enough so she felt very much in charge. She was becoming the competent lawyer she'd always envisioned. What else did anyone need?

A tap on the door. "Maggie, what's keeping you? You could have made up the Statue of Liberty by now!"

"Patience, Ben. Patience. When I come out I'll be gorgeous. You'll find me irresistible."

"It'll never be put to the test if you spend the whole night in the bathroom."

"I'm coming, Ben. I'm coming."

She walked out, finally, and Ben whistled. Turning in front of him, she was pleased to see he still found her pretty. But his appreciation was that of a dispassionate acquaintance. She and Ben would never be more than platonic friends again.

THEY REACHED ANNE SMITH'S HOUSE fifteen minutes later. Smiling graciously, Anne opened the door for them, offering her cheek to Ben, then to Maggie. She led them to the blue-carpeted living room where a plate of crackers and cheese awaited them on the coffee table.

"Sit down," she said. "I'll go get drinks. What will you have, Maggie?"

While Anne disappeared to get Maggie's gin and tonic and Ben's beer, the two sat by themselves in the living room looking through the delicate windows to the trees beyond. At dusk the forest around the house had a lacy look. In the twilight Maggie had the impression that Anne's house and grounds had been granted space on a sort of tree-by-tree basis, and if the owner was ever to leave, the forest would reclaim its own.

Maggie couldn't resist craning her neck expectantly, looking for Cooper's car through the trees. Nor could she squelch the conflicting emotions that churned inside when she spotted a familiar Wagoneer turning into the driveway.

CHAPTER SEVENTEEN

MAGGIE SAT UP STRAIGHTER on the couch, staring through the window at the approaching vehicle. She could hardly wait to see him, to be in the same room with him once more. What would he say to her?

Ben said, "Cooper's here, eh?"

She'd almost forgotten Ben was present. It took an effort to focus on him again. "Yes, he's here."

Ben watched her curiously. "You look changed, Maggie."

"Do I?" Her eyebrows went up. "What has Anne told you about us?"

He shrugged. "Probably only a fraction of what she might have." Studying her, he added, "Wouldn't you think it odd, Maggie, my knowing Anne as well as I do, that the two of us not mention you and her brother? But we haven't wanted to pry or ask questions." He grinned. "You two are welcome to your private problems. We have our own."

Maggie smiled.

"However, I've never met Cooper. Anne didn't give me a dossier on him—what he looks like or even what kind of car he drives." He looked out the window. "One question answered—he drives a Wagoneer. Seems appropriate."

They stood as Cooper and Jesse approached the house. In a quick aside Ben said to Maggie, "Don't worry. You and Cooper were hardly the focus of our discussions. We've spent most of our time on issues that concern us." As the front door opened he added, "Anne never mentioned that her brother had a son."

"He doesn't," said Maggie.

They heard Cooper and Jesse welcomed at the front door, and then the two were standing at the entrance to the living room.

Over the polite confusion of introductions and greetings, Maggie caught Cooper's eye, and the smile he gave her blocked out everything else. In her mind the words, "across a crowded room" came to her as though someone was singing the song exclusively for them. Never had she had such a feeling of being alone with a man in the midst of a thousand others.

The spell was broken. Maggie observed his beige sweater and white shirt with dark brown slacks, and noted how well the clothes suited him. Though she'd never thought of Cooper as handsome exactly, tonight he appeared to be more than that.

Only half listening to Anne's introductions, she tuned in just as Ben was presented as Anne's Father Confessor. Surprised to hear Ben described thus, Maggie threw him a quizzical look, but Ben merely grinned.

Moments later Cooper was standing next to Maggie near the fireplace, looking down at her with his easy smile. "Well, Maggie. I'd begun to wonder if the motel was keeping a paid-up room with nobody in it. They kept insisting the room was still rented out, but they couldn't assure me it ever had an occupant."

Before Maggie could answer, Anne handed her a tall glass cold with ice cubes and beckoned the others toward the kitchen. "Ben, I need you and Jesse to help me carry in the plates."

As Maggie started to follow, Anne quickly shook her head. "No, no. You're the guest of honor. Just stay here and entertain Cooper for me. There are already plenty of us in the kitchen."

Knowing she'd been outmaneuvered, Maggie sat down on the couch, unresisting when Cooper sat beside her.

"My notes must have been stolen from the doorknob," he began, the gray eyes holding hers, "since each time I brought one the previous day's note was gone."

"I know. I'm sorry," she murmured, breaking the visual bond between them and wishing she could deny the effect of his sitting so close. She could feel his presence acutely, as though she were in a magnetic field that set all her nerve endings tingling. "I wasn't going to call you, Cooper. You must have known by the way we left it last time."

"I didn't know, Maggie," he said quietly. "Quite the opposite. I was sure you wanted to call, whether you ever did it or not."

"Be sure all you want," she said, bristling as once again he seemed determined to read her mind. "I made it clear we couldn't continue this relationship. You just don't respect my decisions." Even as she spoke she knew she was lashing out at him because of her own inner turmoil, yet she couldn't seem to help it.

Regretting her impatience, she reluctantly let her eyes return to his face, and was caught as always by the qualities she found there. Damn his strength and patience! Why did they always overpower hers?

"Maggie, respect is implicit in my every dealing with you. The fact that I waited for your call instead of forcing myself on you... Hadn't you wondered why I didn't simply appear? It's all respect, Maggie, every move I make implies respect. But I know you, too. You're fighting yourself." When she turned away to look out the window, he put his hand on her shoulder and said, "Why?"

She squirmed as though to shrug off his hand.

"Many reasons. Too complicated to tell you here, but—" They saw Anne approaching. "I'll tell you sometime. . . ." Her voice trailed off as Anne announced dinner.

Maggie stood up, starting to follow Anne to the dining room. Dinner. Beyond a doorway she could see the beautifully set table with its bowl of fresh flowers and long-stemmed wineglasses. Anne had gone to a lot of trouble. But why, exactly? She touched Cooper's arm tentatively as they started up the two steps that led to the dining room. In a soft voice she asked, "Did you put Anne up to this?"

He grinned. "Of course."

Over their meal, the five talked in general terms about such things as how warm the weather had been for late April, and how the wintering deer had already moved toward higher altitudes. Cooper said his meadows were unusually wet for this time of year.

"The meadows." Anne passed him a dish of fresh carrots. "Do you remember how we used to search for Indian arrowheads around the edges of the meadows, Cooper?"

"Arrowheads?" Jesse broke in. His thin face wore a look of eagerness. "I look for 'em everywhere, but so far I've only found two."

"I'll bet it was exciting when you found those two, Jesse." Maggie smiled at the boy and he nodded. "Like finding treasure, huh?"

"I'm afraid Cooper and I already cleaned most of them out," Anne said, laughing. "We went on arrowhead hunts every Saturday, remember, Coop? We used to crawl along in the grass, pawing and searching and turning over rocks for hours at a time." She shook her head ruefully. "But it wasn't I who had all that persistence, was it? It was you!" Her glance took in the others. "Every Saturday, after an hour or two I'd say, 'Let's quit, Coop, we're never going to find any today,' and he'd say, 'Sure we are. Come on, Anne, you've gotta have patience.' Then he'd run off without giving me a chance to argue. He was big even then and I had a hard time keeping up. But every Saturday we had this running argument—me fussing that we'd already found every arrowhead there ever was, and him insisting we hadn't, and why couldn't I remember that we'd found some of our finest specimens right after I'd said we ought to give up?" She smiled. "So I'm not sure we left many for you, Jesse."

"Nor did we get every one," Cooper added. "If you want them bad enough, Jesse, they're still there."

Maggie saw the look he gave the boy and thought, *he hasn't changed at all. If you want something bad enough*... She shivered. Was she like one of those arrowheads to Cooper? Perhaps.

A feeling of inevitability settled over her, as if her life might no longer be in her own hands. But that couldn't be true, she thought. She was still master, still in control. Or was she? In a sudden panic, she stared across the table at Cooper, who was saying something to Jesse. If she was really in control of their relationship, what was she doing at this table?

"Show you where to look," he was saying, "but I can't do your looking for you. You see, Jesse—" he smiled "—I don't want arrowheads that much anymore."

"Remember how we used to talk about the Indians?" Anne went on. "And how we thought they might be watching us picking up their arrowheads? We never agreed on that, either. You thought they'd be happy to have their handiwork retrieved, and I said, 'They never intended to have kids sneaking around picking up their stuff. They'd want it left where it fell.'

I always had a feeling some Indian might sneak up behind us and shout, 'Put that down, you brat!' ''

''The Indians had been gone almost a hundred years,'' Cooper said.

''It never seemed that long to me. If we could still find their weapons, I always imagined an Indian might not be far behind.'' She laughed. ''Now I'm admitting what a coward I was as a girl.''

Maggie caught Ben watching her with open admiration. ''You a coward, Anne? Not likely.''

''Well, I did have my moments of bravery.'' She moved her plate to one side. ''Like the times I waded through hip-deep snow alone, trying to make it to the school bus. I had visions of myself as a heroine then. The snow kept falling into my boots, and I wondered if I could keep going. But I did, because I knew if I stopped I might freeze to death, and I alone was responsible for my making it.'' She stood up to take dishes to the kitchen. ''It stands you in good stead, later, having had that kind of responsibility.''

''I envy you your childhood,'' Ben said, pushing his chair back. He gathered an armload of dishes.

Maggie rose, too, and in a few minutes the table was cleared and Anne was setting out dishes of vanilla ice cream and spooning raspberries and Cointreau over the scoops.

''Yum,'' Maggie said, dipping her spoon into the syrupy raspberries. ''Are these fresh, Anne?'' Then remembering it was April, she quickly said, ''What am I thinking of? Berry season is months away.''

''That was another thing we used to do,'' Anne added between bites. ''Cooper and I picked wild berries.'' She gave an apologetic wave with her hand. ''I guess I'm in a reminiscing mood tonight.''

''You aren't boring me, Anne. I'm hooked.'' Ben adjusted his glasses. ''Hooked and envious. Everything you did as a child was the antithesis of everything I did. I was a city kid, first in New York, then Los Angeles. Until I was five, I thought trees always came in pots. I didn't live in a tough neighborhood, but the tough kids found us nevertheless. I could see I was never going to match them physically, so I learned to fight with my tongue." He grinned. "I became good at it."

"Yes," Anne agreed. "You did. You can talk an apple out of its skin. Why else would I have entertained you every night in the hospital...and then taken you home on top of it?"

He grinned at her. "You needed psychological counseling about Ted—admit it."

Anne threw him a look. "Ben, would you like coffee?"

"Let's put Ted up to a vote," Ben said. "Whether or not he's too small town for you, Anne. He—"

"Coffee, Ben," she repeated. "Do you want it or not?" Her face had reddened and she stood up quickly—too quickly, Maggie thought.

"This is a closed topic?" Ben asked. "I figured you'd want some brainpower on this perplexing subject." Anne went on serving, tight-lipped, and Ben finally shrugged. "Sure...coffee. Whatever you say."

Anne turned her back on him. "And you, Maggie?"

"Thanks." Tension had entered the room, made even more perceptible as Cooper got up to follow Anne out to the kitchen. Jesse drifted away from the table toward the family room.

"Sometimes you talk too much," Maggie whispered across the table to Ben. "Don't you know her well enough to—"

"I know her better than you. She's hypersensitive, that's all."

"She has a right. Maybe she doesn't want to discuss

her private affairs in front of Cooper, Jesse and me. Just because she confided in you doesn't mean we should have a public debate."

He shrugged. "Anne is a wonderful woman, too good for the local-boy-almost-made-good. She needs second opinions."

"But she doesn't want them," Maggie whispered. "Come on, Ben, play it smart. Don't wave her confidences around in public."

"You know all there is to know about love and courtship?" he challenged. "You're the expert? Come on, Maggie, lay off. You're the most determined spinster I've ever met! You'll be single long after—" He stopped, aware that Cooper was coming back with coffee cups.

Nodding as Cooper placed a cup and saucer in front of her, Maggie added nonchalantly, "Well, Ben, you may be right, that's an interesting opinion." She shrugged. "But I wouldn't bet any money in Vegas."

THE ATMOSPHERE WAS STRAINED as they drank their coffee. Ben and Anne resolutely made all their comments as if the other weren't present, and Maggie gave up hope that anything would come of their friendship. Angry at Ben herself, she also wondered how she was going to get along with him for their remaining weeks of work. He seemed so ready to make cutting, personal remarks without any provocation.

It was Jesse who finally eased the tension. "Aren't you going to ask them about the picnic?" he asked during a lull.

"What picnic, Jesse?" Maggie asked, smiling at the boy.

"He's got it all planned," Jesse said.

Cooper smiled. "All that reminiscing, and I almost forgot. Mrs. Winslow has promised a picnic lunch for tomorrow so all of us can explore the Old Place meadow. I am to tell her tonight how many."

"Tomorrow?" Anne asked distractedly. "I'm afraid I have too many patients admitted right now. Sorry, Cooper. No."

Ben, seemingly indifferent to Anne's response, declined on grounds of being too busy with a report.

"And you, Maggie?"

From the first moment she'd known she wanted to go, wanted to be with him again on his ranch more than she'd ever wanted anything. But she'd been through this before and her old resolves were still in place. *No, Cooper I can't... I can't.*

And then she noticed Ben waiting for her response. Ben, who would taunt her forever about being an old maid. Ben. He was the wrong reason, of course. But he gave her an excuse.

"I'd love it, Cooper," she said graciously. "I'll be there. What time?" She tried not to look triumphantly at Ben.

"The picnic starts whenever you arrive, Maggie."

ON THE WAY HOME it was Ben who broke the silence between them. "Can you accept an apology, Maggie?"

She pretended ignorance. "For what?" He didn't deserve her help.

"You know for what. Come on, don't frost me. I'm trying to be civilized. And I do mean it. That stuff I threw at you was a deliberate spike, mostly because I'd gotten the same from Anne." He sounded genuine.

"My Lord. Anne didn't say that much."

"I'm tuned in to her excessively. You can see it, can't you? I'm vulnerable, dammit. She's got me pinned down."

"Then be sensitive to her, Ben. If she doesn't like

public discussions, for God's sake, don't drag her through them."

"I'm not ready to alter my modus operandi. It goes against my philosophy. I don't do it for any woman. I've always said what I thought."

"Anne isn't any woman," Maggie said quietly.

Ben swung the car onto the main boulevard without comment. They were almost in front of the motel when he said, "This has been a helluva strange assignment for both of us, hasn't it? This trek through Mount Shasta?"

She nodded in agreement. She and Ben had certainly managed to find parallel paths.

ON SUNDAY MORNING Maggie was dressed in a ridiculously short time. She stood in the center of her room trying to decide what to do. Seven-thirty was not "picnic hour" by anyone's definition. Still, she thought, she was ready. She might as well go.

Stopping at a roadside all-nighter, she lingered over coffee and a doughnut, willing away the time.

On the way to Cooper's ranch, Maggie castigated herself. The seven miles from town had focused her objections once more. Cooper Smith was a pretender. Hadn't Anne revealed it? He pretended concern for the people of Mount Shasta but he pushed for skiing because that prime land of his would net him a fortune. He imagined she didn't know about the land, and she wouldn't tell him. But she knew. Oh, yes, she knew, and it was about time she stopped thinking of him as Saint Cooper. He was no more saintly than anyone else.

He was just a world more attractive, and he excited her, and it was just physical and nothing more, and that was why she was going out there today, pulses all pounding and eyes dilated with hope. A physical, elemental, animal attraction. That's all it was.

Cooper laughed when he saw her. He met her out in the gravel turnaround, looking at his watch. "A quarter to nine, Maggie? This is wonderful! Why didn't you just come home with me last night and save some trouble?"

"I didn't think of it," she said, smiling.

"I did. But I figured I was the only one who did. I've imagined your spending the night in my bed at least once every twenty-four hours, Maggie. But it seems to be an idea that's occurred only to me."

"You're a lecher, Cooper."

"No, a lover. Which I'd be glad to demonstrate."

His words provoked a shiver that coursed through her limbs and ended in diffused sensations deep inside. She wanted him to go on tantalizing her, calling forth the almost-agonizing desire she now felt for him. Not love, she reminded herself. Desire.

She smiled up at him. "You're working on me, aren't you, and it's pure lust, Cooper. But I'm responding, so am I any better?" She let her gaze go past him to the house. "It's only nine o'clock in the morning and now you're stuck with me. You must have chores."

"I do. But they won't take long. And I'm not stuck with you. I want you here, Maggie." He put his arm over her shoulder. "You've never seen this whole place, have you? The barn and the guest cottage? Why don't we have Jesse show you around?"

"I shouldn't have come like this," she said.

He held her away from him, exasperated. "Maggie, why can't you for once in your whole short, sweet life, just do what your heart desires? Why can't you let go?"

She reached up to touch his cheek. "I think that must be what I just did. Else why in the world would I have appeared at eight forty-five in the morning?"

Soon Jesse, with an apple in his hand, was leading Maggie at a quick pace toward the barn. Swinging the corral gate wide, he waited until she'd gone through and then carefully closed it.

"But there aren't any animals in here," she said. "Why do you have to close the gate?"

The dark-eyed boy turned to her in surprise. "We always close the gates. On a ranch it's something you do. Have you ever seen Cooper leave a gate open?"

"I haven't been on the ranch that much, Jesse."

"Well, you'll see he never does."

They had reached the mammoth old barn, an unpainted wooden structure of indeterminate age. The siding had long ago turned a silvery gray, and small reddish-colored stains marked the presence of nails long since rusted. As Jesse swung the huge door open, Maggie was aware of a great black interior in which she could see nothing. Straining to orient herself, she stepped into the cavernous room and was met by an effluvium that momentarily took her aback: decades of animals and dust, the bittersweet pungency of cut hay. As her nose accepted the strange smells, Jesse switched on a light.

The inside had been modernized. To her left, bales of hay were stacked neatly halfway to the ceiling, while straight ahead a large enclosure contained a preserved antique buggy and new racks of saddles and tackle. On the right she saw small animal stalls, two of them currently occupied by cows.

Jesse bit into his apple. "Those two are about to calve," he pointed out. "That's why they're kept in here."

"Do you get to play with the baby calves?"

"Play with them?" He seemed puzzled. "No, but I help when they're being born. Cooper couldn't handle it without me."

"I'm sure he couldn't. You must be a big help to him."

"Yeah. He always calls me, even if it's the middle of the night, and I get up and come down here. He says one man can't do it." Taking another bite of his apple he said, "I'll show you my room upstairs."

Maggie said okay, though she hadn't noticed any stairs, but now she saw them against the wall next to the big doorway. Jesse led her up to a landing, pushed a door aside and stood back to let her into a pine-paneled bedroom. It was clean, carpeted and bright, with large curtained windows overlooking the corral and beyond. Furnished with a bed covered with a bright plaid bedspread, a wooden bureau and small desk and chair, it could have been a boy's room anywhere. Only the faint odor of barn reminded Maggie of the essential purpose of the building.

Waving an arm, Jesse said, "Cooper built this room—did it just before I got here. The bathroom's through there."

"It's a very nice place. I can see why you like it. But aren't you a long way from the house, Jesse?"

"No, I don't think I am. Besides, it's neat out here. Cooper asked me where I wanted to stay, and I said here."

"So you could have privacy, I'll bet."

"Yeah, and because it's mine. Nobody's around to bother me."

"But Cooper wouldn't bother you if you were in the big house, would he?"

He considered, munching his apple. "I guess not. He tells me stuff but he doesn't bug me." His face brightened. "He got me a new fishing pole for my birthday and he's teaching me to cast with flys. You ever done that, Miss McAllister? It's tricky, but I almost have it now. I could tell I'd done it right when I hooked a fish a few days ago. Except at the last minute he slipped off. Cooper says I've got the technique down and the luck will come next."

"Do you go fishing often?"

"Some. When I'm not in school or we're not working. We have a lot of work to do, you know." He said it with pride. "We're planting the garden next week. I'd show it to you, but there's nothing to see."

He had turned and was heading back down the stairs. "I'll show you the guest cottage, now, where Ed sometimes stays. Cooper built that, too. It's a whole house."

They walked across the corral and exited on the other side. With a strong arm, Jesse heaved the apple core out among the grazing cattle, and led her along a small path to a house half-obscured by trees. Even from a distance Maggie could see it was charming. Breaking the silence, she asked, "What do you want to do, Jesse, when you grow up?"

They had come to a small gate, which he pushed aside for her. Holding it until she'd gone through, he finally answered. "I want to live here and just do the things he does."

LATER MAGGIE WOULD REMEMBER Jesse's tone of voice more than his words. As he led her through the small cottage, handcrafted and beautiful in every detail, Maggie was thinking about the boy and the things he'd said about Cooper. And that tone of voice. The pride. Had she heard only pride in his words, or did the tone reveal more? She saw Cooper's handiwork and heard the boy talking, and after a while she knew: Jesse worshipped Cooper Smith.

The revelation consolidated Maggie's feelings. Returning to the main house, they walked in silence because Maggie was no longer trying to communicate with him; she was deep in thought and only half-aware he was still with her.

How odd that a trip through barn and cottage had turned into another glimpse at the character of Cooper. With sudden insight, Maggie realized it no longer mattered whether he owned land at the foot of the mountain or whether he was part of a business conglomerate supporting the skiing.

Whatever happened with his land—profitable or not—she was beginning to understand this man. If he said he supported skiing because it would help the town and not hurt the mountain, that's the way it was. Cooper had integrity, fundamental and all-encompassing.

She'd just seen the side of him he ordinarily kept to himself, and it told her all she needed to know: he was incapable of ulterior motives. Her last claim to finding real flaws in Cooper Smith had just vanished. From now on she'd find it even harder to resist him.

In a spirit of joy, Maggie met Cooper back at the main house and found him waiting with the picnic basket packed by Mrs. Winslow.

She smiled. "Ready?"

"Ready, Maggie." He handed her a blanket to carry.

"Jesse, you want to come on the picnic?" Smith asked.

Maggie added, "Come with us, Jesse."

But he said no, he thought he'd let them go alone. Then he cocked his head and gave Smith a sideways look. "Can I take the gun and go shooting?" His posture said he already knew the answer.

"You can't. What would your next choice be?"

"Ride the horse down to the four corners."

"Has he been ridden this week?"

"No."

"Then start him out slow. No racing for the first mile."

"Okay. But I'll gallop on the way back."

"On the way back. But the road only."

"Yeah," said the boy, and ran off toward the meadow.

Maggie turned to face Cooper, her eyes aglow. "I wanted him along, but I guess I also didn't. Not very nice of me."

"Don't worry," Cooper grinned. "No way would he have come. Jesse's always too busy around here, and he's never been keen on a lot of talk."

"Sometimes I can get too much of it myself," Maggie murmured suggestively, "when that's all there is."

Cooper turned to look at her, and Maggie caught the surprise in his expression. But he made no comment, and a moment later he was holding a gate aside, letting her pass through to the road that led to the Old Place meadow. Closing it again, he said, "Maggie, I'm glad you've come."

CHAPTER EIGHTEEN

THEY WALKED TOGETHER up the old road, the rutted tracks of infrequent vehicles only faintly visible in the hard-packed earth. Grass grew between the grooves and the forest encroached on the pathway, tiny saplings of pine and cedar timidly sprouting as close to the tire tracks as they dared.

"There soon won't be any road here at all," Maggie said, bending to touch a small, dark, perfectly formed cedar.

"One would think so," Cooper answered. "I find myself letting the little ones grow. But there always comes a time when I have to bring one of the larger vehicles up here, and then—" He shrugged. "It's hard for a small tree to survive under the wheels of a one-ton truck."

Maggie swung the blanket in her hand, reveling in the perfect day. As long as she'd been in the Mount Shasta area, she'd never grown entirely used to these deep, azure-blue skies or the buoyant feel of the air. She took a deep breath, absorbing the fragrance of pine sap. Understanding Cooper as she now did, she sensed the whole world as slightly altered—but better.

She glanced sideways at him. He was so in his element; rays of light striking the chest exposed by his open-throated blue chambray work shirt, a lock of sandy hair falling over his forehead. His muscular body moved up the road effortlessly with the easy strides of a man used to hiking long distances. He carried the picnic basket as though it weighed nothing.

"Mr. Smith," she offered, and he turned to her with laughter in his eyes.

"Ma'am?"

"How far are we going?"

"It's only a mile to the meadow. There are other meadows, higher on the mountain, but I'm taking you to mine. The Old Place meadow is special. If I never took you anywhere else on earth, Maggie, I'd want to take you there." Under his breath he added, "I've been waiting six years to share it with someone—someone I cared about."

She fell silent, letting his words wash over her.

Beyond a bend she saw an outsize wooden gate that crossed the entire road. As they came closer, Maggie could tell it was very old: the slats were no longer perpendicular and the timber had turned that same silvery gray as the barn.

"My grandfather built this gate," he said, reading her thoughts. He pulled back a rusted iron bolt and it swung wide. Walking through, Maggie caught her first glimpse of the meadow. Framed between a cluster of furry spruce and a broad cedar, she saw open grass bathed in sunlight.

As they moved between the trees she felt cushioning pine needles underfoot and spotted wisps of grass struggling to grow in the shade.

But emerging into the clearing, Maggie realized this wasn't the kind of meadow she'd expected, for it had no roundness, no discrete definition. Instead, random groupings of trees created many small meadows that seemed to change shape and size as Maggie and Cooper moved closer. And in the distance, looming high above a ring of trees, the white-capped Eddies rose in lofty unconcern.

In the grassy center of one of these meadows, Maggie stopped walking and slowly turned in a circle. Wherever she looked, different vistas opened before her, each an artistic arrangement of tree and grassland, of light and shadow.

"How beautiful!" she breathed.

"I knew you'd be happy here."

"I've never seen so much... loveliness."

"Nor have I. For me it's an idyll, Maggie. I know of nowhere else like it." He reached his free hand toward her and traced her eyebrow under his finger.

For an instant, with his palm in front of her eyes, she let her lids close, feeling his featherlight touch without the distraction of sight. She wondered that his large hands, so familiar with tractor wheel and pitchfork, could also stroke her skin with such sensitive lambency. She shivered, her pulse quickening. It was heady enough to be near this man. But when he touched her...!

She looked up into his eyes, now moodily gray, and felt as though he'd caressed her everywhere. At that moment, she also became aware of a distant susurrus of running water, and the sound and her own stirrings within blended into a sense of restless motion.

"Listen," she said.

He nodded. "It's the creek that runs through the meadow. Usually it's quite small, but you heard us say last night that the runoff began early this year. Parts of this section are almost afloat in water. We'll have to walk carefully, now, but if you step where I step we may manage to keep at least the tops of our shoes dry."

He began moving again, leading her across stepping stones of spongy grass toward the upper meadow. "We'll have our lunch up there." He indicated a distant clearing. "That's where the brook comes onto my land before it goes wild."

As they walked on, the sounds of rushing water grew more distinct until at last they reached the stream itself, energetic and noisy, belying its small size.

Then Maggie saw the pond. Just below a miniature rock pile, the stream poured into a tiny lake whose periphery was outlined in rocks and parts of a fallen log. Along its lower crescent a small, rushing waterfall took the stream out again, sending spray and bubbles into the air until the water disappeared into a deep, grass-covered crevasse.

Maggie was enchanted. "A little lake!" she exclaimed.

He set his basket down. "I built it years ago with a few scoops from my tractor. The stream was there, and I'd always wanted a pond, so one day on impulse I just brought the tractor up and made one."

Maggie shook her head, laughing. "The man isn't satisfied with streams running through his property. He has to have ponds, as well!"

He smiled. "When my grandmother bought this land, she always said it was a shame they didn't have a lake. For years the family couldn't afford a tractor, and when they finally got one it was kept busy on more important work. As a boy, I vowed if I ever owned this ranch I'd build my own swimming hole. But when at last I got around to it, I no longer wanted anything very big. This little pond seemed about right."

Near a small cedar, Cooper spread out their blanket. Feeling exuberant, Maggie took off her shoes with the intention of wading in the stream and left him to test the temperature with a finger.

It was freezing, the coldest water she'd ever felt! Wading was out of the question.

But there on the patch of grass a moment of devilry overtook her, and scooping up a small, cold handful, she crept up to Cooper where he knelt on the blanket opening the picnic basket. Intending to sprinkle a few drops on the back of his neck, she accidentally let it all escape and run down inside his shirt. "Oh!" she exclaimed, her dark eyes growing wide in surprise.

He whirled on her in a sudden motion, taking her wrists in a strong grip and pulling her down beside him. She tumbled against him, aware of the breadth of his chest and the hardness of his upper arms.

"That's April water," he said, "that is now running down my back! You'll pay, Maggie!" His gray eyes narrowed and he tightened his fingers, his grip so strong it left her breathless.

She gave him a look of her own. "You prefer August water, Cooper? Let go of me and I'll come back and do it in August."

"Will you?" he asked, still holding her. "Is that a promise?"

"If you want me, Cooper."

"I want you," he said, deliberately changing her meaning. The fields of gray held her with an intensity that sent tingling anticipation coursing through her body, and his hands hinted at power and energy that promised something she was almost afraid to imagine.

"I do want you, Maggie," he repeated, his voice vibrant with warm expectation. "We both know it." He released her wrists and lifted her chin. "I wanted you a week ago, and the hunger has been with me ever since. Nothing has changed. Nor will it. But it's hollow—pointless—when only one of us feels this way."

"How do you know what I feel?" she demanded.

"It's clear enough," he said, letting his hand fall and moving away from her on the blanket. "I don't need a written explanation, Maggie. Some things are fairly evident just by what you do."

"What I do—" she began angrily. "How can you be

so sure how I feel just because I won't...because I didn't... make love to you?"

"Maggie, had you wanted my love you would have taken it. It was there."

For once she felt he underestimated her. Always before he'd credited her with the noblest emotions, saw more in her than she saw in herself. But today... now...he was ready to believe she felt nothing for him. Or that she felt very little.

"You don't think I care for you. Is that it, Cooper?"

He shrugged. "I believe what I'm shown."

"But I've shown you, I've—"

"Shown me what, Maggie? What have you demonstrated that I've failed to notice?" The gray eyes were full of skepticism as he leaned back on an elbow, still farther away from her. "What might be going on in your head that has never found expression in your body?"

She stared at him, aghast. "You don't know, Cooper? You honestly have no clue?"

Again a little expression of skepticism. "Maggie, I know how I feel. But so far you've kept a pretty dark secret of what you feel."

"But you always say you know me!" she cried out. "You search my soul deeper than I search myself, and you come up with answers, and you say that's what I really am. You tell me about myself all the time. Why is it you've got no inkling of how I feel about you?"

She thought she saw the hint of a smile in his eyes, but she wasn't sure. And his words belied the notion entirely. "You have a tongue, Maggie, and God knows, an endless supply of words. If you want me privy to your feelings, why don't you just describe them?"

"Oh, Cooper, I..." She faltered, put off by the distance between them. "I can't just say it into...into the atmosphere."

"Will this help?" He moved closer and took her in his arms. "Now can you tell me, Maggie?"

"I. . ." She started and stopped, her reticence returning. Yet what was she afraid of? Hadn't she decided this very morning that Cooper was everything she'd wanted in a man, that her last doubts about him had vanished, erased by the testimony from Jesse? Why should she hold back any longer?

She pulled away a little, freed one arm so she could wrap it around his waist, then drew him in close. It would be easier if she didn't have to look at him. "I guess I haven't quite expressed it," she murmured against his chest, "and I suppose you might not know." Her voice faded away.

"Might not know what?"

"That. . .well, that. . ." She faltered again, letting out a little sigh. She hoped he might help her, but he didn't. Finally, taking a deep breath, she plunged on. "Oh, Cooper, I want you to make love to me!"

He made no reply, but she felt his arms tighten around her shoulders. Then one hand began an unhurried stroking of her back.

Warm pleasure pulsed deep inside her. She pressed against him, needing him, his strength and his reassurance.

For long moments he caressed her with his hands, and then at long last he drew away and looked into her eyes.

She glimpsed beyond his head the water, a glimmering, pulsing ribbon in the sunlight. The day was warm—unseasonable for spring, tilting toward summer she guessed—and the air was alive with crystalline specks that sparkled in the sun's rays. As she looked at his strong masculine face, the eyes soft and full of desire, she sensed the contained energy in his sinewy body and dropped her eyes. He overwhelmed her.

"Maggie, look at me."

She did and saw for the first time a change in his expression, a flicker of uncertainty.

"What is it?" she asked.

"I shouldn't have done that," he said. "I'm sorry."

Now it was her turn to be puzzled. "Done what, Cooper?"

"Forced you like that. Pushed you to the wall until you asked for me. I'm sorry, Maggie. I thought it was the right thing to do, but now I don't." He sat up straighter and dropped his arms so he no longer held her. "I excused it, telling myself you had to express what you felt or you'd never be quite sure. But it was wrong, because I was implying something false. I already knew how you felt. I've always known. I think, after all, I tricked you."

"Perhaps," she said.

"I don't want you this way, Maggie. I'd never have you under false colors."

She said, "Are you always the one to decide these things? Is our relationship not in my hands, too?"

He didn't answer.

"Sometimes you take on too much," she said. "Too often you decide everything for both of us, and I won't have it that way. I have a say in what happens to us, too." She moved closer to him. "Maybe you did trick me, but I alone said the words I said, and they would never have come out if I hadn't meant them." She reached up to touch his cheek. "I do want you to make love to me, Cooper."

Taking her again in his arms, Cooper silently stroked her eyelids with his fingertips.

In those silent moments while Cooper touched her lightly and almost contemplatively, Maggie felt a wordless communication, a giving that asked little and demanded less. It was more than she'd ever thought possible from another human being.

Then he gave her no more time for contemplation. Instead, he buried his face against the curve of her throat and his mouth found the delicate flesh near her chin. He kissed her where the throbbing pulse quickly betrayed her.

She turned toward him, wanting all of him.

"Maggie," he breathed softly, and the next instant his mouth covered hers, warm and soft at first, then more insistent. Kissing her, he pulled her closer to him, bringing her breasts tight against his chest, moving his hand along her back again in long, languorous strokes.

She coiled her arms around his neck, holding him. With an urgency that belied the gentleness of his nature, he explored her mouth, offering her exquisite sweetness and an awareness of the insistent need that comes with long denial. Then, in one slow motion he pulled her with him so that they were no longer sitting upright, but lying together, their blanket the cloudless sky.

She felt the sun warm against her skin, felt deft fingers undoing the buttons of her blouse. Still kissing her, he pulled the plaid blouse free of her shoulders, and then with searching fingers cupped her breast within its lacy bra. She longed to have him remove the bra, longed for the feel of his fingers on her bare flesh, his thumbs stroking her nipples, which had risen to absorb his touch. The soft wetness of his kiss and the caressing of his fingers brought fire to her insides and a need that burned within her, a longing more urgent than any she'd ever known. "Oh, Cooper," she moaned. "Cooper..." Though she wanted to cry out, "Cooper, take me," she could not yet bring herself to say the words. In a haze of exquisite feeling, she felt herself yielding...yielding....

And then, because she began thinking too much, she suddenly fought her way back, remembering the character of the man who held her in this near state of grace. With awful clarity she knew that he, more than any man she'd ever known, would expect more from her than she was—a soul-deep honesty, an abiding unselfishness. And though she'd changed a little, she was still a world away from what he'd expect. She, Maggie, was still Maggie, thinking mostly of herself, because until now she'd always had to. It was ingrained in her; she would never change.

She pulled away from him. After today he'd want—no, expect—a kind of devotion of which she was incapable. She cried, "Oh, Cooper...I'm so uncertain."

But he seemed not to hear. Instead he drew her back against him, his hands caressing her silken shoulders, his lips once more seeking the soft curves of her throat. When she could fight her own desire no longer and found herself pulling him tighter to her in throbbing acquiescence, he undid the front hooks embedded in the lace of her bra. Putting it aside, he lowered his head to the small, rounded curve of her breast and formed his lips to the pink bud, teasing it to a flowering that brought pleasure flowing upward from her thighs. Maggie's muted moan broke the silence of the meadow.

Moments later her fingers lingered on the top button of his shirt, and undoing it easily, she slowly released his other buttons one by one until the golden hairs of his chest shone in the sunlight and the shirt found its place on top of her bra. Then she wrapped her arms around him, feeling his bare, muscular body against hers, cradling him against her as she might a child.

"Cooper—" she laughed softly, in a voice velvet with desire "—you have the shoulders of a god."

His quiet laugh echoed hers. "I've been called many things, Maggie, but never that."

For a moment he looked down at her, studying her intently, his eyes feasting on her delicate features, his expression so full of desire she could scarcely bear to hold his gaze. And while he absorbed her visually, his hands pulled away her skirt, then removed the last bit of lacy cloth that covered her.

With maddening control he caressed the curve of her hips and then found the secret valley between her thighs, gently stroking the sensitive flesh until she screamed out to him to stop. "No, Cooper, that's not what I mean. Don't stop! Please don't. . . ."

He cried softly, "Maggie! Maggie!" in tones so heartfelt she shuddered. Gripping her against him passionately for a moment, he held her as though he would never let her go, and in the tightness of his grip she could feel his heart pounding and the warmth of his skin, almost feverish. In that same spirit of desperation, he kissed her throat, gently brought his lips to the valley between her breasts, tasting her, caressing her, then finally carried his kisses downward until his face was buried in the most secret places of her body.

With a response she could no more contain than she could slow the tides of the ocean, she fumbled with the snaps of his jeans, released the zipper and eased the fabric downward, feeling for the hardness of him, the part of him that promised to bring her pleasure beyond any she'd ever known. And she found what she'd been seeking.

"Maggie!" he cried again, and with an elemental moan he brought himself to her, entering her with an abandon that was joy and relief and urgency all expressed in one joyous thrust.

Together they moved, her desire glowing like metal heated in a smithy's fire, the electric current he brought to her inner being almost unbearable, yet so intense she wished it could be with her forever. Her arms twined around his neck, tight and full of passion, and she brought his face to hers and kissed him as deeply as he had kissed her, probing the sweetness of his mouth with her tongue, feeling his response against her own lips.

Unable to help, she wrapped him in her legs, bringing him still closer, but in some faraway part of her mind she was also aware of the sounds of the brook. Somehow they melded with the pleasure she was feeling, so that rushing water and Cooper and her own fiery needs became one.

In the depths of her consciousness she felt herself beginning a trip downstream, swept away irrevocably, as powerless as a leaf in swirling water. "Cooper... love!" she groaned, and the stream moved faster... faster...carrying her with it.

With her fingers against his back, she pulled him ever closer, knowing she might be leaving the imprint of her passion against his flesh. But the stream—her love—rushed on.

The warm sun touched her bare legs, fell against her hair, joined her own hot breath in bathing their united flesh in heat. She could feel the rivulets of liquid that crept between them, feel them as one more aphrodisiac for their impassioned bodies.

And then her consciousness joined the rushing brook once more. She was swirling downstream faster and he was with her, their togetherness part of this flood of motion—harmonic, effervescent and inevitable.

She heard him groan helplessly against her throat, until the tide of their feelings grew and became a vast roar. The water took them faster, faster. She was approaching a precipice. She couldn't stop a rush over the top, and oh, God, she wanted to be part of the waterfall, to let go.

And then it happened, and he was with her. Down, down, in a tumult of spray and frothing water and liquid relief. They'd made the journey together, and now they were still together, floating in idyllic warmth and tenderness. Sensation was fading but pleasure wasn't.

They lay in the warm sun in a time frame that had no meaning, in which only the aftermath of pleasure seemed to have reality. Her elation became tenderness and she stroked his damp hair, aware of the sweet muskiness that clung to him, feeling his shoulders strong under her head.

With the meadow surrounding them, she reflected that he was a man of the earth: elemental, decent, his strength arising from the work of his hands, his soul born of communion with the land. She sensed strongly that he was enduring, dependable—as permanent, even, as the mountain. It gave her joy, and even more...hope. For she knew then that he might have strength enough to redeem her. Here in his arms she wanted nothing more.

"Maggie, my own," he said, rising on an elbow to gaze down at her tenderly. "I love you. And I feel I've been touched by heaven."

CHAPTER NINETEEN

THEY RELAXED on the blanket until Maggie began to feel chilly. A breeze had come up just as the sun went under a cloud, and though Maggie snuggled against Cooper, both were aware of a temperature change.

He pulled her to a sitting position, handing her her clothes. "It couldn't last," he said. "The sun already gave us more time than I expected."

He watched as she started to put on her bra, but then stopped her, laying the bit of lace aside. "Let me look at you once more, Maggie," he said, and turned her toward him. With both hands on her rib cage and his palms crowding her breasts, he held her appraisingly.

Under his scrutiny she warmed, feeling his eyes taking her in, sensing his approval as his gaze went from the firm mounds and pointed nipples to her throat and then to her face. He made her feel womanly and revered.

"I want to hold the sight of you until you're with me again. You're beautiful, Maggie."

No answer was possible, so she said nothing but stored his words to savor.

Gently he let his thumbs roam over her nipples, and then produced her bra. With sure fingers he fitted it to her and hooked it in front.

"You do that like an expert," she teased.

"I would do it every day if I could."

"But I wouldn't let you. Just on Sundays and birthdays. . . and on days when you'd been especially good. And Mr. Smith, you're going to see nothing but goose bumps if I don't hurry up and get my clothes on."

Once dressed, they spread out their picnic lunch and ate hungrily. Mrs. Winslow had packed cold chicken, carrot sticks, sliced-cucumber salad and pieces of home-baked, date-nut bread. A thermos held hot tea.

The sun reaffirmed its intention to stay, and Maggie stretched out her legs feeling utterly content. With Cooper beside her, she could ask nothing more of the day.

Later, as they walked back down the road, Cooper asked, "Have you got any free time this week, Maggie?"

She shook her head. "I'm afraid not."

"Then I've an idea for next Saturday. Do you ride? Because I thought we'd take horses to one of the lakes on Mount Eddy. It's a day's trip with spectacular views—and you've so much left to see."

"Yes, I do. . . all right. But I'll provide the lunch."

"Agreed."

Not long afterward she studied him in her rearview mirror as she drove away, a tall man standing where she'd left him, partly obscured by swirling dust.

As she reached his gate, a sudden, unaccountable sadness settled over her, wholly unreasonable. She couldn't explain it: they'd shown each other more of themselves this afternoon than she'd thought possible, and wondrously, each had been content.

What, then, could go wrong? She didn't know. But the uneasiness remained.

MAGGIE WORKED HARD for the next three days. Gordon Hamilton was back in town, and Maggie was happy to introduce him to Ben, hoping Hamilton would transfer some of the subtle pressure from her to him.

The two men seemed to understand each other, though Ben asked her later if Hamilton didn't seem somewhat more zealous than necessary.

"He takes this campaign personally, if that's what you mean," Maggie said.

"That is what I mean. Gets pretty worked up, doesn't he?"

"I guess he's what you'd call a born crusader."

Behind on her reports, Maggie spent part of each day assembling and organizing her notes. Yet in some ways she wished she was further behind than she was, because she could see that her job would not last much longer. Another week and a half—two at the most. Though Cooper called her often in the evenings, she found herself unable to tell him she'd soon be leaving.

It was Friday when everything fell apart. Walking down her motel stairs that morning, Maggie saw that somebody had left the previous day's *San Francisco Chronicle* near the landing. She might have stepped right over it and gone on had she not noticed Hamilton's name on the front page.

Startled, she picked up the newspaper and sat down on the steps to read it. In bold type the headline proclaimed, "Environmentalist Gordon Hamilton Declares Candidacy for U.S. Senate."

Her eyes widened as she read the story under the caption. Hamilton was described as "the well-known environmentalist leader," whose qualifications—apparently due to his success thus far at keeping the skiers out of Mount Shasta—were said to include leadership, dedication to preserving the environment and an ability to get a job done. The reporter had collected statements from Hamilton's supporters who spoke of a "popular demand" for his candidacy.

Maggie turned to the inner pages to finish the story. Hamilton was described as "reluctant," but "willing to answer a call,'' and ''not ready to begin campaigning until his job in Mount Shasta is finished.''

She scowled at the pages, finding it increasingly difficult to go on reading. Her own thoughts kept interfering: So this explained Hamilton's pleasure a few weeks ago at being called ''the great environmentalist.'' Thinking back, she realized the young man who'd found her in Hamilton's office that night must have known all about it; he'd backed off so quickly at seeing her there. Furthermore, Hamilton's forthcoming candidacy explained his excessive vehemence and his readiness to give speeches on every occasion.

She laid the paper on her lap, lost in thought. So he was using her, using her and the situation and all the other environmentalists. Pretending the great issue was saving the mountain when all along the only issue was politics and his own private ambition.

For the first time she wondered if Gordon Hamilton really cared about the mountain at all. As she sat there musing, an unwanted thought crept into her consciousness: wasn't she doing almost the same thing... using this job to further her own ends? She shuddered, realizing that she and Hamilton might be very much alike. Hamilton had already paid an excessive amount in legal fees just to launch his political career. And she had accepted some of that money and kowtowed to him and closed her mind to all opposing arguments... for the sake of her own career.

God help us, she thought. *We're birds of a feather!*

Disgusted and ready to crumple the paper into a ball, Maggie stopped when her eye fell on a strange sentence toward the end of the article.

> Hamilton, who for the past five years has been a professor at the College of the Siskiyous, main-

tains that his stance has changed since the controversial incident of four years ago.

Maggie read the sentence again, puzzling over it. Some kind of veiled reference to . . . to what, she wondered. What had happened four years ago that he now wished to disavow?

Maggie rose from the steps and glanced at her watch. She had an appointment in five minutes, but she was tingling with curiosity. On impulse, she dashed back up the stairs and started to unlock her door. She could cancel the appointment on some pretext and go to the local newspaper archives instead.

She wavered, her key in the door. No, she decided, summoning an image of herself as a professional. Satisfying her personal curiosity would have to wait.

She kept her appointment, admitting only later that she might just as well have canceled it. Burning to run to the newspaper office, she had hardly heard a word the man was saying.

Two hours later, she was sorting through old newspapers in a small back room of the *Mount Shasta Herald*. In a town this size she knew any substantial controversy among the town's citizens would doubtless make the paper. Four years ago. Approaching her quest scientifically, Maggie began reading headlines in the January newspapers and continued until she'd covered the entire year. Fifty-two weeks, a lot of papers to cover, but as she finished reading December's papers she knew she'd been wrong. None of the headlines concerned Gordon Hamilton at all.

Dispirited, Maggie met the editor, bluff and slightly red faced, coming out of his office. "Find what you were looking for?" he asked.

When she said no, he continued, "What kind of story was it? What were the issues?"

Maggie shrugged, not sure what they were or whether she ought to mention Hamilton. She was, after all, still working for the man. But how likely was he to hear about this?

As the editor waited, Maggie's natural caution vanished and she blurted out, "Did Gordon Hamilton get in a fight with some people in this town? About four years ago?"

He frowned, scratching his head. "There was something...but I'm not sure...let me see. Land. Something about land. He was trying to buy a parcel, I think. But there was a misrepresentation..."

Maggie felt tension growing in her stomach.

"Ah, yes...that was it. About March of that year, it must have been." His eyes seemed focused on some distant event. "There was a lot of talk about it, him and that company that was supposedly behind him... something about zoning." The editor's face creased in a broad smile. "Let's look for the story under 'Zoning Disputes.' That would be second section, first page."

A few minutes later the editor had found it. The phone rang just then so he handed the paper to Maggie and left.

With growing excitement Maggie learned that Gordon Hamilton had tried to buy a large parcel of land near the mountain, indicating to the zoning committee that the land would be developed by Cascade Developers. The company had a good reputation and the board was agreeable to a zoning change. Maggie could discern harmony in the first article.

But in subsequent articles the mood changed. Skepticism began to appear among board members and she could sense growing defensiveness in Hamilton's statements.

The final article revealed indignation and hostility on both sides. One of the board members had discovered Hamilton was bluffing and had never approached anyone from Cascade Developers.

> Hamilton is in fact about to build condominiums that will be substandard in both size and quality. These plans, which have been placed in the hands of a second-rate builder, indicate to me that Hamilton is ready to start construction on three hundred chicken coops!

With held breath, Maggie read quickly, trying to find out who had discovered Hamilton's deceit. At first there was no mention of names, but in the last sentence of the article the board member was revealed. It was Cooper Smith!

Stunned, Maggie sat on the small chair in the archives trying to absorb what she'd just learned. So Hamilton had once tried to deceive the town. No wonder there was so much animosity between him and Cooper.

She imagined the scene, Hamilton standing before the board with his pretenses and his lies, and the board members facing him down. Not a pretty picture, she thought.

And then another scenario came to her. Her standing before old man Meiers with a lie almost as bad, her hands shaking and Meiers throwing over Ben on account of it. Shaken, she knew then that the difference between her and Hamilton were miniscule, that under their innocent fronts, both were wolves at heart.

The editor came back. Trying to hide her feelings, Maggie said noncommittally, "I guess that's all I need—not exactly what I imagined." Giving the man a distant smile, she left the office and headed for her next appointment.

THAT NIGHT MAGGIE SAT in her room, despondent. "I'll see you tomorrow," Cooper had said, and Maggie had agreed, knowing in some remote area of her brain that it would never happen.

Saturday. Tomorrow was Saturday, and all week she had worked in a kind of suspended animation waiting for that day. Until this morning, most of her thoughts had circled and whirled and always come back to the heady prospect of finding herself once more in Cooper Smith's arms. The knowledge was always there, no matter what else she was doing.

But today everything had changed, and she hadn't the heart to tell him. He would just have to find out and hate her for her cowardice, for being too weak to let him know face-to-face.

She was at a crossroads with Cooper now, and both of them knew it. They'd stepped over the threshold into full intimacy, and she could either go forward with him, giving up the career she'd set for herself, or retrench and hang on to the gains she'd already made. But she knew her personality was too well formed and she could never turn back. Like Hamilton, she had created a format for her life that excluded all disrupting influences—even love.

She sighed, trying to see into the darkness beyond her window. She'd never acknowledged it before, but yes, she was in love, and perhaps had been for longer than she knew. Cooper Smith's essential goodness had won her heart; God knows that part of her was locked in forever. But he hadn't won over her soul or whatever it was that determined her character. He hadn't conquered that indomitable part of her that pushed on so relentlessly, exacting dues and demanding that she not veer from her course.

Success would always come first for her. It was inevitable. A need for success had brought her to this point and nothing had ever really changed. Wasn't she, then, exactly like Hamilton? Driven to make his fortune on cheap building, he had, when thwarted, merely turned his ambition in another direction—toward politics. She hated him, but they were members of the same subspecies: the unrelenting and the driven.

She stood up, turned on the light and reached into the closet for her suitcase. Sorry for what she was about to do, Maggie began emptying her bureau. She couldn't face him again, not even once, lest she cave in. The only way she'd ever get out of Cooper's life was to leave, and she had to leave first thing tomorrow.

CHAPTER TWENTY

MAGGIE CONTINUED PACKING until her drawers were empty and all her toiletries were arranged in her cosmetics bag. The room had a sterile look without the small items she normally left scattered around—her hairbrush, a book on the bedside table, dark glasses on the bureau, a sweater draped over the back of the chair.

Surveying it, she felt terrible. The room had been home for a month—more of a home than she'd had in years, because she'd grown to love the town and felt aligned to it, a sentiment she'd never held for Newport Beach. But more than that, she felt aligned to him. God, it was going to be hard to leave!

And what about that other part of it, the job she'd prided herself on so much? Thorough as always, she began a last search for forgotten items, opening bureau drawers one last time and looking under the bed, her hands occupied while she tried to sort out her feelings about her assignment. How would she reconcile leaving before the job was finished?

It went so against the grain, her giving up suddenly like this. From the first she'd meant to turn this assignment to her advantage, and now she was running out on it, and a part of her said no! She couldn't leave yet! The internal argument went on relentlessly. Hadn't she already done most of what was to be done here? Couldn't Ben handle the rest?

Oh, he could, she knew it, but that wasn't the point, was it? She'd always wanted full credit, and now here she was, settling for less.

She shrugged, trying to convince herself, and awkwardly got back up again. There would be other assignments, other challenges, and surely old man Meiers—who'd already praised her tapes—would see she'd done the larger part of this one pretty well. Maybe one just had to balance things in life.

Well, she was doing it, weighing the completion of this job against becoming sidetracked from her life's work, and the two didn't weigh out. One more day with Cooper Smith and she'd be permanently lost.

Finished with her packing, Maggie put on her nightie and glanced at her watch. It was after eleven, too late to call Ben. Tomorrow. She'd call Ben early, just before she left.

IT WASN'T EASY to sleep that night; Maggie was aware of the passing hours nearly all night long.

At six in the morning she finally got up for good, rising tiredly to shower and dress. Just before seven, ready to walk out the door, she dialed Ben's number.

A sleep-heavy voice answered.

"Ben," she said, "I'm leaving. I just wanted to let you know."

"Leaving? What do you mean? Who is this?"

"It's Maggie, Ben. Come on, how many calls do you get at seven in the morning? I'm sorry to wake you—I really am—but I'm leaving town, and I had to let you know. I'm going right now, or I wouldn't have called so early."

He was fully awake now. "You're leaving for how long? What's this all about?"

"I'm turning the job over to you. You know the

people we're still scheduled to see and what has to be done—we went over all that Thursday. But something has come up and I can't finish the assignment. So I'm running out on it, Ben." She let regret alter her voice. "I guess that's how you'd describe it—running out. But I don't have any choice. Honestly."

"Huh," he said. "Well. I'm not sure what I'm supposed to say. Congratulations, Maggie, on your better assignment?" He seemed to be thinking. "Or, tough luck, kiddo, I understand. You haven't made it very clear." When she didn't help him, he added, "And I can see I'll get no explanation, either."

"I'll explain, Ben. But I'll have to tell you later, back home. I can't talk about it now."

"Okay."

"And one last thing.... About eight o'clock, will you call Cooper Smith? Tell him I had to leave town but that you've got a note for him. I'll bring it over in a few minutes and slip it under your door. And Ben, if he says anything, tell him I feel terrible, will you? Really bad." She started to cry. "I can't...can't talk, Ben. Goodbye."

Hastily, Maggie wrote the note, trying not to smudge it with tears.

> Dear Cooper, I don't expect you'll understand what I'm doing, after what we had together last Sunday. It was so good. Too good. And maybe that's one of my problems. I care for you too much. But caring means commitment, and I'm not sure I can change enough—or give up enough. Does this make sense? No, it probably doesn't. I'm not very good at explaining. All I know is, I had to stop us while I still could.
>
> Maggie

An hour later she was halfway down the canyon and headed for Sacramento.

THE LOS ANGELES AREA looked worse than Maggie remembered. She arrived home on one of those days when the temperature hovered at an unseasonable ninety degrees and the smog settled in reddish brown over the foothills.

It was early afternoon when she stepped off the plane at John Wayne Airport. The minute she was outside, hot air struck her face like a blast from a furnace. Walking across the Tarmac she was aware of a thickness in the atmosphere, as though she was breathing in more contamination than oxygen. And no wonder; everywhere she looked cars were moving, a perpetual and restless sea of cars.

Expensive as it was, Maggie took a taxi to her apartment.

She unlocked her door and stood there a moment, taking it in. Nothing had changed, not even her memories of the place. Her furnishings reflected her personality and fit her life-style as she remembered it—fast paced, efficient, uncommitted. Anything in the room could be replaced without regret. All the lines of her furniture were simple, practical. But this was what she'd chosen and it had always suited her.

Maggie took her suitcase into the bedroom and sat down on the bed. She put her head in her hands, thinking. In a moment she'd have to call old man Meiers and let him know she was back . . . and try to explain why she'd left. She was sure she could make it sound reasonable, but she would never try to explain everything—that in working for Hamilton and trying to discredit Smith, she'd spent a month betting on the wrong horse. Meiers would never care about that.

Besides, what did it matter anymore?

MAGGIE PLUNGED INTO HER WORK at the firm with a vigor that left her little time to think. Sooner or later thinking evoked memories and memories brought pain—and the pain was Cooper Smith.

Now that she'd decided to make legal success her paramount goal, there were things she could do to help herself along. One of them was working long hours.

Another was volunteering for disagreeable jobs and making the most of them. Eventually her colleagues would notice and give her credit. But somewhere in her psyche she began to see other reasons for this tack—reasons that had to do with atonement. In an odd moment as she sat at her desk, the thought had come to her. If Cooper Smith had known how she got the Mount Shasta assignment he would have considered her actions tainted.

For the first time in her life she felt more than mild regret for something she'd done. When Ben got back she knew she'd have to say it at last, that she was truly sorry for having connived behind his back.

A few days after her return, old man Meiers called her into his office. Sitting there behind his enormous walnut desk, he looked smaller and balder than she'd remembered. But his expression had all the old energy as he pushed back his glasses and smiled. "I've been reading the transcripts of your tapes, Maggie. They're good. Very thorough. You've done a workmanlike job up there. What would you say the chances of success are, eh? The hearing will be coming up late this summer."

Maggie hesitated. Now that Gordon Hamilton was out in the open, her opinion of the environmentalist position had altered so radically she could no longer be objective. "I don't know, Mr. Meiers." It was the truth, and she wasn't quite sure why she'd told it; an attitude of uncertainty would do her no good. Then, to her surprise another bit of truth came out. "There are formidable arguments on the other side. And formidable opponents, too."

Meiers had picked up a calendar, and now he put it down in surprise. "This is your opinion after all that work up there? Well. . . this is a revelation."

She hadn't pleased him, she could see that. But suddenly she didn't care. "Perhaps you've taught your fledgling lawyers too well. I remember once your saying that one can always find an argument for either side of a case. While I was up in Mount Shasta I found both arguments."

To her surprise the old man smiled. "Well put, my dear. This should make you admirably qualified for the final argument when the time comes. In the meanwhile, welcome back."

Maggie had thanked him and left his office strangely dissatisfied. Somehow garnering Meiers's praise hadn't moved her much at all.

FOR THE NEXT WEEK Maggie worked on small, boring assignments: a will, an ugly divorce settlement, a probate. Staying in her office extra hours not only produced fast results, but it sopped up the unbidden thoughts that threatened to upset her. Images. A glimpse of blue sky, a certain look in a pair of gray eyes.

Once she even asked herself what he must be thinking, how he'd taken it the morning he'd learned she had not only forsaken the trip to the Eddies, she'd actually left town.

No, no. She couldn't think about that! With an effort, Maggie focused again on the situation at hand. She could see that while she'd been gone, younger attorneys had grabbed the larger cases, and it would take a certain amount of energy to get back into preferred work—and maybe a little skulduggery, too.

But something had unaccountably changed. While she welcomed the hard work, any kind of deviousness left her cold. She no longer had the heart for it.

As the days passed, Maggie's unrest spread beyond those aspects of life in a big firm. When she went home she felt dissatisfied, and when she accepted dates it was worse. All around her life seemed diminished, as though she'd returned from Shangri-la and nothing here compared favorably.

One Saturday she went out on her little porch to lie in the sun. Dressed in a bikini, she stretched out on her lounge chair with a book, determined to let the sun bring its balm to her skin. . . to burn her, even, so she'd no longer feel such inner coldness.

She had only begun to read, working to get into her story, when the doorbell rang. She sat up, surprised. She wasn't expecting anyone, and solicitors weren't allowed into the complex. With a glance at her bare legs, she hurried into the apartment for a robe. Annoyed at the interruption, she called through the door, "Who is it?" deciding that she'd get rid of whoever it was fast.

A familiar voice called back, "It's me, Maggie," and she swung the door open to Ben.

THEY SAT ON MAGGIE'S SOFA and talked. Ben had arrived back the night before and would have come to see her immediately had it not been so late.

"What was going on between you and Cooper?" Ben asked.

"What do you mean?" she evaded, not wanting to confess everything just yet. She was afraid if she said very much she might break down, tell him how miserable she was or even cry. She held on to herself. "What made you ask?"

Behind his glasses Ben gave her an odd little look. "I

think you know." He cleared his throat. "The situation didn't quite work out as you wanted, Maggie, and I'm sorry. But after you called, I'm afraid being awakened so early had its effects and I fell asleep again. When I got up it was late, almost eleven. I looked at my watch and couldn't believe I'd slept that long.

"For a moment I forgot I had that phone call to make, and then I remembered. But when I dialed Smith, Jesse said he'd already left. At that point I knew I'd blown it for you and didn't know what to do next. So I thought I better get over to your motel room and leave the note on your door."

Ben paused in his story, leaving Maggie with a sense of dread. She guessed what was coming next and didn't want to hear it. Oh, God, she didn't want to hear it, not after what she'd done to him....

"You saw him," she said tentatively.

"I sure did. He was just coming down the stairs. I guess he'd pounded on your door and had waited there quite a while. He was walking down those stairs like he was dazed, like someone who's been knocked on the head and wakes up to find himself in a strange country. He had that distant kind of look."

She thought, *Oh, no....*

"Then I had to give it to him. You handed me this great assignment, Maggie, telling the man you'd not only stood him up but you'd split and were now hundreds of miles away. It wasn't what you'd call a preferred job. Having to hang on there while he reads the note in this black stillness."

Tears came to her eyes. She could think of nothing to say. She just sat on the couch feeling miserable, hating herself.

"Did he say anything?" she asked finally in a choked voice.

"Not a word," Ben said. "Nothing at all that I remember."

Silence hung between them, thick and unpleasant. Ben turned toward her after a while. "Do you have some coffee, Maggie?"

"Oh, yes. Yes. I'll make it." She stood up, grateful to be moving, almost hurrying to do something, anything that might help shake off what she felt.

From the living room, Ben said, "Oh, he did say something, Maggie. I just remembered. He said, 'Thanks, Ben.'"

TWO MONTHS PASSED without change. Maggie's only source of pleasure when she thought about Mount Shasta was learning that Ben might soon be going back to see Anne. At least something good had come out of that experience.

It made her a little easier to see Ben happy, perhaps the only source of satisfaction she had these days. It also surprised her that someone else's happiness might seem so important.

IN MID-JULY old man Meiers called Maggie and Ben into his office. "Sit down, sit down."

The two threw each other looks of mutual surprise before settling into chairs. Meiers seldom talked to his attorneys in pairs, as far as Maggie knew. It had always been one or everyone.

"One of you has to go back to Mount Shasta," he opened without preamble. "The final hearing on the injunction will be held in four days and I want to be represented by at least one of you in addition to my trial staff. They'll need. . ."

His words faded out of Maggie's consciousness. She wanted to go, suddenly—she *had* to go on account of Cooper. She had to know how he was, what he was doing, just ask a few questions, maybe not even see him. She could be discreet, it wouldn't take much....

Then she saw Ben's face. He had moved forward and was sitting stiffly with his mouth slightly ajar.

"Whoever it is will be there to coach the trial staff on personalities, issues..."

Maggie saw that Ben had moved again; he was almost off the edge of his chair.

"So I want you to decide between yourselves, since it makes no difference to me." He stopped talking and silence fell among the three of them. Ben moved back in his seat and stared steadfastly out the window, focused on something beyond old man Meiers's head.

Suddenly a voice broke the silence, and Maggie realized almost abstractly that it was hers. "Why don't you let Ben do it?"

Ben swung around, throwing her a surprised glance.

She went on, propelled by something she didn't try to understand. "I don't see how I can get away right now, and Ben knows everybody up there as well as I do. He...he'll do a good job for us, Mr. Meiers." She had the vague feeling she ought to look around to see who was talking.

"Well...what do you think, Ben? You want to go?"

"Yes. Yes I do." Ben nodded. Maggie could see the suppressed smile behind Ben's somberness; his lips were taut, turning his mouth into a thin line.

She thought, *Go ahead and smile, Ben.*

"Well, then." Meiers coughed. "You want to put that on the calendar, Ben? I'll let you make your own arrangements." He opened a notebook. "Unless you two have questions, that's all for now."

Maggie left Meiers's office quickly, not wanting to talk to either of them. She'd had her say and that was that, and even now she wasn't quite sure why.

She'd almost reached the door of her office when Ben caught up with her and grabbed her arm. "What made you do that, Maggie?"

Refusing to face him, she answered with a shrug.

"I never expected a move like that. I thought I'd have to fight you for it. But I wasn't about to fight, either, so I figured if the old man gave it to you, so be it. But I've got to know. How come you gave that assignment to me?"

There had to be a reason, she thought, but could think of nothing except a fleeting image of morality disembodied; a principle or something of the sort, which came to her just before she spoke. But it wasn't so unusual anymore. It happened to her all the time. And it wasn't something she could explain.

Ben let go of her arm. "So you don't have a reason, then. It's just another of your weird moves."

He was about to leave when Maggie finally answered him. "Oh I do, Ben. I owed you one, remember? Or maybe two—for what I did to you in March and for your speaking to Cooper for me. I guess I'm still one short, but...well, another time. Take your trip." She moved through her office door. "And give my love to Anne."

"Just Anne?" The blond eyebrows went up.

"Just Anne," she said firmly. "Nobody else up there will care about my love."

A week later, Maggie learned the injunction had failed.

CHAPTER TWENTY-ONE

MAGGIE SIGNALED BEN to come into her office, and then she closed the door.

"What happened up there, Ben? Tell me the details. Is Meiers pretty mad about it?"

"He may never quite understand the situation." Ben sat down in the leather chair facing her desk. "I tried to explain the mood up there, the way most of the people feel, but whether I did an adequate job—"

"It's one of those things you have to see for yourself, isn't it? I mean, talking to the townspeople face-to-face. We weren't helping them, Ben, you know that. Skiing was... well, the town needs it."

"So I gathered. In fact, I got that impression from the start. But the judge summed it up so our final arguments sounded hollow." He ran a quick hand up the side of his cheek. "He did say a lot of good things about us, incidentally, about our being thorough and presenting a good case. But in the end he claimed he had to deny the injunction for the good of the town. I wasn't too surprised."

"And Hamilton?"

Ben smiled. "I wish you'd been there, Maggie. It was an Academy Award performance. I'd become skeptical about his sincerity before I left, but after the judge's decision it was one big Charlie Chaplin act: hand over the brow, the big scowl, a lot of pacing up and down. He might as well have been wearing the big, floppy shoes. The guy was ludicrous."

Maggie laughed. "I guess I never told you I was sick of him, too. But I had worse problems, Ben. I'd decided we were fighting a hopeless battle. The longer I was up there the more logic I found on the other side."

"Thanks for filling me in."

"What else could I do? Are we supposed to be harping on the negatives—damning our own case out loud?" She shook her head. "I don't think so. And I was having enough trouble dealing with it myself. God, I'm sick of working on stuff I don't believe in!"

For just a moment Ben regarded her in silence. "This is the first time I've ever seen you emotional about your work, Maggie. You'd better watch it. You'll lose your effectiveness. We're advocates, not crusaders."

Are we, she wondered, and wanted to tell him he was wrong—it was about time they cared which side they were on. But Ben would have laughed. She changed the subject.

"How was Anne?" she asked, knowing she was inquiring about the wrong person. *Tell me about Cooper,* she wanted to cry out, but the words wouldn't come and she couldn't force them. Picking up a pen, she idly traced the embossed words on a piece of letterhead.

"That's the subject I've been saving for last," he said, and Maggie looked up to catch his quick smile.

"Something good, Ben?"

"Very good, and you're the first around here to know. In two months I'm quitting the firm, Maggie. By October I'll have my own practice in Mount Shasta."

She stared at him, openmouthed. "Mount Shasta?"

"I could hardly commute from here, could I? And that's where I'll be living. In early September I'm marrying Anne Smith."

ANOTHER MONTH of dullness passed with Maggie increasingly unable to push aside thoughts of Cooper Smith. It had worked so well at first, the plunging into her work so she couldn't think or feel. But now the memories had a way of pressing in on her so she could no longer fight them. She kept seeing him everywhere: his intense eyes, his features and the strength they implied. His sense of justice intruded on her, affecting her every move.

And noting the change in Ben was part of her pain, too. He smiled more and had about him an obnoxious air of contentment. Even his thin face seemed less pinched these days. Every time she saw Ben she was reminded of what she was missing.

Yet she knew it wasn't work, but the lack of Cooper in her life that depleted her energy. Without him there seemed so little point in doing anything well. What did it matter what all her fellow lawyers thought?

Sometimes it even seemed pointless knocking herself out to please old man Meiers, who might never be hurried into offering her a partnership. Was this how you got one, or was partnership merely a function of time that those who hung in long enough were eventually rewarded?

Once-forbidden thoughts crept into her awareness. *I'll go see him! I'll just go up there for two days and tell him I'm sorry!*

At last she decided to do it. Three weeks from now she'd take a long weekend and fly to Sacramento. She began counting the days.

THE LETTER CAME the next Tuesday.

Once Maggie saw that it was from Mount Shasta her heart began to pound and blindly she dropped onto her living-room couch. Even seated she was trembling, her breath coming as fast as if she'd run up a long flight of stairs.

Mount Shasta! It had to be him! She could hardly get the envelope open.

The phone rang just as she broke through to the inner sheets, and holding the letter in a shaking hand, she stared at the instrument, unwilling to pick it up. She felt that her future hung on this piece of paper and whatever else the world offered was unimportant.

Only long habit finally drove her to answer the phone. A man she hadn't seen in a long time asked her for a date. But Maggie shook her head. With Cooper's letter in her hand the idea was unthinkable. "I'm terribly sorry," she said, "but I'm tied up that evening. Otherwise I'd love to. Maybe we can get together another Saturday." Breathless, she let him know she had no time to talk.

Then she spread the letter out. Cooper had written longhand on plain typing paper.

> Dear Maggie, I've waited a long time to write you, imagining I would soon get some additional word from you. I've always been easy to reach. But your long silence made me mull over our relationship—if, indeed, we still have one.

The words brought tears to her eyes. She wanted to cry out to him, *We do, Cooper, we do!*

> I'm not exactly sure why you left that Saturday, Maggie. You left so much unsaid. But I'd guess it has something to do with trust. That you haven't learned to trust me, or anyone, and that once we became close you feared losing something—your identity, perhaps?

Whatever. But now I know all my reassurances were to no avail. Your defenses were too strong.

Knowing what your work means to you, Maggie, I can only hope you do well, and that it will prove enough.

I'm sorry. I had imagined a different ending for us.

Cooper

Maggie put the letter down, stricken.

It was over. Whatever she'd had with this man was now finished.

She sat staring at the wall, seeing nothing, willing herself to feel nothing. The worst that could ever happen to her had happened. . . again.

From some dark well of memory she remembered how it felt the day her father left, how she cried, the emptiness in her stomach. . . no, not just in her stomach but everywhere. She remembered her loneliness, how lasting it had been, surrounding her for days and weeks. . . and still there after a year.

Oh, Lord, Lord. Was she to feel all that again? She turned her face into the back of the couch, stifling the sobs that broke from her throat and then racked her body. *Oh, Cooper. . . Cooper. . . .* In her mind's eye her hands reached out to him and her face turned up to his. She sought from the ghost in her heart the comfort only he could give.

But there was nothing there.

Feeling as if she might drown or die, Maggie sat abruptly upright. She was an adult now and nobody could help her but herself. Nobody. She had to do what she could. Fumbling for the phone, she dialed blindly and asked the information operator for the number of the man who'd called minutes before.

Taking a deep, restoring breath she waited, hearing

the man's voice come on the phone. But it was the wrong voice, the wrong timbre—someone she didn't wish to hear, after all. She shook her head, saying quickly, "Sorry, I must have the wrong number."

MEANINGLESS WORK added to Maggie's despair. Sometimes after she arrived in her office, she just sat there, asking herself whether it was the work itself or the attitude she brought to it that gave her job so little appeal.

She didn't know.

Realizing it would help to keep busy, she often daydreamed instead, reliving her moments with Cooper, remembering the things he'd said. Her memories brought more pain than pleasure, yet she dwelled there anyway. One day she recalled with a sense of shock what he'd said just before they fell asleep in their little shelter on Mount Shasta. "I hope you don't wake up some day and find you've lost other things that you didn't know were important—until they were gone."

Maggie picked up a pen and began doodling on an envelope. "Gone," she wrote. "Gone, gone, gone." She ignored the tears that started down her face.

A FEW DAYS LATER Meiers walked into her office and handed her a file. "Read this, Maggie, and take some action, will you?"

The case involved a Mexican family who'd refused to pay their rent, drawing first a number of threatening letters from the landlord and now a move for eviction.

Maggie read it quickly, finding the matter uncomplicated. She would simply petition the court for a hearing and the matter would be disposed of in the landlord's favor.

But something in the case caught her eye. The landlord had written numerous letters, more than customary, and she began to sense he was reluctant to take his case to court. Maggie wondered why.

On an impulse, she picked up the phone. Moments later she was talking to a woman with a heavy accent. "Yes, he say we owe rent," the woman said. "But *Dios mi*, the plumbing...it no work. It never work good, now not work at all."

"Have you asked the landlord to fix it?"

"*Si, señora*, ask, ask, ask. No fix. Toilets not work. Have to go to neighbor." An audible sigh came over the phone. "I got money, but I no pay. Not with no toilets."

Maggie listened, disheartened. The woman sounded sincere and even brave. She'd told of trying to locate the landlord's address, then going there by bus and not finding him home. And all the while the plumbing had remained broken.

The file in Maggie's hands took on life and personality. Her call over, Maggie pushed it to one corner of her desk, staring at the name on the outside. *Burlington v. Rodriguez*. She'd been told to do something for Burlington, but now she had only contempt for the landlord and her sympathy went to Rodriguez. She shook her head, doubting herself. Lawyers weren't supposed to get personally involved, but she'd done it, and almost without knowing where the idea came from or how it seeped into her conscience, Maggie felt the warm presence of an unseen ally: Cooper Smith would have defended Rodriguez!

Maggie shoved the file under other work. Files got buried all the time; it was an occupational hazard. When Ben walked in just then, she forgot it altogether.

Maggie saw Ben's expression before she saw anything else, a change so startling she could hardly believe he was the same man. His smile was quick and lively and he exuded enthusiasm. "Just two more weeks, Maggie, and then I'm up there with Anne."

"You look illegally happy."

"I am. I hadn't known a woman could alter my life this way." He placed his hands on her desk and leaned toward her. "An idea just came to me, and it's worth mentioning." At close range Maggie could see that a few additional pounds had added just enough flesh to soften the sharp angles of his face, and with a start she realized Ben was almost handsome!

"Skiing's going to come to that mountain, Maggie. It's inevitable. And when it does..." He reached across the desk and touched her hand. "Look, kiddo, there'll soon be plenty of work for two lawyers!"

"Thanks, Ben." She smiled. "You couldn't have said anything nicer."

BEN WAS PULLING OUT in a few days. His work had dwindled to the small chores of handing his cases over to others, and seeing him in the halls these days, Maggie could swear he walked with springs on his feet.

"Anne will be coming down to meet my family," he said one morning, poking his head into Maggie's office, but she thought no more about it until she passed his open office door on the last day and he called out, "Someone you know is in the lobby. We're meeting Anne downtown for lunch."

Maggie stopped and shifted the document she was carrying to the other hand so she could rest her palm on his doorjamb. All Ben's personal items were stacked neatly on his desk and he was tossing papers into the wastebasket. He looked organized and happy, and she envied him. "Your old secretary?" she asked with a smile.

"Why don't you go see?"

"A surprise, eh? All right, I'll go find out who

you're showing Anne off to now." She started to leave but came back. "I'm really happy about your wedding, Ben. I wish I could make it."

He grinned. "Me, too."

Caught by his happiness, Maggie sauntered to the lobby lightheartedly, expecting a former employee of the firm. Old secretaries were forever coming back and looking up Ben, claiming they missed his sense of humor.

She rounded the last corner and glanced around quickly, searching among the plaid-cloth chairs.

And then she saw who was there and froze. The deposition she was carrying hit the floor with a thud, and she saw Cooper's head turn and his eyes find her.

"Maggie!" he said, pleasure lighting the gray eyes. Quickly he put down his magazine and stood up.

Transfixed, she stood staring at him, letting the deposition lie there forgotten as he came toward her. In that instant all her longings for him surfaced and she wanted nothing more than to rush into his arms.

Yet something held her where she was, some inner restraint that operated subconsciously, and a voice that came from somewhere else said calmly, "Hello, Cooper."

He reached her and held out his hands. "Well, Maggie. Ben said he'd send you out." His voice was as she'd remembered: warm and resonant, and his face exactly as she'd seen it night after night in her mind's eye. She found herself reaching for his hands, unable to do anything else.

His hands! How large and warm they were! She shivered, needing him to hold her but too reserved to move any closer.

"What...why are you here?" she asked, then wished she'd thought of another way to start. If he'd come to see her, he would have found her immediately.

"I came down with Anne," he said, those eyes absorbing her as toweling takes up water. "We're here to meet Ben's family."

"Ben's family?" She tried not to care that his presence had nothing to do with her.

"His parents decided it was time we all got together."

She nodded. Family celebrations, and then there'd be the wedding, and she couldn't attend and go through it, not with Cooper there.

"Anne's partner gave her these few days so we had to come now. We'll be visiting in Ben's home. But Maggie—" He seemed in a hurry, rushing to get his thoughts expressed. "I want to know about you. Are you happy?"

She yearned to tell him the truth. Regrets surged through her mind aching to be expressed.

It's been so bad, she thought, *I ought to tell him. I've missed him so much.*

But she couldn't.

She shrugged, summoning an indifferent smile that took almost more will than she had. "Yes, Cooper, I'm happy. And you?"

He never answered the question. Instead he said, "And your job, Maggie. Are you getting the kind of work you want?"

"Not exactly." She felt a little safer talking about this, so she told him about Rodriguez and her distaste for helping evict an obviously mistreated family.

"And now you have a decision to make," he said.

She paused, then shook her head. "There's no decision, Cooper, nothing I can do. I'm just stalling, but eventually I'll have to—" she became defensive "—I'll have to see they're thrown out, okay? They'll be put outside the building with their stuff on the sidewalk. That's the way it is in a big law firm. You take the cases they give you and you handle the side where... dammit, where somebody's paying."

"Like the skiing on Mount Shasta," he said, and she thought she heard an edge of bitterness.

"Yes, like Mount Shasta. That's a perfect example, isn't it? Ben and I were hired mercenaries. What else would you call us? We went up there to do a job—a job for money—and we lost, and that's supposed to be the end of it for us." Her tone softened. "But you know it wasn't the end for me, don't you? Because after I met you I was half hoping it would come out the way it did."

She turned away so he couldn't see the tears glistening in her eyes. Quietly she said, "You stand for honesty, Cooper. You always have, and there it is. I've been honest with you. But this isn't getting us anywhere, is it?"

"I don't think there's anywhere for us to get, Maggie." She heard the regret, but he was no longer holding her hands, and she felt separated from him by a chasm too deep for either of them to cross.

She knew there was nothing left for her except to say goodbye, yet she couldn't quite do it, so she stood one last minute, near him but not looking at him, sensing that he was doing the same.

In the distance she saw Ben coming, and she knew she had to escape. The last thing she ever wanted to do was break down in front of Ben and cry.

"Cooper," she began, picking up her deposition to cover her misery, "I have to get back to work now. You do understand. I...why don't you write me sometime?" She was already backing away.

"I don't think so, Maggie. It wouldn't help us."

"Goodbye, then." Without looking at him again, she fled, and desperate to get out of public view, hurried to her office, closed the door behind her and collapsed on her big leather chair.

She felt as if she might never move again.

In some distant place she heard the wail of a siren and closer at hand the office air conditioning came on with a whoosh, but neither sound had even the slightest meaning for her. Maggie was locked in a private, soundproof place.

Even the knock on her door, when it came a few minutes later, took several seconds to perceive. Before she realized someone wanted to come in, the knock had come twice. She sat up straighter, baffled. If she did nothing, perhaps it would go away. But then the thumping came a third time.

Maggie tried to collect herself. From old habit she responded, as reflexive an act as answering the telephone. Quickly blotting her eyes with Kleenex and coughing to clear her throat, she fought for composure. At last she called out a husky, "Come in!"

It was Cooper standing there like a specter.

She stared, once more unnerved, and felt the shock that sent tremors through her body. She could think of nothing to say but, "Oh!"

Quickly he crossed to her desk, holding out photographs. "I meant to give you these pictures I snapped that day, but you rushed away. Here, Maggie, you should have them. I won't be needing them anymore."

She looked down and saw herself posing in his meadow with Mount Shasta in the background. She couldn't reach for the pictures, couldn't touch them, never wanted to see them again.

He laid them on her desk. "I have to go, Maggie. Ben is waiting. Look up, Maggie."

She raised her chin, hoping tears hadn't left streaks on her face.

"Anne sends her love. She wanted you to know."

"Yes," she said, and then, "Thanks. Tell her . . . tell her to enjoy this next month."

"And you—you be happy, Maggie." He touched her hand lightly, smiled, then turned and went through the door.

As he disappeared around the corner she felt despair settle over her with the finality of death. In one day she'd said her last goodbye to Cooper Smith twice.

THE FOLLOWING WEEKS were almost unbearable. Torn by regret about Cooper and distaste for her work, Maggie wrestled with the only problem that had a solution. Her negative feelings about *Burlington v. Rodriguez* grew stronger daily, and unable to ignore her conscience any longer, she asked to be taken off the case.

Meiers seemed surprised but made no comment at the time. It was only later, in the hall, that he stopped her. "You going to be having big bouts of conscience about all your cases from now on?"

"What do you mean?" she asked, looking down at the short, rotund man.

"I mean the Rodriguez thing. Do you see any money coming from the Mexicans?"

She gave him a look, not answering.

"You may not like the notion, but law firms exist to make money. I hope I've made the situation clear."

"Perfectly," she said and recognized the moment as a turning point in her life. From that second on, Maggie divorced herself mentally from Meiers, Meiers, DeCaro and Kosinski.

CHAPTER TWENTY-TWO

"ANNE, IS THAT REALLY you?" Maggie asked a few days later as a familiar voice said, "Dr. Smith here."

"It's me, Maggie. My goodness, we haven't talked in ages! I can't believe this. How are you?"

Warmed as always by the voice of her friend, Maggie hung on to her office phone tightly, making light of her job and hurrying past the news of herself, herself being, currently, not a very hopeful subject.

"But you, Anne—are you nearly ready for the wedding? It's only a week away, isn't it? You must be going crazy about now. I'm so happy for you."

Anne laughed. "I should be going a little crazier, I think, but my patients keep getting sick at inopportune times, such as just when I'm about to run out and buy something for my trousseau. But Ben's parents, bless them, have got the reception pretty well organized. And Ben and I have written our vows and the minister has them. And the church—Ben has taken care of all that." Maggie could feel the other's smile. "At times life up here seems so normal I almost forget I'm a near-bride."

"When do you come down, Anne?"

"Day after tomorrow. And then at Christmas I intend to forget I'm a doctor for three whole weeks. I hope when I get back I won't know which end of a stethoscope to use!"

"Anne, I should let you go. But I just wanted to tell you I'll be thinking about you. And that I can see how well your life is going to work out. Ben has changed so much he's, well, if he wasn't still funny sometimes, I wouldn't know him. He's a hornet become a lamb. You've managed—"

Anne broke in. "Why did you say you'd be thinking about me?" No answer. "Why did you say it, Maggie? Aren't you coming?"

"I. . . I don't think so."

Anne's dismay was genuine. "You're not coming? But you must. . . you *have* to! Maggie, I'd counted on your being there. I'd planned to ask you to be in the wedding party, but we're only having one attendant each—Ben's sister and my brother. Are you—" She broke off. "I'm sorry, I shouldn't press, but it is disappointing."

As Maggie tried to assemble her thoughts in a way Anne would understand, her friend said, "I guess I know why. It's Cooper, isn't it? But if you don't come to this, Maggie, how are the two of us ever going to see you again? Cooper's apt to be around, anytime. Oh, Maggie. . . ."

As Maggie listened to Anne her eyes wandered to the window, to a couple walking by on the street hand in hand. It occurred to her suddenly that she was being selfish, that because of her own heavy emotions she was putting a cloud on Anne and Ben's big day. She was a friend to them both; they would expect her there.

"Look, Anne," she said into the strained silence. "You're right. I can't duck him forever. He exists, I exist and I might as well get used to the fact that we share a common world. I'm glad I called. I am coming. Now go buy something, you've only a few days left!"

THE PRESBYTERIAN CHURCH in Whittier was small and filled with people. Maggie came in quietly and sat down by herself, alone in a back pew until others filled in on either side of her. She waited through the hurried footsteps of latecomers, through silence, and then through a heraldic trumpet joyously proclaiming that the ceremony had begun.

Moments later, Cooper stood facing her at the altar. Odd, Maggie thought, how he seemed to stand there alone. She didn't see Ben, or the minister or the maid of honor, only Cooper Smith in a gray-and-black tuxedo, his large shoulders on a level nobody else's reached, his eyes finding hers and holding them.

Maggie smiled, and Cooper smiled back.

All her control vanished. She stayed in her seat by sheer will, held there by social convention and the looks and gasps that would follow her if she ran down the aisle into his arms. But in her mind she did it, jumping from her seat and skimming the white satin streamer until she found herself taken in by him and held close.

Later she would remember only Cooper, and momentarily, the way Anne looked walking down the aisle in her low-waisted white satin dress. The rest of the ceremony went by in a haze; the minister's words, music, vows, singing, the organ, Anne and Ben kissing. And Cooper standing looking at her.

Only at the end did Maggie really look at Ben. He was starched, grinning, well-combed and terribly happy.

For an instant, Maggie considered skipping the reception. If the wedding had been hard, the reception would be harder. Cooper would stand near her and she'd break down. He would talk to her, look at her with those gray eyes and make her forget the past months. But then she'd have to go back to life without him. That was the trouble.

In the end she opted for the reception, settling for a poor bargain: a few minutes' pleasure swapped for months of new pain.

It was dusk and the garden of Ben's parents house

had been turned into a fairyland of colored lights. Lanterns swung from the branches of trees. Flowers were everywhere: a bouquet on every table; a great centerpiece of gladiolus on the buffet; roses, pansies and stocks in beds around the periphery.

An expanse of scrubbed driveway had been turned into a dance floor, and in a raised area above the floor a small orchestra had begun to play Strauss waltzes. Maggie smiled when she came around the corner of the house and heard the music. Anne and Ben weren't kids, as anyone would know hearing the sounds from that orchestra.

For a few minutes Maggie stood hemmed in by people, waiting in line at the guest book but scanning the crowd for Cooper. She was so ambivalent, she thought, hoping to see him like this and at the same time dreading their encounter.

Handing the pen away as she finished, Maggie left the sign-in table and drifted toward the buffet. But she never quite got there because Cooper put his hand on her shoulder. She spun around, knowing it was him, all her senses alert to him. The masculine smell of his after-shave wafted down to her and his hand seemed to burn where it touched her. When she looked up, his strong features filled her entire line of vision so that all others dropped out of focus. Everything stopped.

"You look lovely, Maggie. Have I ever seen that dress before?"

She glanced down at the skirt of her yellow chiffon dress, its delicate material so fine it seemed hardly to touch her body. She'd bought the gown especially for tonight, swirling in it before the department-store mirror to see how it would look when she danced. If she danced. She'd been amused that it made her feel rather seductive; the neckline scooped tantalizingly to reveal the upper curves of her breasts. As she'd stood contemplatively before the mirror, the salesgirl had peeked into her dressing room with the comment, "Wow! That sure makes you look sexy!"

Maggie smiled, her eyes returning to his. "No, it's new."

Across the yard the music swelled and threatened to end conversation. Cooper put out his hand to her. "Will you dance with me, Maggie?"

She nodded, and for as long as the piece lasted, Maggie floated across the dance floor in a cloud of happiness. Cooper's touch was light, his dancing superb. They turned and touched and moved together as if they'd been a dancing partnership all their lives.

When the orchestra stopped momentarily, Cooper kept his arm around her waist, pulling her close exactly as she'd imagined in nights of restless dreams.

She looked up at him. "Anne looked beautiful coming down the aisle, didn't she?"

"I don't know," he said. "I was looking at you."

He said it somberly, sending a thrill of hope through her. Did she still mean this much to him?

When the orchestra began a waltz, they moved again in flowing unison, Cooper holding her at a distance while the yellow chiffon dress swirled around her legs with ballerinalike grace. She had no idea how long they continued; dancing with Cooper was forever... and could have been only minutes.

At some point they stopped, and spotting a vacant table in the far corner of the yard, he seated her there, his hand lingering over hers before he asked, "Food, Maggie?"

She nodded, not caring at all whether she ate, but deciding he probably did.

She watched him stride through the crowds, a man taller than most, singular in every way, she thought, remembering how he'd looked to her that first night in Mount Shasta. Then, too, he'd been someone apart.

When he came back with two brimming plates she felt herself floating again. She would make these minutes last because soon they would be over and whatever else there was in her life would once again be all there was.

Seated, he leaned toward her. "You must be happy, Maggie. You couldn't look this beautiful if you weren't."

"Tonight I'm very happy." She smiled.

"But your work—that isn't going well?"

She shrugged. "Remember I told you about the Rodriguez case? The Mexican family a landlord was trying to evict for nonpayment though he hadn't repaired their plumbing? Well, I told Meiers I wouldn't work on it and we had a little standoff; he reminded me that the firm wasn't getting any money from the Mexicans and did I understand his meaning.

"I said I did. Oh, I certainly did. Now I've got some decisions to make."

Cooper listened gravely. "The Rodriguez thing—why did you side with the Mexicans?"

"I thought you'd understand, you of all people. Because it was so unfair, their being thrown out when the landlord abused them. Why do you ask?"

He looked at her searchingly. "I wanted to hear you say it, Maggie, to see if I'd gotten it right. You're still working for Meiers, yet you went with your emotions. It's hard to imagine." He shook his head.

"Don't taunt me, Cooper. Yes, yes, yes. I went with my emotions."

He smiled. "I don't think you'll be working for Meiers long."

"Perhaps not. But I have no alternatives, either, and if I quit I'll be drifting." She looked past him, seeing the people and the festivities for the first time. Everyone looked happy, and suddenly she felt anchorless and even lonely. She'd hoped he might suggest she move to Mount Shasta, but he hadn't. He'd offered nothing, suggested nothing.

She saw the moment for what it was, a fantasy, a respite from reality. Cooper was here for a minute—five minutes, an hour—and then he'd be gone and her disrupted life would have to begin again. Contemplating her future had spoiled the present. There was no point in extending this fairy tale. She stood up abruptly. "Cooper, I have a headache. I think I'll go home now."

"But you haven't eaten...and there's more dancing."

"Why?" she asked. "What are we trying to prove?"

"I have nothing to prove," he said solemnly, standing beside her. "I thought perhaps you did."

She shook her head. "I'd like to go now."

"Before you leave, Maggie, I want to give you something. It's in my car. Come out to the street with me."

Leaving the festive sounds, the laughter and the music was easy. For Maggie they'd become audio cruelties, taunting and hurtful. She wanted to get away from all of it, and mostly from him. He could only hurt her more.

They stood beside his Wagoneer. Briefly he took her shoulders and looked down into her eyes. Would he kiss her, make all her hurts go away? Could she yield to him if he did?

"I'd like to kiss you, Maggie," he murmured, "but as you've already pointed out, what's the point?"

And then he was in the Wagoneer, rummaging. At last he brought out a package and handed it to her, saying, "You should have this...to remember me by."

She turned away from him, tears in her eyes. Cooper Smith had given her back the trophy with the golf balls.

CHAPTER TWENTY-THREE

SITTING AT HER DESK Monday morning, Maggie wasn't sure what her next move would be. She only knew attending the wedding had been a mistake, that it had added to her unhappiness and done nothing to solve her job uncertainty. Yet of one thing she was sure: her days in the law firm were almost over. From now on she'd have to be her own boss, work on cases of her own choosing.

She leaned her chin on her hands, thinking. She'd lost the only thing in her life that mattered—Cooper Smith, and yet in some ways she hadn't lost him entirely, because he'd left her changed, his value system incorporated into hers permanently.

Didn't one own, in a small way, all those people who'd become part of oneself? With or without Cooper she'd begun to see herself as a person she liked—better yet, respected—and that was comforting. Without him she might be lonely, but the company she had in herself would finally be worth having.

She thumbed through a legal directory, wondering if there were firms in Los Angeles small enough to let her be her own person.

Los Angeles. She shook her head. Why was she considering Los Angeles? She'd never really liked the city very much, had she? The crowds, the cars, the smog. What did it hold for her now that she'd seen a better place? For the past four months she'd imagined herself living somewhere else—dreamed of it, hoped for it.

Then why was she considering setting up her life in Los Angeles?

Abruptly, Maggie reached for her telephone. "Air California? Please reserve a seat for me on a round-trip flight to Sacramento."

THE SEPTEMBER TEMPERATURE in Sacramento was in the high nineties, a far cry from the fresh coolness of late March, and Maggie's rented car cost a little more, too, but none of those things seemed important to her.

Driving north from the airport, she was aware only of the vast, open fields and the distant mountains, purple in the haze of a hot late-summer day.

She felt free. She'd never had such a sense of escape, as though she had been released from prison with money in her pocket and an unlimited future.

And yet, she thought, easing her foot down on the accelerator, there was little reason for her feeling of liberation, and her future was anything but certain. She was going back to a place she'd known only a short time to throw herself at the feet of a man she'd known well an even shorter time—someone who might or might not still want her.

But it didn't matter. Everything felt right. She glanced down at the trophy lying beside her map and grinned, remembering their good times together.

A few hours later, Maggie was in the canyon that led to Mount Shasta, looking eagerly left and right. The richly green conifers that climbed the banks in every direction offered cool respite from the September nineties. Though waves of hot air shimmered off the pavement in front of her, she spotted the cool lake waters to her right, and then the Sacramento River rushing downhill to join the lake. Insects bumped against her windshield, but in the distance the sunlight glistened off pine needles and highlighted the jagged outlines of the forest. High overhead an azure-blue sky held a single white puff of cloud.

Gradually the air cooled as she climbed higher, and through a cleft in the mountains Maggie at last got her first glimpse of Mount Shasta. With a sense of shock she realized the mountain had changed, its splendor dimmed in a transformation from white to brown. Only small patches of white lingered as a reminder of past glory. The sight saddened her; she, too, was left with mere remnants of what she'd had last spring.

But by the time Maggie reached the main street of Mount Shasta her optimism had returned. The town looked as old as ever, but endearingly so. Everywhere the place had a fresh-washed look, as though unfiltered sunlight had heightened every color. She felt a million miles away from the smog at home.

Continuing north on the freeway, she had just cleared town when she noticed a brown edge to the horizon. At odds with the sparkling air everywhere else, the little patch of brown lay thin and flat and ominous. She considered it for a moment, idly wondering where it came from. But as the freeway took a broad turn and her appointed off ramp loomed ahead, more important thoughts crowded her mind. Only a few miles from him now, her heart began to accelerate. How would Cooper react to her sudden appearance after so long? Could she ever convince him that she'd changed, that she was now returning to him on trust?

For a moment she had a feeling of despair. What if this was a fool's errand and Cooper rejected her outright, as he'd certainly be justified in doing. Or worse, what if he'd found someone else?

Maggie turned off the freeway onto the Old Deetz Road, willing this trip to turn out as she hoped. She'd just reached the railroad tracks when an odor rushed in through her open window.

She smelled smoke. As she approached Cooper's ranch, it grew stronger. The acrid smell bespoke burning wood, and she shivered, suddenly apprehensive. With each half mile its intensity increased.

She reached the gate with its familiar sign, Red Cedar Ranch, and drove through, her eyes making a continual sweep to see what might be burning. But she saw nothing, only the farmhouse in its grove of pines and the meadow off to her right. Cattle grazed in small groupings, their neck bells jangling periodically as they moved.

Stopping her car with mixed feelings of hope and apprehension, Maggie quickly got out and then paused, collecting herself. She touched her freshly washed hair, knowing it looked its best. Her lipstick was fresh and her orange silk shirt was as becoming as anything she owned. But would it be enough, she wondered tremulously, starting up the little path to his house. Would all of this be even half enough?

Midway up the path she stopped, struck by a sudden thought. Where was the Wagoneer? She turned, trying to find it, her hope plummeting as she realized another car was parked near the road to the barn but the Wagoneer was gone. How could she have failed to notice? The lipstick...the hair...what did they matter if Cooper wasn't here? And worse, who *was* here?

She continued on, her mood altered to dull disappointment. *Damn! Damn! You asked for this, appearing unannounced.* Pausing at his door, she tried to summon her courage. *You had this coming, Maggie,* she told herself.

Two knocks and a short wait, and she found herself facing a woman she'd never seen before—a gray-haired, matronly woman. Maggie asked if Cooper Smith was there, but the woman said he wasn't, wiping her hands absently on the blue apron that covered her flowered dress. The gray hair was pulled back from a surprisingly smooth complexion.

"Can you tell me when he'll be back?" Maggie took a deep breath, noticing that the odor of smoke was getting stronger.

A troubled expression crossed the woman's broad face. "I wish I could. He just left, but he's off doing something I'd rather he wasn't. He—" She seemed uncertain about continuing, then added, "Shall I tell him who stopped by?"

"Yes. Tell him Maggie McAllister. I don't know whether he ever mentioned me."

The woman nodded. "He did. About three months ago he spoke of you a lot. I'm Mrs. Winslow, I. . ." She stared down the road, distracted. "The smoke's getting worse, isn't it?"

"It makes me nervous. What's burning?"

"A forest fire, back toward the Eddies. That's where he's gone. They called from the Forest Service to say someone had gotten trapped and they didn't know anyone closer who knew those roads like he did. So he went." Like a deer disturbed by a human scent, Mrs. Winslow lifted her chin and sniffed. "I wanted to tell him not to, but he—"

In dawning horror Maggie broke in, "He went into the forest fire?"

"He said he had to." A look of entreaty searched Maggie's face. "I wish you'd been here to stop him."

"I couldn't have stopped him. He does what he wants."

"I know."

As the phone rang inside, Mrs. Winslow gestured her up the steps.

Maggie waited in the kitchen while Mrs. Winslow said hello, then listened, her expression turning grim. After several seconds she said, "She's not here, I'm sorry." And then, "I can't tell him. He's already gone."

Momentary silence hung in the kitchen as Mrs. Winslow hung up the phone. With an unconscious gesture she wiped dry fingers across her apron, not noticing that Maggie waited without taking her eyes off the other's face.

"What is it?" Maggie asked when she couldn't wait any longer.

"The Forest Service. They called looking for Anne, but she's probably back at the hospital by now. She was here when Cooper left. Then they had a message for him, too. It makes me so mad, I—" She picked up a soiled pot and began running water into it. "I wanted to tell them to go out and find him before he gets too far—they've got a Forest Service helicopter. Then I remembered it was down in Dunsmuir right now."

"Tell him what?" Maggie pressed.

"That the man he's going out to rescue probably set the blaze himself." She threw Maggie a quick, angry look. "He's risking his neck for a criminal, that's what he's doing."

Maggie's hand went to her mouth in disbelief.

"A low-life skunk, and Cooper's out there trying to get to him in time."

"Who?" Maggie asked. "Did they say who the man was?"

"Oh, yes, they said." Mrs. Winslow's mouth curved down in derision. "They said before he left, even, but Cooper never let that bother him, he just got his stuff together as fast as if it was you."

"Well who is it?"

"You probably wouldn't know him." Mrs. Winslow's hands paused in her cleaning of the pot. "It's a man who's lived in this town five or six years, a college professor. But I don't trust him—never liked him. His name is Gordon Hamilton."

THE NEWS STRUCK MAGGIE harder than a physical blow. Inwardly she felt herself reeling back, stunned at the implications of what she'd heard. It was shocking enough that Cooper had dashed off into a fire, but to rescue Gordon Hamilton....

Maggie could only stare at Mrs. Winslow and try to collect herself.

"I do know him," she said finally. "I don't like him, either." She watched the housekeeper scrubbing the pot as if to remove the top layer of metal, her knuckles white with effort.

"Mrs. Winslow—" Maggie touched the woman's arm "—isn't there something we can do?"

"Something the Forest Service could do, but not us. They'd know how to take the shortcut to Dead Fall Lake, which is where Hamilton is, or just this side of it. Cooper's going the long way, he said, because the road's better." She brushed a loose strand of hair off her forehead.

"But isn't there a map somewhere?"

Lifting a dripping finger from her pot, Mrs. Winslow pointed. A half-folded area map sat on the drain board. "He was looking at that before he left. But it's not going to do either of us any good. We couldn't find our way on those logging roads."

"Maybe not," Maggie said. "But I'd like to at least look."

FIVE MINUTES LATER Maggie was in her car with the map. How she'd managed to pilfer it without Mrs. Winslow's knowledge was a tribute to her former conniving self. She'd made up a story and slipped the map into her purse when Mrs. Winslow's back was turned.

But this time, she told herself, her motives had been pure.

Once out of sight of the ranch, Maggie drove as fast as she could, glad to be back on paving so she could make better time. She'd studied the map carefully and found Dead Fall Lake. Now she had only to make the correct turnings on the smaller lines, which she assumed were the logging roads the housekeeper had mentioned.

At a four-way crossing about two miles from the ranch, Maggie turned left instead of heading back toward town, speeding on the nearly deserted roads with a sense of urgency that made her pulse race. As long as she could follow the small lines she'd be able to save nearly seventeen miles, she guessed, and perhaps enough time to catch Cooper before he got into the fire area.

Yet as she drove north and then west on the back roads, a sense of foreboding overtook her. The burning odor was getting even stronger and she wondered how much time she'd actually have. She'd entered an area where the forest had thinned, a valley broken by occasional thickets, in which she sometimes had almost unlimited visibility.

Suddenly, not as far away as she'd imagined, she saw a wall of smoke rising. It was black edged with gray and seemed to be curling south and a little east, as though coming to meet her. She tried not to look at it.

The map lay on the seat next to the trophy, folded open to the right area so Maggie could consult it quickly without coming to a complete stop. Picking it up, she slowed as she came to a crossroads. Ahead lay the paved road, to left and right the way was dirt. And like the map, all roads were nameless.

A quick look convinced her the route was still straight ahead, and she sped up, conscious of time passing with awful speed. As she drove boldly over the pockmarked road, Maggie took stock of what she was doing, knowing that besides her battle with time and danger she had entered another arena with unaccustomed recklessness—the arena of the heart. She might, after this harebrained mission, still be rejected, and she thought about it, imagining Cooper ordering her home. But now she no longer let it concern her. Her only purpose at the moment was to keep Cooper out of that fire.

Around her, the quality of the air had changed for the worse. Dense and acrid, an occasional wisp of smoke blew by her car, and the sun no longer shone as brightly as before.

Suddenly, for no reason she could imagine, the paving stopped. Dismayed, she rolled up her windows and continued over dirt, pushing the car less successfully, but still going faster than she should.

Another few miles and the road branched, one fork going toward the Eddies, the other back out over the valley. Without looking at the map, Maggie headed south toward the Eddies. And toward the smoke, too, she noticed.

A rut in the road jolted her car to one side unmercifully, and Maggie slowed, pausing once more to study the map. With a finger she traced her route over one small line, then another. As far as she could tell she was still on a correct heading, the lines like a maze, leading to Dead Fall Lake.

But after a mile or so of bumping and swerving, Maggie came to a three-way fork, and consulting the map once more she saw that the fork was not depicted anywhere on the sheet. Maggie laid the paper back on the seat, accepting a grim fact: her map had just become worthless.

For an instant she stared out through the windshield, studying the terrain ahead. Dirt roads in three directions, all angled differently, and she at a loss as to which one to take. She now understood Mrs. Winslow's assessment of the logging roads. They were indeed tangled threads accessible only to those who regularly drove them.

And they were in terrible condition, too. On all three she could see foot-deep ruts and rocks that weren't rocks, but boulders. Trying to see where each led, Maggie finally chose one of the roads, and after bumping along a half mile felt rewarded when it angled the way she thought it should.

For the first time she saw flames sparking through the smoke. Even through her closed windows smoke crept into the car, fouling her air. Outside, the sun had disappeared under a layer of black.

Had it not been for Maggie's faith in her sense of direction, she would have turned back. But she'd seen Dead Fall Lake on that map, knew its general location at all times, and believed that by following the right heading she'd eventually intercept Cooper Smith.

Seeing an enormous boulder ahead, Maggie jerked the wheel right and braked, and to her dismay heard stone grinding on metal. The car lurched, dropped into a rut, and came to a near-stop. "The roads," she muttered, swearing. "I can't be defeated by the roads!"

The car bucked as she urged it out of the depression, and the motor coughed angrily when she tried to gun it back to a reasonable revolution. But it finally responded, and once more the car moved ahead, now on a section of road somewhat smoother than before.

Yet conditions outside weren't better, but worse. Floating by her window were black, wind-driven particles, some still smoking. As she plowed ahead toward flames, the wind came harder and the particles grew thicker. The air in her car turned so foul Maggie wondered how long she'd be able to breathe it.

As fearful as she now felt for herself, Maggie was

driven by an even greater fear: what was happening to Cooper?

Recklessly she plunged ahead, her mission turned into a near-obsession as she tried to put down panic but felt it just below the surface anyway. Perspiration turned her hands clammy and dampened her silk shirt. She knew she ought to turn back, faced with nothing ahead but smoke and flame and the terrible road. Yet a vision of Cooper in worse circumstances drove her on blindly.

Caught once more by a grinding rut, Maggie at last looked behind her to find a spot where she might turn around. And that's when she knew it was too late. A grass fire had started in the yellowed weeds she'd just passed through, and with dawning horror she realized turning back was purposeless. She was now surrounded by flames in all directions—and those behind were closer.

With a sense of futility, Maggie continued forward, for the first time acknowledging the possibility that she might not live through the day. She'd only pressed on another quarter mile when her road was crossed by another like it, and understanding at last that she was powerless to do anything for Cooper, she searched the road to her right, hoping it might lead away from the fire.

At first, knowing her own state of mind, filled with fear and suspecting she was hallucinating, the object she saw there seemed to be insubstantial, nothing more than a mirage. But a second look brought her a better sense of reality, and Maggie knew the vehicle coming toward her was no mirage.

It was Cooper's Wagoneer.

CHAPTER TWENTY-FOUR

WITH A GASP OF RELIEF, Maggie jumped out of her car, waving. She stood in the dust, breathing the thick acrid air, feeling the hot wind and seeing flames so close she should have been terrified, yet she felt nothing but joy. She'd found him!

The Wagoneer slowed and stopped in front of her, and Cooper got out, his face a study in astonishment as she started forward.

"Maggie!" he shouted, bounding across the distance that separated them. "My God, Maggie, what are you doing here?" Not touching her, he stood momentarily immobile, staring down at her with his hands hanging loose at his sides. "Maggie, are you crazy?" His eyes went beyond her, scanning the fire, and then stopped on her face with a look that said he was anything but glad to see her.

Stunned at his reaction, she began, "Cooper, I wanted to—" but stopped when she saw he wasn't listening. His attention was on the fire, and then he was heading for the Wagoneer, gesturing for her to follow.

She turned away momentarily, hiding the tears that had sprung to her eyes. That one look had been enough; Cooper was finished with her. She tried to gather enough composure to follow him.

From behind she felt her arm grabbed, found her feet moving as he propelled her toward his vehicle. "Get in! We can't wait!" And even before she was settled he'd started the engine with a roar. In the distance a lofty pine ignited with a whoosh, its flames shooting upward like a skyrocket.

In seconds they had passed her car and were bumping down the road in the direction Maggie had been going. Now something else occurred to her, and Maggie grabbed the door handle shouting, "Wait! I forgot something!"

He hesitated, giving her a quizzical look, then continued on. "Not now, Maggie."

"But I left the trophy on the front seat. Let me jump out and get it!"

"Maggie, for Pete's sake, there's no time—even for the trophy."

"But it may burn!"

His eyebrows went up. "You're worried about the trophy and not the car?" For a moment it appeared he might laugh.

"I've got insurance on the car."

"I don't believe it," he said, shaking his head. He gave her a quick look and pushed the Wagoneer harder, making no further effort to talk to her.

In the seat beside him Maggie felt unrelieved isolation, made worse by his physical closeness. That he had already shut her out was all too obvious, and given time she'd decide what to do—but not now. Leaning toward him she shouted above the engine noise, "Do we have to go up there, Cooper? Why are we doing this? It's Hamilton—he's the cause of it all."

"I know it's Hamilton. I knew it before I left." Both hands were on the wheel, wrenching it hard to avoid first a gully, then a two-foot boulder. Maggie careened sideways and grabbed for the door handle.

"But you didn't know the Forest Service called again, Cooper. They called—" She took a deep breath and regretted filling her lungs with smoke. "They called right after you left and told Mrs. Winslow to warn you. Hamilton is under suspicion. He probably set the fire!"

Only the slightest movement of his shoulders signaled that he'd heard.

"But he doesn't deserve to be rescued!" she cried. Up the road she saw a hit-and-miss pattern of trees aflame, some with sparks twinkling on every limb, others untouched.

"He deserves the same chance as any human being. The moral judgments will come later."

For the first time Cooper turned to face her. "It's you I'm angry about, Maggie, your coming out here like this and risking your life. Why did you do it? Why didn't you think?"

"I wanted to stop you, I—"

"You knew I wouldn't want you here, dammit! You've made me choose, Maggie, choose between letting a man die and putting you at risk, and now you've forced my hand—pushed me into taking a chance with you! If I could still send you back, I would!"

"Then take me back to my car!"

"It's too late for that. There isn't time. Even when I found you there wasn't time. God knows what would have happened if we hadn't met!" His grip tightened on the wheel, angry hands that were less hands than fists. "You don't know the safe roads out. I had to bring you, dammit to hell. There wasn't any choice!"

She'd never heard him swear before, never seen anger like this in any man. He frightened her, and she sat still, trying to think of some way to reach him. In a distant recess of her mind a voice whispered, *It's not as bad as you thought.*

She said quietly, "I'm me. . .Maggie. And I make mistakes."

His jaw, already hard, tightened more. "Don't you

think I know? Oh, I know you, Maggie. But why did you have to make this one?''

She couldn't answer. Hypnotized by the spectacle beyond her window, she watched the fire move in an irregular pattern, a trail of grass burning next to weeds that were still green, a tree smoking and its neighbor unsinged. High in the trees she could see the wind and the black fragments that rode the air cushion, some dropping, some blowing on past. She guessed they were still on the fringes of the main body of fire.

Beside her Cooper growled, ''You can thank God Hamilton's close. Just pray he's got enough sense to stay put!'' His eyes never left the road. Still driving with relentless concentration, he pulled the wheel continuously and the Wagoneer lurched and bounced between boulders big enough to damage the frame. Accelerating without respite, the vehicle plunged into deep gullies and climbed out of them, roaring.

With one hand gripping the handle on the door and the other the edge of her seat, Maggie hung on. Outside their vehicle she could see flames crawling between the trees and their peril growing, and though she tried not to focus on it, there was nowhere else to look.

She felt claustrophobic, trapped in the car with the whole world outside hot and threatening. Cooper ran the air conditioning, but it gave little relief and the smoke was inside, thick and choking. She wanted to get out, to cut and run down this narrow path of clear roadway until she'd left the whole awful nightmare behind. But she knew she couldn't. She sat still. Instead, from the corner of her eye she saw trees catch and flame up like torches. Fear took over. Pulse racing and heart pounding, she felt dizzy and fought back by staring at the floor.

What if they died rescuing Gordon Hamilton, a man suddenly contemptible in her eyes? What if she lost everything because this other man—the man she'd chosen to love—was unwilling to simply let him go? The Wagoneer lurched wickedly, and tightening her grip, she turned to look at Cooper. Bent over the wheel, tendons taut on the back of his hand and eyes hard on the road ahead, he didn't look like a saint. Yet he was, she thought, and in spite of her fear she relaxed slightly. If she was going to die, at least it would be with him. Anyway, she no longer wanted to live without him.

Lost in her thoughts, the peril retreated momentarily and Maggie was surprised to find them slowing. "There he is!" Cooper shouted, and Maggie looked but didn't see Hamilton, only his car parked in an area of charred grass. A few feet away a red gasoline can lay on its side.

"Where?" she asked, and Cooper pointed as he scrambled out the door.

In a few lengthy strides Cooper reached the car, and then Maggie saw Hamilton—or saw his shoes, because only that part of him was visible, poking out from under the car.

As Cooper bent over, shouting, "Come on, Hamilton!" Gordon struggled out by himself, inching backward. Wild-eyed, he stood up shakily and Cooper began to lead him toward the Wagoneer. Hamilton's trousers hung off him in shreds, and his face was black, whether from charred grass or burns, Maggie couldn't tell. Only his eyes were white, and they were wide open and terrified. Maggie jumped out of the Wagoneer and held open the back door.

Fumbling his way inside, Hamilton was a pathetic figure, insane with fear and now, Maggie saw, pain. He scrambled into the back seat, moaning.

While Cooper ran back to the driver's seat, Maggie seated herself and turned toward Hamilton. His face was contorted beneath the black and nothing remained of the dignity he'd once had. Even the whitish wings at the sides of his face were almost obscured by dark smudges.

"I'm burned," he groaned. "Let's get out of here." Sitting hunched over, he seemed hardly aware that Cooper had already started the engine and the Wagoneer was turning in a large arc.

Maggie's contempt lessened in the face of his obvious misery. "Are you burned all over?" she asked.

"No, no. Just my legs. Oh, God, my legs."

Driving the car faster now that they were headed downhill, Cooper said nothing. With terrifying energy he pushed their vehicle back over the rocks and gullies, throwing it into a higher gear and forcing it faster than Maggie thought possible.

But she knew why. The fire had increased in intensity, the places once vacant now filled with flames, so that they were headed down a path between two walls of fire. Had she not been thinking about the man in back she might have buried her head in her arms and refused to look.

"Hurry!" Hamilton shouted, looking out the window, and Maggie could see his terror now verged on hysteria.

"Shut up, Hamilton!" she shouted. "Keep your panic to yourself! Don't look. Close your eyes if you can't stand it."

"But the flames!" he screamed, and then he folded inward, clutching his lower body. "My legs. Oh, God, my legs!" He kept darting fearful looks at the fire outside, and Maggie could see he was on the edge of breaking, that he might do something rash that would kill them all.

"What happened, Gordon? How did you burn yourself?" *Talk,* she thought. *Keep talking.*

"The gasoline...it exploded, went up my pant legs when I...when I lit it." He wheezed and a rivulet of perspiration ran down his face, leaving a tiny white streak. His eyes went to the window and with a distorted expression he grabbed the door latch.

"Get your hands off that handle!" she shouted. Then, more quietly, "What were you doing with the gasoline?"

"I wanted to show them," he blubbered. "Wanted...my God, we're burning up!"

His shout drew Maggie's eye to the window. Ahead the road had narrowed and now they were running a gauntlet of towering flame. Maggie, too, wanted to scream in hysteria. But she didn't. Instead, in a deadly soft voice she said, "Be quiet, Hamilton!"

With that clarity that comes of finding oneself beyond help, of knowing that screaming will be of no use, she held back any sound and found herself sinking into near calm. In one or two seconds they'd be gone and this would all be over.

The Wagoneer tore into the narrow slot, plunged through it and beyond, and then, to her astonishment, kept going, still careening off rocks and dipping down into deep ruts. Maggie's eyes focused once more.

The terrain had opened up, a land of intermittent trees, all of them standing tall and black; of burnt grass; of smoke boiling up from the ground, each black funnel a witch's caldron.

They drove a few more yards to a wide spot clear of any vegetation, and then Cooper stopped. Wordless, he ran his arm across his forehead, leaving his sleeve wet and a partially dry track across his face. "The fire's gone beyond us," he said.

"We're safe, then?" Maggie asked.

He nodded, his fatigue drawing his features downward. "Yes...."

"I'm burned," Hamilton moaned from the back seat. "Get me to a doctor."

"We still have a way to go," Cooper said, starting the engine once more. "Hold on back there."

Maggie turned to him again, once more sorry for the fragment of a man hunched on the seat. "Why did you light the gasoline, Hamilton?" *Keep him talking.*

"I said—" he sucked in air "—to show...what would happen when too many people came. They... they're gonna let skiers...come." He stopped to breathe, his face distorted with pain. "People. They'll ruin the forests."

"Like you just did," Maggie added, unable to stop herself.

"Didn't mean to...to let it get so big." Once more he bent over his legs, holding himself stiffly.

For the first time Maggie focused on his charred pants, and now she noticed that in places where the cloth had disappeared, areas of Hamilton's legs were horribly burned. She shuddered.

"How long to the main road, Cooper?" she asked. But before he could answer she saw dust ahead, and realized a vehicle was coming the other way.

Cooper squinted. "I think I see the Forest Service." He leaned closer to the windshield. "It may be Forest Service Rescue."

CAREFULLY THEY TRANSFERRED Hamilton to the rescue truck, arranging his legs straight ahead of him on the bench in back. Contorted with pain, Hamilton's face was almost unrecognizable. Maggie stood near the doorway watching the men lay a blanket over his lower body, and felt compassion for what he'd already been through. Worse, she knew more was coming.

The Forest Service vehicle moved away slowly, its driver compensating for the bad road. Wearily, Maggie and Cooper got back into the Wagoneer, and for a few moments neither talked. Cooper leaned his head back against his seat, eyes closed.

Maggie stared out the window at the landscape, so changed in only a few hours. Beyond the freshly burned area, she could see black smoke still boiling upward and flames sparking occasionally among the churning clouds.

She sighed. "So needless. My rental car's gone, too, I'll bet."

"It probably is."

She thought of her suitcase and the trophy, lost with the car, and wondered why any of them mattered. They were just things, part of the waste, stupidly destroyed like the forest. She sighed again.

"We can have them make another trophy," he said.

"It doesn't matter anymore."

Hearing an engine somewhere overhead, she tilted her head back and saw a small plane circling the densest part of the fire, then saw orange liquid falling into the flames.

"The borate bombers are here," Cooper said. "Thank God. Now it won't be long."

He turned toward Maggie. "And what are you doing here? We never got that question answered."

"Was there ever time?" she asked.

He shook his head. "You've put me through a lot, Maggie, but never anything like this."

"How can you say such a thing, Cooper? How can you say *I* put you through it? You were hell-bent to rescue that man. I had nothing to do with it!"

"You've missed the point, haven't you, Maggie? Like you always miss the point. It was your being here that made it hell, nothing else. Your life in my hands and my knowing I had to bring out Hamilton or live forever with the knowledge I'd let a man die. But you. . . you're the element I couldn't handle. Your life at risk, Maggie. At the end I almost turned back."

"I never saw you even slow down."

"I did. But only in my mind. My hands and feet kept the car moving."

"Why did you care?" she asked angrily. "You've always been willing to let me go. Even down in Los Angeles you were willing. The way you handed me back my picture. You knew we were finished."

"Were we?" he asked.

"I. . ." She turned to him in confusion. "I don't know. Maybe not. I came up here, didn't I?"

"To see me?" he asked intently. "Did you come to see me, Maggie? Was that what brought you?" The smoky eyes searched hers with patience and calm.

"Yes," she said, her voice flat. But she knew there was no other answer. "Yes, I did."

"Then we weren't finished."

"But—"

"We were never through, Maggie. It's only you who didn't know it."

"But you acted. . . you seemed so. . ." She couldn't go on with the face of the man she loved so close, his eyes so warm and his hand now touching her cheek.

"Maggie, you fool, you sweet, wonderful fool. Do you know me so little that you don't understand what I was doing? Didn't you know that I loved you, that I loved you almost from the moment I met you and have never stopped all this time?" His hand went to her chin, lifting it gently. "Look at me, Maggie, and try to understand."

She forced herself to search his eyes, to lose herself in their depths, to perceive the love that was there for her to read.

In the distance the borate bomber droned, its sound the only noise reaching them from the dead land outside. They were parked in outer space, the home of the charred and destroyed. Yet she felt nothing but a sense of life and hope.

"Love can never survive one-sided," he went on. "And I had run to the end of my tether showing you how I felt. After that it was only you who could bring us back, Maggie. You, understanding at an intellectual level what you needed. What was important to you. In the end you had to get there by yourself."

"But you took a chance..." she began.

For the first time he smiled. "It wasn't much of a chance. I knew you pretty well."

"You're arrogant!" she cried out.

"No," he said. "Confident." He stroked her hair. "You loved me, Maggie. I've felt it all along. But you had to change, didn't you, to make it work? Funny how blind you were."

"Oh, God," she said, and buried her face in his chest. "What have I done to you? What have I made you suffer?"

"Suffer?" he asked against her hair. "It wasn't that bad. You don't suffer while there's hope." He brushed her hair back with tender fingertips. "Nothing I couldn't survive—until today."

"Cooper," she breathed, wrapping her arms around him. "Cooper, I do love you. Oh, Lord, how I love you!"

For answer he pulled her closer, holding her against his chest, cradling her head with one hand.

She could feel his pulse, feel the strength of him, sense his presence as a power that would protect her, keep her safe. In a small voice she murmured, "To me you are like the mountain, my darling. Enduring. Forever."

"My Maggie," he said, and let his fingers run through her hair. "It will always be true. Always."

They sat in silence, a joining that was spiritual and almost better, Maggie thought, than what they'd had in the meadow.

The droning airplane disappeared and they were alone in their silence. When it seemed they'd sat so long pressed together that they might never part again, he tilted her face so she had to look at him. His hungry eyes absorbed her, and Maggie could see he was about to speak.

Instead she quickly put her finger to his lips, smiling. "When I move here next month I'll have it all, won't I? My man and my mountain."